The Banned Underground

The Mystic Accountants

Will MacMillan Jones

Safkhet Publishing

Safkhet Publishing, Cambridge, United Kingdom

first published by Safkhet Publishing in 2012

1 3 5 7 9 10 8 6 4 2

Text Copyright 2012 by Will Macmillan Jones
Cover Art Copyright 2012 by Kim Maya

Will Macmillan Jones asserts the moral right to be identified as the author of this work under the Copyright, Designs and Patents Act 1988. Kim Maya asserts the moral right to be identified as the cover artist of this work under the Copyright, Designs and Patents Act 1988.

ISBN 978-1-908208-08-8

All characters and events in this publication, other than those clearly in the public domain, are fictitious and any resemblance to real persons, living or dead, is purely coincidental.

All rights reserved. No part of this publication may be reproduced, stored in or introduced into a retrieval system, or transmitted, in any form or by any means, including but not limited to electronic, mechanical, photocopying or recording, without the prior written permission of the publisher.

A CIP catalogue record for this book is available from the British Library.

Printed and bound by Lightning Source International

Typeset in 11 pt Crimson

Production Crew:
Cover Art   Kim Maya
Managing Editor William Banks Sutton
Copyeditor   Charlotte Choules
Proofreaders   Kim Maya Sutton, Nicholas Polizzi

 The colophon of Safkhet is a representation of the ancient Egyptian goddess of wisdom and knowledge, who is credited with inventing writing. Safkhet Publishing is named after her because the founders met in Egypt.

DEDICATION

When the Publisher asked me to write this dedication thing fer this book, I asked around all the characters here... well a few of them... alright, just me husband. But Ben only said that no one were goin' ter argue with what I said anyway. (He's right there, bless 'im.) The publisher thought that I were goin' ter say summat nice about the author, who he thinks is a pleasant, hardworkin' an' inventive bloke. We, his characters, have a different view. He shouts at us when we don't do what he wants us to; he sulked at me fer days just 'cos "I completely messed up his plot lines," what is a total lie; an' how his computer works wi' him is completely beyond me, I can tell yer.

So, this book is dedicated ter his family. How they put up wi' him, I don't know. Probably they are happy when he's yellin' at us, since he can't be off yellin' at them at the same time. Or maybe he can, I don't know. But we 'ere all reckon that they have a lot to put up wi', and we would feel sorry fer them if he ever let us alone long enough ter be bothered.

The author's partner did ask me if I could turn 'im into a frog fer a while, but Ben warned me off. "Remember, she's not the one at that keyboard," Ben said, so I didn't. Anyway, there yer are. It's fer that long suffering lot, the writer's family. And, Mister Publisher, if he takes any reprisals out on me, I'll be comin' round ter see you, so best get diggin' that garden pond yer wife wants. Yer might be needin' it.

Grizelda

The Cast

The Banned Underground

Fungus............................A bog troll, with an enquiring mind.

Haemar............................A dwarf lead singer with great expectations.

Felldyke...........................A drummer who hangs around with musicians.

Scar..................................A keyboard player with an unsound sound balance.

GG...................................A guitarist, imprisoned for playing progressive rock records to the King under the Mountain.

Dai...................................A dragon. A heavy drinker, and therefore, the bass player.

Eddie...............................A taxi driver who saw the light, courtesy of a right hook.

The Goodies

Caer Rigor.......................An association of witches who would like to be good-natured.

Grizelda..........................A witch with a permanently bad nature, constantly surrounded by frogs. Known as Aunt Dot to her family.

Ben..................................In the wrong place at the wrong time. As ever.

Chris & Linda.................Family to Grizelda, nuisances to the rest.

Erica & Imelda................Witches on the make

The Not Quite So Good

The Tuatha......................Legendary beings with an equally legendary capacity for drinking, fighting, and telling bad jokes.

The Edern.......................Could have become High Elves, with mystical powers and aloof attitudes, but settled for international merchant banking and bad attitudes.

The Dwarves

Lord Lakin ....Undisputed ruler of the Helvyndelve, pining for a throne
Waccibacci-san................A pine throne maker.
Daran & Milim ....Guards. Enough said.
Assorted dwarves............Lacking enough beer, or pizza. Or beer.

The Baddies

Caer Surdin......................An association of dark witches and warlocks.
The Grey Mage ....A local dark lord and qualified tax accountant.[*]
Ned ....The assistant dark lord, learning his craft, and trying to be crafty at the same time.
The Watches ....Apprentices to evil. That's what happens when you chose taxation or taxi driving as a career.

The Worse Baddies

Ben Buddhists.................All dressed alike, probably to avoid identifying the guilty.
The Mystic Accountant..Wants to take over the whole world, starting with Wales.

Also Appearing

Assorted dwarf guards....desperate for a drink, a pizza, and a good fight, In any order.[**]
Abused traffic officers.....Abused, but that's a normal state for traffic officers.
Various police officers. ...Perfect, wonderful guys.[***]

---

[*]   Interchangeable terms, according to some.

[**]   Or was that the entry for the traffic police?

[***]   Won't hear a word against them, not while they know where I live.

Accountancy gets a very bad press. The practitioners of this arcane and intricate art are much more than just bean counters. The author has been an accountant for many, many years without feeling any compulsion to count the number of baked beans in a can.*

The profession would get much more respect, if the general public only realized how many dark wizards used accountancy as a cover.

No frogs were harmed in the writing of this novel.

---

* 463. Google it.

Chapter One

England. The Lake District. The most beautiful place in the world.[*] However, this region – beloved by photographers across the world – has a downside. Occasionally, it rains. This fact is especially known by the assistant photographers whose task, in return for meager wages, is to carry all the gear and *not* drop it in the mud, under any circumstances, on pain of death.

Accordingly, unusually, and most remarkably, that evening it was raining. The waters hammered on the houses of the towns and villages, forcing visitors to take shelter in the various pubs.[**]

Much photographed and adored by the professional photographers, and hated in equal measure by those who had to carry the equipment, the mighty Lakeland Fell of Helvelyn stood tall against the storm. The delicate tracery of the attached Striding Edge laughed at the rain, while the lashing water made sure that the paths became a nightmare to traverse while burdened down with the gear.[***]

Down the slopes into the next valley of Borrowdale lay the ancient Bowder Stone, rumored to be the location for various supernatural beings and, in fact, the front door to the Helvyndelve. The ancient dwarven halls of the Helvyndelve lie beneath the frowning fells of Helvelyn and quite a few other mountains too, of course, as the Helvyndelve is enormous. On a night such as this, who would have been surprised at the sight of a large group of eldritch beings, dwarves, trolls, half-elves and so on swathed and huddled against the rain, gathered together there? Their conversation could have been – should have been – mystical, magical, occult, or paranormal, or indeed all of them at once:

"I don't care who you are, if you ain't got a ticket, yer can't come in," said security.

"But I'm with the band!" said the first in line.

---

[*] Yes, all right, I know that you think the bit of the world you live in is better, but you are only the reader, so your opinion doesn't count. If you happen to be the publisher or the author's bank manager, then yes, clearly a mistake has been made and will be corrected in the next edition.

[**] The locals, used to the rain, found their own excuses for being in the pub.

[***] Four cameras, two tripods, assorted lenses, and most importantly, lunch.

"They all say that," replied security, in the form of two dwarves clad in full body armor and bad attitudes.

"I've got a t-shirt on."

"All it says is 'Let me in cos I'm with the band'," pointed out security.

"See?" insisted the would-be concert-goer.

"£9.99 at the supermarket. Everyone's got one." The dwarf opened his cloak and revealed a badly-fitting t-shirt stretched over his armor.

"Come on. Some of us behind you are getting soaked waiting out here!" came a complaint from further down the line.

"Not my fault they didn't put up any awnings," replied the ticket-less one.

"Show us yer ticket, or go away," insisted security.

"Alright, I haven't got a ticket."

"Should have said so. Then you could just have bribed me straight off, instead of standing out there getting wet."

There was a chink, as several coins passed hands. A derisive snort and several more joined the first set vanishing into security's secure pockets. The line moved on.

Inside the Gate Chamber – a large, dimly-lit cave underground beneath the Bowder Stone – more security awaited the intrepid visitors.

"Helvyndelve Security. Please leave your spears, swords, staffs, wands, knives, and other weapons at the desk, to collect on your way home," said the banner.

"Good bit of spell casting that, Milim," said the first underground guard, another medium-sized dwarf who was also fully armored.

"Getting the banner to talk like that saves us a lot of work, Daran," replied his colleague, through his enormous beard.

"Pity it has a Yorkshire accent though."

"Can't have everything. No, sorry sir, got to leave that over there. Collect it on your way out."

"But it's cultural!" objected the gig-goer.

"It's also banned completely in most countries," Daran insisted.

"It's recommended for police use in the others."

"But not here, so leave it."

"Guard?"

"Well done sir. Identifying me as a guard wins you a prize."

"Great! What did I win?"

"The right to be not gratuitously assaulted, until you're on the way out again."

"Guard? I've got a press pass!"

"Press past me and you will know about it. Get in line with the others."

"Guard?"

"Yes sir?"

"Says you have to leave your weapons here."

"That's right."

"I'm an expert in unarmed combat."

"Then just leave your arms with the other weapons."

Daran and Milim watched the guest – empty sleeves flapping – join the wanderers down the dimly-lit corridor into the heart of the Helvyndelve.

"I dunno, Daran, it's not rocket science is it?"

"And he's armless now."

"Don't that make 'im more dangerous than before?"

"Oh, cos he's an expert in unarmed combat?"

"I never expected The Banned Underground to get a house this size. The Chamber of the Throne's goin' ter be packed out," Milim said to Daran.

"Lord Lakin spent a lot on the advertising for them. Witches Chronicle, Modern Warlock, What Witch, The Craft Magazine, New Shaman, Investment Banker International."

"Investment Banker International?" queried Milim.

"Get a lot of the Edern reading it. Regular order at their Fairy Hill."

"Always been a bunch of bankers, that's true. Is the Lord expecting any trouble?"

"Don't think so, really. The Tuatha can't make the gig. Erald, their boss, has got them on some sort of team building exercise in Wales. It's his latest management thing. He got it from that Lord Telem of the Edern."

"What's it supposed to do, then?" Milim wanted to know.

"I saw the brochure lying about. It's supposed to, uh 'encourage coordinated action; enhance teamwork; develop leadership skills; teach the art of 'elegation; reduce dependency on others; encourage self-reliance'."

"What does he want to teach that lot those things for?" Milim asked.

"Improve their efficiency?" Daran wondered.

"The only thing they'll ever be efficient at is drinking. And if they get any more coordinated at the bar, no one else will ever get served."

"Talking of which, let's get the doors locked and get a round in before the hospitality bar closes and the gig starts."

"With Fungus the Boogieman and The Banned Underground playing, the bar will never close."

Milim and Daran closed the magical doors and locked them with the traditional spell – "and bloody well stay shut!" – before following the last of the latecomers down the western passage to the Chamber of the Throne.

Despite how much money had been spent on the advertising, the drinks, the other drinks, the further drinks, the emergency drinks, the essential drinks for when the emergency drinks ran out, and the last ditch secret stash of drinks for real emergencies (such as running out of drinks), *and* the customary catering, ("you want onions or chips wiv yer burger, luv?") the backstage area was not so well equipped (except for the drinks).

The Banned Underground were enjoying the hospitality room, a curtained off area ten square and dusty feet behind the dais at one end of the enormous Chamber of the Throne, which lay deep below Helvelyn itself. The ancient, mystical, and woodworm infested Throne of the Mountain King occupied much of the space, but there was plenty left as a stage for The Banned Underground.

Popular in many quarters, and unpopular wherever bar tabs remained unpaid, the band (all dwarves with one exception,) were:

Haemar: lead vocals

Scar: keyboards

Felldyke: drums, percussion, empty beer bottles, etc.

Gormless Golem (aka GG): guitar

And, on saxophone, a five-and-a-half foot high, luminous green bog troll called Fungus the Boogieman, according to the fly posters presently being removed from various local car parks.

"I wanted those M&M things, with all the yellow ones taken out," grumbled Scar, engaged in his favorite hobby: complaining.

Fungus was peering through the hastily-erected curtain, which hung behind the dais on which the throne rested.* His shades kept slipping down his nose in the heat but he would not discard them.

His thoughts were interrupted by the sound of Haemar gargling.

"Do you have to do that, Haemar?" Fungus demanded.

"Just lubricating me throat before the gig," Haemar replied, unconcerned.

"Can't you use *WD-40* like any other singer?"

"This water is free. Look, it even runs free."

"Down the wall, near the power socket," observed GG who was fussing around as usual.

"Any normal singer would use beer," said Felldyke, the almost-spherical drummer, who could be observed with a beer in each hand. Extra bottles stuck out of the special pockets he had sewn into his stage clothes. Spare drumsticks were rammed into every conceivable spot and some of them were made of wood instead of chicken.

"I'll do a sound check for the kit," Felldyke said. He walked out through the curtain and sat down at the drums. A hammer, carefully thrown from the audience, banged off his helmet and he listened respectfully to the echoes.

"That'll do," he said.

"Where's Gormless Golem?" asked Fungus, seeking his errant guitarist.

"He's round the back somewhere, fiddling with the cables and amps," replied Scar. "He plugged my organ in first but wasn't happy with me sound balance."

"Only cos you fell over on top of 'im," said Haemar, discarding the water and opening a whisky bottle.

"Tell you what, we've got a great crowd," reported Fungus, excitedly. The Throne of the Mountain King lay on a dais in the enormous cavern, about nine hundred feet underground at the heart of the dwarf mansion. It was full of jostling dwarves, trolls, the occasional elf and some witches and warlocks.

"Who cares?" said Haemar. "Who's got the money?"

"Security, for security while we play," Fungus said over his shoulder.

"Can't trust that lot. Security guards are the biggest thieves around," worried Scar.

"Where's the set list?" asked Felldyke.

---

* After a hard day of being sat on by Lakin, the Lord of the Helvyndelve, the throne needed the rest.

"What do you want to know for?" asked Scar.

"So I know what to play."

"Felldyke, you play the same beat to every song, so what difference will it make?"

"Where's GG?" asked Fungus, bringing his head back through the curtain and, again, dislodging his sunglasses.

"Here, Fungus," called Gormless Golem.

"What have you been doin' back there?"

"Setting up the amps and cabling. Tell you what, with all this rain outside, it's a bit damp back here."

"It'll dry out when we get going," promised Fungus, unconcerned.

In the chamber, the noise of the excited audience took on a new quality. The dais shook slightly as a group of heavily-armored dwarves tramped onto the stage. Several were wearing protective earmuffs, although the bright pink, fluffy material clashed rather with their fetching grey metal helmets.

The guard captain drew a deep breath.

"Right you stupid lot, shut up," he yelled.

"Why do you think we are stupid?" called a nearby member of the audience. The guard captain glared back.

"Yer paid to get in, didn't yer?"

Lakin, Archlord of the Helvyndelve and hence King under the Mountain, then leaped onto the dais to the cheers of the crowd. He was a tall dwarf (that is, tall *for* a dwarf) and dressed completely in gleaming black ceremonial armor. He waved his arms in the traditional way, until the crowd quieted down.

"Tonight, we are going to hear The Banned Underground!" Lakin announced.

As this was printed on the tickets, it came as no surprise even to the drummers in the audience. So they stayed quiet, listening to the Lord of Helvyndelve. Disappointed in the lack of reaction, Lakin continued.

"As you know, they helped last year in the recovery of the lost Amulet of Kings, which I now wear, and this is their victory gig. So, big it up for... THE BANNED UNDERGROUND!"

The audience responded now, as he left the stage, with a huge roar of approval. Security pulled away the curtains and Haemar grabbed the mic stand, wrapping his trademark scarf around his left wrist.

"Here we go!" he yelled at the audience and The Banned broke into *Going Underground* – their normal opening number.

Soon the gig had indeed warmed up and the crowd was dancing. Well, most of them. The symmetrically challenged (one-legged) Marvin was still complaining... to anyone who would listen.

"He's playing *At the Hop* again," he complained

"Got to admit, they work hard," yelled Daran to Milim, as a fast new number started.

"Dunno this one. What is it?"

"*Easy Livin'*, of course."

"Is everyone 'avin fun?" screamed Haemar from the stage.

The volume of the roar of approval caused Scar to fall over again.

"I'm gonna have to do something about his *un*sound balance," fussed GG, from underneath Scar.

Felldyke started on a drum fill as the band drew breath. Unfortunately, he let go of one drumstick at a crucial point and, as the errant stick whirled across the stage to make a pinpoint landing in the left ear of the captain of the security guard, he grabbed a replacement from his smock. A chicken nugget fell out as well, and made a less-than-resonant sound on the snare drum and had to be discarded. To be eaten later.

"Next, another old favorite," Fungus yelled into the mic, while Haemar rescued GG.

The errant guitarist wind-milled his right arm a few times and careered across the stage, rather worse for wear from a combination of beer and being sat on by a very heavy keyboard-playing dwarf.

Nevertheless, the frantic opening chords exploded out of the amplifiers and assaulted the auditorium.

Gormless Golem bounced off Fungus and staggered back although, to his credit, without missing a note.

Unfortunately, he failed to miss his speaker stack, which collapsed. Some speakers fell onto Felldyke and his drum kit, one large speaker toppled slowly over onto Scar's keyboard, and the head unit, stuffed full of complicated circuitry and *electronics*, fell into a large pool of water which had collected backstage.

"*Jumping Jack Flash!*" howled Haemar into his microphone, announcing the song, while GG took off as the power fed back up the cable into his *Telecaster*, and flew across the stage, (narrowly missing Fungus who ducked in time) to smash into the throne. There was a mighty flash, the stage lights went out, and the Throne of the Mountain King disintegrated.

"Man," said Scar, with feeling, "that Keef an' Mick write smashin' songs!"

Five extremely large guards, each displaying a casual approach to both violence and personal hygiene, formed a stage invasion.

"For your own safety, you will come with us," growled their leader.

"Who's threatening us?" asked Fungus, who was still a little shaken from the experience of a ballistic guitarist crossing his vision at a 3-inch distance.

"Will I do?" asked the guard captain, who had failed to remove the drumstick from his left ear.

"One good thing... " remarked GG as he left the stage slung over the shoulder of one guard.

"Do tell," asked Fungus, jumping slightly under the influence of too many mushrooms, adrenaline from the gig, and the sharp point of a sword in his back.

"At least I wasn't using the *Les Paul.*"

The next morning, The Banned Underground awoke slowly in their cell.

"Oh, my back," groaned Gormless Golem.

"My 'ead," complained Haemar.

"Most of me," chorused Fungus.

"All of me," contributed Scar.

"I think something went to the toilet in me ear," muttered Felldyke.

"Hur, hur, hur," sniggered the guard standing over him.

The band, and in particular Felldyke, woke up very quickly.

"The Boss wants you," the guard told them.

"Springsteen and the E Street band?" asked Fungus, hopefully.

"No. And the street you're on has no 'E's in it."

"Surely every street has two?"

"I don't care what guitar you were using," said Lord Lakin, accusingly: "what about my throne?"

"Will it mend?" asked Fungus.

"I could give it to one of the local schools as a project, like one of those 5,000,000 piece jigsaws, or a scale model of the Blackpool Tower made out of matchsticks," grumbled Lakin. "I could pretend that it is a Tracey Emin performance piece. I could even put up a plaque, saying 'Damien Hirst was here'. But in practice, no it will not mend. It will have to be rebuilt and that will cost a fortune."

"Ah," Haemar commented.

"The ticket sales for the gig will help. And the catering invoices. What's left will just about be met by the bar takings, despite the size of your tab."

"And our fee?" asked Felldyke, cautiously.

"What fee?"

"Ah. Right."

The Banned Underground understood that their management had just stolen the whole take from their victory gig. Sullen expressions fell onto every face.

"There is," Lakin informed them, "another problem."

"Another problem, Lakin?" asked Fungus, indifferently. "What sort of a problem?"

"One that money cannot solve."

The Banned looked momentarily cheerful.

"It is a matter of artistry. I need an artist."

"Scar's been an artist all his life," offered Felldyke.

"Not *that* sort of an artist."

"Ah. Right."

"The ancient and possibly magical Throne of the Mountain King has been shattered and a new one must be created. Since you kindly offered to finance the project from the frankly enormous profits from the gig –"

"When did we do that?" asked Fungus.

"Just now," replied Lakin.

"I don't recall it either," said Haemar, sulking into his helmet.

"You were all asleep at the time," replied Lakin, smoothly.

Behind The Banned the guards sniggered, loudly.

"All that remains is for you to find the master craftsman and bring him here."

"Us?"

"But we are musicians, not detectives," objected Scar.

"Ah," responded Lakin, "but what do professional musicians want most?"

"Beer?" offered Scar.

"Whatever that yellow stuff is that Fungus keeps in his pockets?" suggested GG.

"To be paid," muttered Fungus.

"Correct!" said Lakin, cheerfully. "So, if you successfully come back here with the descendant of the dwarf who created the throne, with him full of purpose to create a new masterpiece, or a replacement throne with a genuine certificate of authenticity, then you have another gig. For which you will be paid. But in the Cavern of a Thousand Knights, this time."

"So," said Fungus, looking gloomy, "we have to go on a quest, to locate a nameless descendant of a probably deceased dwarf, who may or may not be a skilled Magical Throne Manufacturer, and convince him to come back with us here to recreate a throne for you."

"I always knew you were quick on the uptake."

"I thought that we were friends, Lakin," complained Fungus.

"Oh we are, Fungus. That's why I am sending you on this quest, so that I do not have to see you every time I see my broken throne. I would be sure to get upset, having a short temper."

"It's not only your temper that's short. Still, we don't have much choice. Now, I am going to make some conditions."

"I'll listen before I agree. Don't be too long," warned Lakin.

"Sizeist remarks will get you nowhere. We take our instruments as cover for the quest."

"Agreed."

"We'll need a budget for traveling costs an' food an' so on."

"OK"

"I need a last known location for this Clint."

"Clint?" enquired Lord Lakin.

"What else are you going to call a dwarf with no name?"

"But he has a name," Lakin told Fungus.

"Go on."

"Mr. Waccibacci."

"Mr. Waccibacci?"

"Well, to be accurate, it *should* be Waccibacci-san. They *are* of Japanese stock."

"When *were* there ever any Japanese dwarves?" asked GG.

"Oh, a bunch moved over there many years ago, to open new markets, explore fresh demesnes and take the entrepreneurial spirit of the dwarves to new places," Lakin explained.

"You don't expect *me* to fall for that one," objected Fungus.

"OK. We chucked them out for stealing sheep," Lord Lakin replied.

"I thought sheep-stealers normally ended up in Wales," said Haemar.

"Yes, but the guard captain at the time was dyslexic. So he drove them into *whales* instead and it took them so long to get out of the large intestines that they found that they had emigrated. To a Japanese whaling ship."

"And have you any idea where we might find them now?" asked Fungus.

"Wales probably."

"Oh very funny," grumbled Haemar.

"No, seriously. We think that they could be in Swansea. But first, I am sending you to Manchester, to see a dwarf who might have a better idea where they are."

"Why Manchester?" asked Haemar.

"He likes dark and gloomy places, apparently."

"Typical dwarf, then," answered Fungus.

Chapter Two

Many have waxed poetically about the rain in the Lake District. Few have praised the rain on the grey streets of Manchester. Yet, without the life-giving rainwaters, the streets might actually be black and the mighty Irwell River might lose that particular shade of bright green, which has inspired so many to leave and seek their fame and fortune somewhere else.

In the south side of the city lie many prosperous suburbs and leafy, tree-lined avenues. With a vertiginous camera swirl, we may leave our view of the city center, and focus on the homes to be found here, where the pickpockets are better dressed and the street muggers polite.

Here, teenagers can be raised to understand that robbery is antisocial and unlawful, unless carried out while wearing a suit and having 'Investment Bank Manager' as a job title. In a similar vein, oppressing the poor and disadvantaged is discouraged and left to the experts at the unemployment center.

Neither unfortunate nor especially poor (after their father had been held upside down until their weekly allowance had fallen from his pockets) were Chris and Linda. Siblings, they were superficially alike, although at 13, Linda was showing the early signs of too many visits to burger bars, and at 16, Chris was getting used to other types of bars. He affected a mean, moody James Dean-ish appearance, spoiled only by an excess of pimples. Linda was blonde, of which we shall say no more.

Rubbing his bruises from the shake-down, their father attended the front door. Normally, the postman was reliable in his failure to deliver the post, but today his normal routine visit en-route to his long-standing girlfriend had been curtailed. Linda had received two letters!

"At least arriving on the same day cuts down the effort," moaned the postman. "But if you keep receiving letters, I will start delivering your bills as well, instead of just leavin' them in the sack for a week or two and using them to light the fires back at the sortin' office."

Ripping open the envelope with her fingers, for none of the other family members were comfortable with Linda wielding sharp knives, she gasped.

"It's from Aunt Dot!" The teenagers' aunt had been their host last year on a memorable holiday.

"When did she learn to write then?" asked her dad.

"My sister has always known how to write, thank you very much!" Cassandra, their mother, could be very waspish when she wanted, which was all the time, really. Tall, slender, and fierce-faced, she could inspire terror in anyone she met.

"Yes, but there's a difference between theory and practice. And she's never practiced," her husband pointed out.

"She wrote that spell book last year," Cassandra protested.

"No she didn't. You know it were ghost written. Remember, she asked you for the phone number of the exorcist afterwards."

"Never paid him either, did she?" Chris reminded his mom.

"How do you know?" Cassandra asked.

"He rang her, threatening her with repossession."

"How did she get out of that?" asked Linda.

"Her frog spell, I think. She keeps him in her kitchen now, as a flycatcher."

"Not now she won't," said Linda, reading her letter.

"Why?"

"Cos she's moved. She says that she got a promotion after that do in the Lakes last summer and had to move to Swansea."

"That's promotion? Going downwards, surely," objected her father.

"Only on a map. Apparently it was a good career move."

"Where is Swansea?" asked Chris.

"South Wales."

A silence greeted this, in part as neither teenager, typical products of the state education system, was entirely sure where the proud principality of South Wales actually was.

"And she wants us to visit, well, me and Chris to visit," Linda continued.

Looks of sadness failed to pass over either parent's faces.

"Good idea," commented their mother.

"When do you go?" asked their father.

"How long for?" queried their mother.

"Have you got those holiday brochures still, luv?"

"The last time you sent us to stay with Aunt Dot, mum was in the hospital," Chris sulked.

"That dreadful pain's back again. Ring *Casualty*."

"*Casualty* is a TV show, not a place, mum."

"Are you sure?" asked Cassandra.

"Yes, mum."

"Well, make it the undertakers instead then, just in case it is serious."

"She's paid for the train tickets, too," said Linda, still immersed in her letter.

"We'll help you pack," said her dad.

"Who sent the other letter, Linda?" asked Chris.

The sound of ripping paper was repeated.

"This one's from Fungus, the musician we met at Auntie's last year."

"No wonder the paper's green."

"And smells of mushrooms," remarked Cassandra, pulling a face.

"Is that what the smell is? I thought it reminded me of something for a moment," reminisced the teenagers' dad.

"Guess what?" asked Linda.

"I hate guessing games. And riddles," Cassandra muttered.

"Only cos you always lose."

"Well, it's the unfair questions. What have I got in my pockets? How is anyone supposed to guess that and get it right?"

"Cheat. Like you do anyway, mum."

"Never mind that, what's in the letter? Besides the used mushroom that just fell onto the floor?"

Linda carefully read the writing, which resembled the musings of an arthritic spider.

"Oh no."

"What?" demanded Cassandra.

"He's coming here. With The Banned Underground," Linda said.

"Wicked!" enthused Chris.

"Then, he's going onto… "

"Stop the suspense. Just tell us."

"Swansea."

"Excellent!" enthused her father. "You can all travel together."

"Dad, Fungus is a luminous green bog troll, and the rest of the band are dwarves."

"So? They'll be practically normal on the railways. Especially in First Class among all those politicians."

"They'll only have standard saver tickets."

"Well? Who's goin' to notice them among the football crowds?"

"He says here that they've a gig booked at Manchester U for Friday and then tickets to ride to Swansea for Saturday," read Linda.

"Do they run trains to Wales on the weekend?"

"A slow train apparently," said Chris, looking over Linda's shoulder at the letter.

"Is there any other sort?"

"They did build that high-speed rail link, Dad."

"Then why is it still quicker to drive to London?"

"Sometimes there's a delay."

"That's the line to get served at the buffet at Crewe I expect. Even the drivers take so long to buy a buttie* that the food sell-by-date has expired before they reach the tills."

"I thought that was the reason for the road work on the M6. To encourage people not to drive," pointed out Cassandra.

"Anyway, they want to crash here before and after the gig, then have a lift to the train station at Stockport for the trip to Swansea," Linda told her family.

"When are they arriving?" asked Cassandra in alarm.

The doorbell rang.

"Now? The post was a bit slow," Linda replied.

Haemar stood at the door of the average suburban semi-detached house, one finger on the bell, when the door opened silently; he took a hasty step backwards.

"Cor, you don't half look like yer sister," he said at once to Cassandra.

"Oh, you know her?" asked Cassandra, with deceptive meekness.

Haemar, who knew Grizelda well, was not fooled.

"Everyone 'round our way knows her. And is shi... terrif... full of respect for her."

"Well, just so you know –"

"Yes?"

"– she's the nice one in the family," smiled Cassandra.

Haemar took another step backwards. He knew that, traditionally, quests involved being in mortal peril, but he had not been prepared for Stockport. Outside, in the street, negotiations with the burly, greasy-haired taxi driver were at an advanced stage – akin to the Israeli/Palestinian peace talks – and with every prospect of lasting as long. At the back of the taxi, Scar and Felldyke were unloading The Banned's gear as quickly as they could, while the argument developed further.

"Look," said Fungus, trying to be reasonable, "we agreed a price before we set off."

---

*   Northern English word for sandwich.

"You never told me we were coming all this way. I'm out of my area now, an' can't get a fare back. So I'm charging you for both ways," the taxi driver insisted.

"But you've only driven us one-way." Fungus protested.

"Get in the bus then, an' you can come with me for the trip back."

"But then we'd be back where we started from," objected Fungus.

"Just goes to show," put in Gormless.

"What?" Fungus and the driver both glared at him.

"You can travel ten thousand miles and still stay where you are."

"I'd rather walk five hundred miles and make some progress," panted Scar, invisible behind an enormous bass drum.

"Don't fancy walking all that way with the kit, though," said Felldyke.

"Well, obviously."

"Cos it would be five hundred more miles to walk back."

"I have a solution," said Cassandra.

Fungus and the taxi driver stopped glaring at each other. With an innate sense of self-preservation, Fungus entirely failed to glare at Cassandra. The taxi driver, veteran of many a battle with impecunious Mancunians (which seemed to be most of them in his experience) maintained the glare.

"I want payment for both ways," he maintained.

"Perfect. You are, I suppose, Fungus?" Cassandra asked.

Fungus bowed slightly, and lifted his infamous *Frodo Lives* baseball cap.

"And you are playing tonight at the U?"

"Yes ma'am."

"Then this chap can drive you all there. So if your two friends put all this stuff back in the bus… "

Felldyke opened his mouth to protest but received a sharp elbow from Scar, so didn't.

"I'm not going to hang around all that time!" exclaimed the taxi driver.

Cassandra displayed a sweet smile, and a right-hook worthy of Mohammed Ali in his prime.

"Well sleep through it then," she advised.

Fungus stepped smartly aside, allowing the (now sleeping) driver to collapse tidily into the gutter.

"You can't leave him there," said Cassandra, "a traffic warden will put a ticket on him. Lock him in the back of his bus, put it on the drive, and then," she smiled widely at The Banned Underground, "I think you'd better all come inside."

Chris and Linda were pleased to see Fungus and the band again. Their parents were less overjoyed to have their house overtaken by a group of itinerant, dwarven musicians, but reacted with true northern English hospitality.

"I'll put the kettle on. You lot, sit down and try not to break anything."

"It's really nice to see you again," said Linda to Fungus.

"What's the Helvyndelve like now?" asked Chris.

"Not as good as it used to be," replied Haemar.

The teenagers looked at each other. At their first visit, the ancestral home of the dwarves had been dark, gloomy, and full of two hundred years' worth of rubbish and used pizza boxes that were waiting for collection. How could it have become worse?

"Well, when Lakin started using the Amulet of Kings, we all thought: 'Great. Free power, rubbish shifted, all that stuff, get the bars and cafés running again,'" started Haemar.

"But it didn't quite work out like that," said Scar. "We all thought 'e was a great bloke, one of us, like. But when 'e got the amulet goin', he changed into the Boss."

"He started playing Bruce Springsteen records?"

"We could have coped with that. Nah, 'e became really bossy."

"'Don't drop litter,' he said," said GG.

"'Clean up that mess,' he said," added Scar.

"He started the shift plan again. He said 'e needed revenues," Felldyke contributed.

"As if the bars weren't profitable enough."

"He restricted drinking times," said Haemar. The entire band fell silent in horror at the memory.

"So," asked Cassandra, "is that why you all left?"

There were some sheepish looks, followed by a lot of nudging and whispering along the lines of:

"You tell her."

"I did it last time."

"We haven't bin here before."

"Well, I could have done it last time if there were a last time."

"Let's all vote for GG to tell her."

"What?"

"Works for me."

"An' me."

"Well," started Gormless Golem.

"Don't tell me!" said Linda. "There was a gig."

"How did you know?" asked GG, impressed.

"It seemed inevitable," sighed Linda.

"Well, we were putting on a blinder of a set. Fungus were on fire on the sax, Haemar's vocals were spot on, an' Felldyke were as tight as I've ever seen him."

"That were your brother-in-law's homebrew did that to 'im though," put in Fungus, to Cassandra.

"But then we 'ad an accident. See, it was raining outside, and the cavern leaked a bit, well a lot, onto the amps. The feedback caused a bit of an accident."

"What sort of an accident?" asked Chris.

"Well, it sort of blew the throne apart."

"Lakin's magical throne? Where the Amulet of Kings goes?" asked Chris, his jaw dropping.

"Yes," confessed GG.

"If he's turned as bossy as you say, I am surprised he didn't lock you up," said Cassandra, sternly.

"He did," answered GG.

Haemar came, reluctantly, to his guitarist's support.

"But someone told him how much it would cost to feed Fungus in jail, so 'e let us out."

"And sent us on a quest to find a Zen master throne builder he 'ad heard about," finished GG.

"How do you propose to find such a person?" asked the teenagers' dad, who, like the spaghetti western bounty hunter, had no name, just an addiction to *Bounty Bars.*[*]

"Well, we'll try first at the uni gig. See, there's a few trolls and dwarves work at the uni these days."

"The lecturers, probably," muttered Dad, who had been to an open evening there.

"There are a couple that do philosophy but they also do security an' lab tech work," explained Fungus.

---

[*]   Other confectionery is available. This footnote is to comply with consumer rights legislation and thereby stops the author and publisher getting some advertising revenues, thereby increasing the cost of the book to the consumer. But your rights were protected, so that's all OK then.

Haemar continued. "So first we try there and then move down to try Grizelda an' 'er new coven – 'e did quite a bit of work there, we know, so that's the second place to look."

"So that's why you have tickets to go to Swansea," Linda exclaimed.

"To be fair to 'im, Lakin did give us a traveling budget," Haemar told her.

"But it's not exactly generous," Scar complained.

"So that's another reason for this gig. We need to raise some extra cash for the trip," said GG.

"Well, we will help out," said Cassandra, at which the gloomy atmosphere lifted somewhat. "We will lend you these two. They can help at the gig and go to Swansea with you afterwards."

The gloom returned quickly at the thought of Linda and McDonald's.

"Grizelda has paid for the tickets and we will put in a contribution for the gig and their food bill."

The mood lightened once again.

"I'll go an' see if the driver has woken up yet," offered Fungus.

"That's OK. I sorted him out myself while I was making the coffee," replied Cassandra.

The Banned Underground shook slightly and drew closer together for protection.

"Don't bunch up," the teenagers' dad advised them. "You make a better target."

Cassandra turned to her children.

"Right, you two, go and pack. And make sure that you wear those magical amulets you brought back with you from your aunt's."

"The Wards of Lingard?"

"Mum, how did you know about them?"

"All mothers have an inborn magical sense for things their children have hidden from them."

"Really?" Chris had more than a trace of concern in his voice.

"Oh yes. And as those ward thingies mess up the satellite TV reception all along the street, it wasn't hard to find them. Lucky the neighbors didn't find out, or they'd have sued us."

The teenagers quickly left the room and could then be heard squabbling as they hurried upstairs to pack.

"We are going to miss them so much," sighed their mother.

"That's all right, they can stay here with you," said Fungus.

"No," replied their father, with a reflex retort known to any parent who sees a chance to offload two teenagers for a long weekend. "It's a family duty now to help you out and we will never shirk a family duty. However difficult. I quite fancy Greece, Cassandra, what do you reckon?"

Then came the sound of thunder. Any radio producer would have sampled the sound for use as a stampede effect but, in fact, it was only Linda and Chris returning downstairs. Each wore a silver chain, with an amulet, around their necks. And other clothes, of course, as well.

"Put those inside your t-shirts," advised Fungus. "We are having the gig at the U, so there will be lots of students about. Can't go wearing jewelry like that too openly."

The teenagers nodded and hid the chains.

"Right then," Fungus said, with some authority. "This is the plan. We go to the uni bar and start settin' up. Felldyke and Gormless, that's your job."

"Why us?" asked GG.

"Well, GG, you're the only one who understands the electrics. And Felldyke is best at setting up the drums. Scar and Haemar, your job is to find the management an' sort out the bar tab, and how we get our share of the ticketing."

"What are you doin'?" Scar asked Fungus.

"As I am the least conspicuous –"

"Huh?" asked Felldyke

"He means he looks like a student," answered Scar.

Everyone in the room turned and examined Fungus. He stood five feet eight inches high, with a faded denim shirt and jeans; his head bore the infamous cap with the *Frodo Lives* legend, shades and sandals.

"OK. I can see that."

"Even though he is a luminous green bog troll?"

"Can't help how I'm made," grumbled Fungus.

"He will pass for what's normal in a student bar anyway."

"MY TASK," said Fungus loudly, "will be to try and find out if any of our kind knows how to find this Zen master. So, I will mingle with the lecturers and technicians, engage them in conversation, and see what I can uncover."

"And not engage in casual drinking in any way," commented Haemar, sourly.

"A foul calumny. If I do any drinking it will be with a serious purpose."

"So no change there, then," muttered GG.

"Just remember we 'ave a gig to play afterwards," warned Haemar.

"I," said Fungus, haughtily, "am a professional musician."

"That's what bothers us."

"What are *we* going to do?" asked Chris.

"You two should stick with Haemar and Scar and keep an eye out for anything suspicious," Fungus told him.

"I thought that you were seeking a master craftsman, not a secret agent or a subversive," said Cassandra, accusingly.

"A student bar is bound to be full of subversives. How are we to choose just one?" asked Haemar.

"He can make magical furniture, so it always pays to keep your eyes open."

"I could see that in a driving instructor," said Chris.

"Or a CCTV camera operator," added Cassandra.

"Can't trust promoters either," Scar agreed.

"So just watch everybody. If I am making enquiries that upset anyone, I'd like to know about it," warned Fungus.

"I think he knows something we don't." Haemar said to Scar, very quietly.

"Doesn't everyone? This is a university bar," Scar replied.

"So we'll watch Fungus as well as watching everyone else."

"We've only got four eyes between us."

"Well Scar, you've got a squint. That should broaden your field of vision a bit. I'm just sayin', that's all. It's not that I don't trust Fungus, of course I do, but there's something worrying 'im we don't know about. And that worries me," said Haemar.

"Let me get this straight. You are worried that 'e may be worried *and* worried that 'e 'asn't told you whether 'e's worried or not worried *and* worried that there may be something to worry about that would only worry you if you knew about it in the first place, so that you could worry about it properly? No wonder people worry about you," reasoned Scar.

"Scar?"

"Yes, Haemar?"

"Shut up."

"Yes, Haemar."

"Come on," ordered Fungus, "time to load up the tour bus."

"What tour bus?" asked GG.

"The taxi minibus. The driver has just agreed to drive us about for the weekend."

"When did he do that, then?" GG wanted to know.

"In about three minutes, when he wakes up," said Cassandra, inspecting her watch and the knuckles on her right hand.

"He's going to be your right hand man, if he doesn't want my right hand again."

"Try him with some of this," said Fungus, with a grin, putting his hand in his pocket.

"Brilliant. A roadie at last," said GG, as a very bemused taxi driver helped load the drum kit back into the Mercedes *Sprinter.*

"What's his name?" asked Scar, lifting one end of a heavy speaker cab and placing it, carefully, on top of the high hat cymbal.

"Eddie," answered GG. "They are always called Eddie. Makes it easy to remember when they keep changing. Ain't that right, Eddie?"

"Der," answered the strangely bemused taxi driver-turned-road crew.

"Now you two take care," the teenagers' father told them, with a faraway look in his eye (maybe the Caribbean...) "Say hello to yer aunt for us, tell her we will come an' visit her new place as soon as we can. You've got yer pocket money, should last yer one week, so we'll be back in two. I've ordered the taxi for the airport, luv."

"Look after yourselves and do not get involved in any more fighting," warned their mother.

"I will look out for them," promised Fungus. For some reason, expressions of relief and trust were absent from the faces of both parents.

"Eddie's ready," called Haemar from the minibus.

"Well, have a nice trip, kids."

The front door closed rather quickly as the teenagers and Fungus walked down the drive.

"Just like last summer," observed Fungus, cheerfully.

"I think that's what bothers us," said Chris.

They all clambered into the minibus and, after a brief argument about who was sitting where, set off.

"Steady, Eddie," warned Fungus, as the bus lifted onto two wheels, negotiating one of Stockport's many scenic roundabouts.

"Hey look," said Haemar, "there's a hat museum.* We could donate Fungus' baseball cap."

"Try it and I'll donate yer head to help show off the exhibits," replied Fungus.

---

* And there is if you go and look. Remember, if you want to get ahead, get a hat.

Chapter Three

Imagine a Dread Portal. Intimidating, frightening. The sort of entrance that will only open with a squeal of tormented souls from the hinges, while the door itself shuts with the leaden sound of closing coffins. Not as alarming as the entrance to your bank manager's office, but not far off.

Knocking on this door should carry a government health warning and be a reasonable cause for subsequent claims to incapacity benefits. The sign over the door, in mock gothic script, tells of the terrors within, beginning with the ancient, horror movie-inspired furniture and wizened denizens tasked with reducing the casual visitor to a state of preternatural fear. And that's before meeting the receptionist:

TGM Accountants and Taxation Advisors

"Ah, Ned. You are a little late for your appointment," commented The Grey Mage, from his seat of power behind his extremely large (and empty) desk, denoting his status as the one who took the money, but did the least work.

"Sorry, Boss. I've bin sat in yer reception fer twenty-five minutes," replied Ned, a tall and skinny apprentice Dark Lord and Senior Taxation Consultant, as he sat down on the visitor's chair in his leader's office.

"No excuse. Now, I have a task for you."

"OK, Boss."

"Last year, we nearly gained the Amulet of Kings from the Helvyndelve, but were foiled at the last moment."

"I remember. I still limp a bit on wet days."

"Now, I hear that the Throne of the Mountain King has been wrecked," informed The Grey Mage.

"Earthquake, Boss?"

"No. Musicians."

"10 to one it were Fungus an' The Banned," mused Ned.

"I bet Lord Lakin *wants* them banned. In the meantime, he cannot fully use the amulet, for it needs to be placed in the magical throne to rejuvenate its powers."

"Which is now knackered."

"Exactly. So, Lakin has sent them on a search for the dwarf who created the original throne, to employ him to make a replacement. Your task –" instructed The Grey Mage.

"Is ter stop them?"

"Yes. Follow them as they seek this anonymous dwarf."

"Called Clint, is 'e?"

"Who knows? But prevent them from bringing the dwarf, or a throne, back to the Helvyndelve. If you can do that, we will soon be able to capture the Dwarf Halls. And take over the pizza franchise from them."

"Yes Boss," said Ned meekly.

"I have found out that The Banned Underground will be playing a gig tonight in Manchester."

"Wow. Bet that took some doin'. Were it mystic scrying? Crystal ball gazing? Did yer summon a demon with arcane knowledge?"

"No. I read the fly poster in the car park at Tesco's, before the attendants took it down."

"Pure magic."

"Don't be sarcastic. For now, it is enough for you to understand this. Our country is in a mess."

"No change there, Boss."

"I will entrust you with a secret. Within the evil wizards of Caer Surdin there is a group of us accountants who have decided that the time is ripe for us to take control of things. First, we have assumed mastery of our craft. Now it is our aim to use that craft to secretly take over the country. Introduce sound economics and proper finances. After all these years, it's time that experiment was tried at last."

"A revolution? That's really cool. Are you, like, Che Guevara?" asked Ned, impressed.

"Nearly. One day I hope to be on a poster, instead of this Fungus the Boogieman."

Ned speculated that this could be so, with the words *Wanted for Questioning* underneath the picture.

"We are patriots, make no mistake about that," The Grey Mage assured him.

"So, even though we're evil wizards, we are actually the good guys here?"

"Rather like Guy Fawkes."

"He wanted to blow up Parliament!" said Ned.

"Sounds like someone who had the good of the country at heart to me then."

"True, Boss."

"Take a couple of the apprentices for back up," The Grey Mage instructed.

"They always seem to get my back up, right enough."

"Use that idiot who drives a taxi, for one. He can provide transport. There's a junior in the tax department that'll do too. Go in disguise."

"Not false beards, Boss. They always seem to fall off."

"Just use clothing. There are some hoodies in the drawer over there. The one marked 'VAT – Do Not Open'."

Ned opened the Drawer of Secrets and pulled out a pink sweatshirt emblazoned with the words: 'Hen Night – Handle with Clare'.

"Perhaps not that one. Try the black ones instead."

The concert hall at the student union was buzzing with excited students watching The Banned set up for the gig. And drinking, of course.

"Put the bass drum down there, Eddie," ordered Felldyke, opening a beer bottle with his teeth.*

"Der," replied the taxi-driving roadie, following instructions.

"How are we doin'? " GG asked.

"Nearly there. Just need you to wire it all together now." Scar told him.

"OK. Where's Haemar?" asked GG.

"Haven't seen 'im, to be honest. Him an' Scar went off with the kids, to look for the promoter," Felldyke replied.

"What about Fungus?"

"He's getting on with his job, over there."

Over there, Fungus was in a heated discussion with academics.

"Yeah, I get that, but is the cat alive or not?" asked Fungus.

"Aye, there lies the rub," agreed an English Lit student who had interfered in the conversation on his way to the bar and now regretted it.

"Yes, that is the question posed by the conundrum," said the lecturer.

"Open the box," decided Fungus.

"No, take the money instead," advised the student.

---

* Don't try this one at home. Felldyke has had four teeth surgically removed (in a fight) and had replaced them with artificial teeth purposely designed for opening bottles, which will not pop out of his mouth when so used. Yours might, so you have been warned. This has been a public service announcement.

"No, I meant open the box to find out if the cat is dead or not," said Fungus.

"Too big a risk. Take the money. What if the cat's dead? All you get is a dead cat."

"Can be good eating in a curry, though," said a dwarf lab technician, who was also involved in the discussion.

"Not if it's been in the box for too long," the student disagreed.

"So there's no real solution?" asked Fungus, disappointed.

"Well, yes there is, but only if you pay me a lot of money to tell you. Over a six week course," replied the lecturer.

The hall was filling up and so the student departed in search of the bar while it still stocked drink.

"Now that it's just us," said Fungus, "I have another question."

"Go on."

"I'm looking for Waccibacci."

"Shame that that student just left us. He's got loads back in his rooms."

"No, not that Waccibacci. I asked about philosophy first to check you out. This Waccibacci is a Zen master who also makes furniture. We are on a quest to seek him out."

"Well he's not in my class," the lecturer told Fungus.

"Probably a graduate, I expect," said Fungus.

The lecturer wandered off in disgust but the lab technician pulled Fungus further into the quiet corner.

"We know about him," he hissed. "He was here about twenty years ago. Got pushed out for correcting the exam questions."

"What's wrong with that?" asked Fungus, surprised.

"You're not supposed to do it while you're taking the exam as a student. Anyway, he moved on. We heard he was helping out at one of them new universities in South Wales. Running the woodwork department in the day and teaching Zen at weekends. No one had an address though."

"Any idea where in South Wales?" asked Fungus.

"Wasn't near most of the mines. Too many negative vibes, he said. Near the coast maybe?"

"Thanks. Comin' to the gig?"

"Thought I might."

"Here's some free tickets for your help."

"Ta."

Fungus returned to the backstage area, pausing only to argue with security who were unaware that he was with the band, until he showed them the t-shirt (£ 9.99 from the supermarket, he told them after they had let him through).

"Any sign of Haemar an' the kids?" he asked GG, before pulling his saxophone from its case and starting to warm it up.

"Yeah, they are 'anging around somewhere. Hall is filling up nicely now, eh?" said GG, looking around the concert hall.

"Yeah. Since they're students I thought we'd start with something a bit different. How about *Milk and Alcohol?*"

"Make mine a double," replied GG, tuning his *Telecaster* guitar.

"Right!" said Haemar to the promoter who, in his expert opinion, was as slippery as a freshly caught eel. Having got his fish on a hook, Haemar was not letting go.

"We want ter sort out the ticketing now."

"Leave it for an hour. There's a bit of a blockage. Not all the receipts are in yet from the outlets," the promoter suggested.

"I can block yer inlet quite easily. Scar, stand by the door." Haemar drew his cultural weapon.

"Hey," objected the promoter, backing off around his desk, "I thought they were for stage use only."

Haemar grinned.

"But all the world's a stage. Got that on good authority." He buried the axe in the desktop, which came apart in a thousand splinters. Notes and coins spilled out of the stricken drawers of the desk onto the floor, although the stricken drawers worn by the promoter spilled something else onto the floor.

The two dwarves shoveled coins and notes into a sack, leaving a tithe on the floor.

"We'll take this, you can keep the rest. And yer get to keep the bar receipts, but pay off our tab."

"Pay off your tab? It's the same size as the national debt!"

"Then get a good accountant," said Haemar on his way out, collecting Scar, Chris and Linda as he did so. None of them were looking back to see three hoodie-clad figures slide into the office behind them.

"I think yer need some creative assistance," Ned said to the promoter, looking with interest at the devastated office.

"Not more musicians!"

"No sir, we're accountants."

The promoter turned white and screamed like a schoolgirl.

"Do you want me to hit him with the abacus* now, Ned?" asked the junior.

"Mebbe later on," Ned advised, watching the promoter twitch.

"Here's Haemar now, Fungus," called GG.

"Has he got the cash?"

"Yep. The bag's fastened to Felldyke's leg."

"Good. Hey you two," Fungus turned to Chris and Linda.

"How do yer fancy being backing singers?"

"Great! But we probably won't know the lyrics," Chris replied.

"And we haven't rehearsed!" Linda objected.

"Then you're the same as all the other professionals here," Fungus reassured them. "I've changed the set list a bit to cope with the audience profile," he added.

"Oh yeah?" asked GG.

"We'll go for as many drinking songs as we can think of."

"Why don't we stick to what we know?" asked Felldyke, opening another beer.

"We are," answered Haemar, wrapping his scarf around his wrist.

The compere strode out in front of the curtain and ducked as a fusillade of empty bottles hit the stage.

"And now, for one night only, The Banned Underground!" he yelled, before jumping off the stage to safety.

The curtain drew back, to reveal Haemar clutching the mic stand, Fungus and Scar arguing, and Chris and Linda hiding behind Felldyke. Luckily, Gormless Golem knew the opening chords to *Milk and Alcohol*, and the band quickly picked up the tempo.

"*Drinkin' Wine*, next," panted Fungus.

"Shame we haven't got a bass player," gasped GG.

"Why, would he make a difference?" asked Scar.

"And who would tell anyway?" asked Haemar, filling his helmet full of water before putting it back on his head.

"Straight on to *Four to the Bar* by the Pirates," instructed Fungus.

"You must be 'Kidd'ing."

---

* An abacus is a more potent weapon in an accountant's armory than a calculator. Not only does it do the math, but also it plays games and is a better hand weapon if the clients are slow paying their fees.

By the halfway point, the audience was both drunk and exhausted from the pace. Even the team of evil auditors had left the wrecked office and had joined in the fun.

"I know we are using them fer our own ends but they can't half play," yelled Ned, as The Banned Underground moved into slower territory with *Shot Gun Blues.*

"'Ere, Ned, see those two behind the drummer? The backing singers?" The junior tax assistant elbowed his leader sharply, to reinforce his point. Ned got the point, but also got the elbow, and then got the hump as he promptly slipped on some spilled beer and fell over. Moments later, the junior started jumping and yelling with even more enthusiasm than the audience, before running off towards the exit.

"What's up wi' him?" asked the assistant assistant, "'e looks like he's got ants in his pants!"

"Funny you should say that," replied Ned. "Useful spell that one. But I see what 'e meant. I've seen them two before. They've got the Wards of Lingard. I bet that's why they're with the band."

"Well, it's not for their singing. Mind you, they seem to know this one." And indeed they did, as The Banned Underground roared through *Jailhouse Rock,* to general appreciation.

Eventually, after four encores, the promoter cut the power off. As the bar was unable to serve more beer, the gig ended.

"Do you do that every night?" asked Chris, who was dripping with sweat and exhausted.

"Not every night," admitted Scar, who was drooped over his keyboard.

"Definitely a high spot tonight," agreed Felldyke, who had fallen off his stool and was flat on his back behind the drums. A professional musician (even if he was the drummer) to his core, one hand was firmly on the bag with the money.

"Der," agreed Eddie.

Fungus was almost beyond speech.

"Eddie, pack up the kit," whispered Haemar, with his dripping scarf draped over his face.

"Der."

"Back to Cassandra's place, and then we go south," managed Fungus.

"Der."

One or two students were lured by the promise of free CDs of the gig (false of course, only illegal bootleg recording had been carried out) into helping Eddie load the gear back into the *Sprinter*. After a brief argument with the satnav (which was convinced that the quickest way from Manchester city centre to Stockport was not down the A6 but via Doncaster) they set off. All were too hyped-up, tired, drunk or "Der" to notice a taxi following them discreetly. Fortunately for the dark wizards, Ned and his assistants were in a rather old and dilapidated *Mondeo*, so it fitted in nicely as a local vehicle.

At Linda's urgent request, the *Sprinter* pulled into the drive-thru for refreshments, causing the *Mondeo* to swerve violently and then head off down a side street to avoid detection.

As a result, the accountants nearly missed the *Sprinter* pulling away, and only just managed to catch up. Behind, in the side street, they left the twitching body of the local denizen who had hoped to remove the wheels from the car while they were stationary. Ned had been creative again.

Chapter Four

The following morning was chiefly memorable for the thick heads all around. The mornings in Stockport may bloom and blossom, with birds singing merrily – if quietly, to avoid attracting the attention of the local Chinese restaurateurs and their catapults, a learned survival trait – but here on the housing estate all was silent. The band members crept quietly around Cassandra's house, drinking large quantities of black coffee, and trembling at the sight of toast.

Outside in the street, the mood was somber also. Ned had made them all sleep in the *Mondeo*, in case they missed the *Sprinter* leaving the drive on which it was parked. The *Mondeo* has many sterling qualities but, as a hotel room for three, it lacked some amenities.

"I need to go," said the junior assistant.

"Can't yer wait?" sighed Ned.

"Been waitin' all blasted night."

"Why didn't yer go before we set out?" Ned wanted to know.

"You wouldn't wait."

"Alright. Best just go over that hedge."

The car door opened, and closed gently. There came a sigh of relief, then a squeal of fear. The car opened less gently and slammed very quickly. Moments later, something bulky hit the door.

"They shouldn't be allowed to keep dogs like that! I could have bin scarred for life!"

"Don't fuss. No one would have noticed," Ned reassured his junior.

"Thanks very much. See what 'appens when you need to go."

"Do yer want something to drink, help yer calm down?"

"Please. I'll use this bottle here... what was in it?"

"I used it when I needed to go," Ned replied.

The car door was opened urgently and various other urgent noises followed.

"Quiet," hissed Ned. "Start the car, they're leaving."

And indeed, the various group members were being loaded by Eddie the roadie ("Der") into the *Sprinter*.

"Now remember to be nice to yer aunt." Cassandra warned Chris and Linda who, being tired teenagers, were not in the best of tempers.

"Long as she's nice to us," Chris answered back.

"Well maybe that promotion has mellowed her a bit," said their father.

"From sadistic to just nasty?"

"Don't talk about yer aunt like that," admonished their mother.

"But last year she got us involved in a war," Chris pointed out.

"Only a small one. Good training for when you grow up a bit more an' get a job."

"Is all employment like a war, dad?"

"Let's see. Long periods of boredom, followed by short periods of excitement when those in charge panic a lot and blame you for everything that went wrong. Yes, I can see the parallels with employment there."

"Maybe I won't join the army after all then."

"Good idea. Become a banker instead and earn more money."

"And you don't get shot at as a banker. Well, only by the police in pre-emptive self-defense, obviously."

"And eating off the land under the stars sounds great in a book, but you should try it when it's freezing cold an' raining, an' the farmers have locked the chickens away cos they know there's a forces exercise on, and then your fire won't start," Dad recollected.

"Hang on, are you talking about Aunt Dot's again?" Chris asked.

"What is there to do there, Dad?" Linda wanted to know.

"In South Wales? There's bound to be some sheep left. And it is not too uncivilized. They do have cinemas, *McDonald's, Pizza Hut*, shops, things like that."

"I bet Aunt Dot doesn't live anywhere near those things. Has she still got that goat?" asked Linda.

"Oh yes. According to that letter you got. I read it all last night while you were out. She still has the self-propelled fridge, although that's having a hard time re-locating."

"The fridge? How? Why?" Chris was confused.

"Well it seems yer mates here had a gig at Grizelda's place, and the fridge got off wi' the bloke from the local electricity company. It keeps sending him smutty faxes now, begging him to come down to Wales."

"Does he ever answer?" asked Linda.

"No. Apparently he's got this new washing machine and sits for hours gazing at it."

"That's weird," said Chris.

"Um..."

"Still, time for you to go. Does yer driver know where he's goin' to?"

"Der," asserted Eddie.

"That'll have to do, I suppose. Oh look, here comes the taxi I ordered."

Cassandra leaped aboard the still moving taxi, the teenagers' father following her as if attached by a chord, (B-sharp probably) with a suitcase on his other arm. Turning the corner on two wheels, the taxi sped off into the distance.

"Goin' fast," commented Scar, pausing in the loading of the tour bus.

"Der," agreed Eddie.

"Probably nicked the fare from that old *Mondeo* taxi over there," replied GG.

"Doesn't seem fair, that," commented Scar.

"Competitive business. Only as good as your last trip."

"I've known a few guitarists like that, too."

"Not looking at me, I hope. I'm reformed, remember? No more prog rock for me."

"I just like to keep an eye on yer," mused Scar.

"Der."

"Eddie's worried that we might be overweight," Scar interpreted.

"Speak for yerself. I'm just under-tall for my size," retorted GG.

"No, the minibus. Look at the back springs."

Indeed, the *Sprinter* was sagging somewhat over the rear axle.

"It'll be alright. Anyway, it's traditional to have a tour bus like this. Overcrowded, overloaded, overindulged," said Scar.

"That'll be those two then." They looked at the two teenagers who were falling asleep in the back already.

"All aboard," called Fungus, hopping into the front. "Are you ready, Eddie? Let's rock and roll."

"Der."

The *Sprinter* moved off in a fashion which belied its name. The arthritic *Mondeo* had no trouble keeping up as they headed out onto the M56 highway, heading for Chester.

"Are we there yet?" asked Chris.

"Shut up," said The Banned Underground in unison.

The satnav barked instructions imperiously until Felldyke rammed a spare beer bottle top into the USB slot, whereupon it sulked for a while (allowing Eddie to successfully negotiate the Sharston Junction without hitting anything or getting lost,) and then was reduced to impassioned pleas to head north – since the quickest way to Swansea from Manchester just *had* to involve Preston.

Lacking a satnav, the *Mondeo* slid behind some other vehicles to remain unobtrusive – Ned taking the opportunity of a quick service station break to change its color by magic, thus avoiding a parking ticket.

"But I liked red. Hid the rust at MOT* time," complained the assistant assistant.

"The last time yer took this to an MOT station, the staff all ran an' hid until yer went away," accused Ned.

"So? Still got me MOT."

"Only cos you knew 'ow to work their computer," pointed out the junior.

"Well, what's the point of trainin' to be an evil wizard if you don't put the knowledge to good use?"

"Look, they're turning left," Ned observed.

"Right."

"No, left. Yer can't turn right on a motorway."

"Can in America," said the assistant assistant.

"This is England, where we do things right."

"So it is right."

"GO LEFT you idiot, before you lose them," ordered Ned.

"Right."

"Oh gods, why did I choose you two?"

"Cos the Boss told you to."

"Right."

"Not left then?"

The assistant assistant, like the reader, was confused.

"Just follow that *Sprinter*."

"Thought we were following a minibus? You're not supposed to run about on motorways."

For a moment, Ned considered following on foot as a serious idea, but then calmed down as the vehicles passed slowly down the scenic A483 towards South Wales.

The assistant assistant, driving, was observing the road traffic signs as they progressed.

"Look, all the road signs are in foreign. Perhaps we are in America after all."

"That's not foreign. It's Welsh." Ned told him.

"Why can't I understand it then?"

---

*   UK vehicle inspection

"Look, it were painted by someone called Allan*," said the junior, from the back seat.

"Must be proud of their work, here. Our council wouldn't let them sign the road."

"That's mebbe why we 'ave no road signs," mused Ned.

A ballistic Honda minivan, horn blaring wildly, encouraged the driver to pay more attention to the road signs as it missed the front of the *Mondeo* by the width of the new paint job on the bonnet.

"Read the signs, can't you?" yelled the passenger in the van as his nose skimmed the front of the *Mondeo*.

Fungus and the dwarves had no difficulties at all with the ancient and poetic language, even when badly painted on the road (by an arthritic road painter who had had to keep dodging cars, tractors and occasional sheep while painting).

"*Araf,*" said the road, and the *Sprinter* obeyed.**

"Who's this Araf?" queried the *Mondeo* driver.

"He learned to write in the same place as Allan, anyway," said the junior.

"Now it says '*ARAFWCH.*' Wonder what it means?"***

"Maybe you pronounce it 'ARAF OUCH?'"**** suggested Ned.

The *Sprinter* driver understood, and obeyed. Accordingly, with only a slight crashing from the rear load space, the *Sprinter* sailed around the corner. The fast-moving *Mondeo*, however, made an existential choice, and carried straight on through a hedge into a very muddy field. Fortunately it failed to connect with the extremely large tractor which was towing a low loader up the field. Slowly.

"Made me say OUCH," grumbled the driver.

"Didn't you read the signs then?" asked the farmer, chuckling as Ned opened his wallet and started counting out notes while the tractor pulled a now very well-disguised *Mondeo* out of the field. Slowly.

"Must have missed them," sighed Ned.

"Didn't miss me hedge though, did you boy?" chuckled the farmer.

"Clearly. Still, we are really grateful, mate."

---

*   Welsh for "exit"

**   Slow down. Now.

***   If you haven't already slowed down, this is your last chance. Honest. Before you crash.

****   No. Although you might say "ouch" afterwards, if you didn't *araf* in time.

"Any time, as long as you bring your wallet."

The *Mondeo* shot off in pursuit of the departed *Sprinter*, showering mud everywhere.

"Come back soon!" called the farmer, before going home to count his subsidies.

"Polite old chap, I thought," said the assistant assistant.

"Glad yer think so, cos I paid 'im wi' your share of the beer money." Ned told him.

"Where's this road go to then?" asked the assistant assistant, after a while.

"That place." Ned told him, pointing to the map.

"Which one?"

"*That* one. I stand more chance of being elected Pope than learning to pronounce that."

"Yer 'ave enough trouble makin' yerself understood in English," grumbled the assistant assistant.

"That's Llanelli," said the junior from the rear, without difficulty.

"'Ow did you learn to say that?" asked Ned.

"Me sister married a lad from down 'ere, an' I used ter come on holidays. Welsh isn't that hard really."

The other two turned to look at him in disbelief, spreading (in accordance with their evil wizarding mission statement) terror and mayhem among the drivers coming the other way, who wished only to peacefully occupy their own side of the road and resented the intrusion of a rusty, mud-encrusted *Mondeo* into their personal space.

After the noise died down, Ned put on a CD and the journey continued peacefully.

"Look, there's the *Sprinter*... Parked outside that pub, in the busy car park. I don't suppose... " suggested the driver.

"Na, too risky," said Ned. "But I bet that there will be another pub along shortly." And there was. A lovely looking place but with no cars outside. The bar was quiet when the three wizards entered except for a group of four characters all dressed in identical shabby black walking clothes, clustered around the dartboard. They seemed to be arguing. The junior assistant headed straight for the bar.

"*Tres crwrw, plis,*" he said, showing off his Welsh.

The rather chubby, bearded publican looked bemused.

"*Tres crwrw,*" the junior repeated.

"Sorry mate, I'm from Essex," said the publican.

"Where's that?" hissed the junior assistant into the assistant assistant's ear.

"Dunno. He sounds like a southerner to me. Better count yer change."

"Three pints, please," said Ned. "Quiet in here today."

"Not as busy as I'd like, that's true. Just that bunch over there. Irish I think they are, but whatever you do, don't get between them and the dartboard."

"Right," said Ned.

"Don't start that again," groaned the junior.

"I'll get another round in but one of yer should watch the road to see if the *Sprinter* goes past."

"We get quite a lot of joggers,"* called the publican, who had been listening.

A couple of hours later, the *Sprinter* roared past the window. There was a rush to the door, a slamming of car doors, and the *Mondeo* left the car park as quickly as it could, which was (it has to be said), not as quickly as it might have managed earlier in the day.

The dark-clad group walked without haste to the window.

"I know we are supposed to be on holiday, Laeg," said the one called Finn.

"Too right we are!" asserted Diarmid.

"The Tuatha are never off duty," Laeg said firmly.

"I am sure that they were from Caer Surdin. I recognized them from when we got involved in that scrap at the Helvyndelve," said Finn.

"Did you now, Finn," said Laeg, slowly.

"Do you think we should call Erald? Since he's our leader?"

"No, but I think we'll turn south now."

"Suits me," said Diarmid. "I know of some great pubs round Llanelwedd."

There was a general agreement and soon the pub again bore a close resemblance to the *Marie Celeste*. The publican, who had been the master of said ship,** heaved a sigh of relief at their departure.

---

*   Could be a running gag, this one. Sorry.

** And was now in hiding from the insurance company.

The *Sprinter* left the main road and rejoined a dual carriageway, then followed the brown tourist signs for the Gower, and before long, the passengers were enjoying the scenic delights of the first registered Area of Outstanding National Beauty in the whole of the United Kingdom.

"Where's Grotbags' place then?" asked Haemar.

"I think it's going to be down that lane," Fungus told him.

"How can you tell?" asked Scar.

"Because she has just crashed her broomstick into that haylage bale, as she was looking at us," replied Fungus, winding up his window to reduce the volume of complaints coming in from outside.

Grizelda of the Third Pentangle (known outside her hearing as Grotbags) straightened her clothing, bashed a dent from the regulation hat, and approached the *Sprinter*.

"Is that a taxi?" she demanded. "I can't stand taxis."

"Der," answered Eddie.

"You bein' funny, lad?" Grizelda's tone became dangerous.

"Der."

"Hi, Aunt Dot! It's us, Linda and Chris," called Linda, from the back of the minibus.

"You've just saved yer driver from a fate worse than frog. Should've yelled out sooner. Who are this lot wi' yer then?"

"Hi, Grizelda," Fungus answered.

"Wotcher," said Haemar.

"Der."

"Snore," Felldyke contributed.

"A star shines on the hour of our meeting," tried GG.

"Oh no it doesn't. It's still daylight. Oh no, please tell me it's not that lot. I had to abandon my last garden, cos it never recovered from their gig."

"Took us ages to get over it too," muttered Haemar. "The catering was lousy."

"Not the only thing that were lousy. An' am I hearing right that you 'ad a bigger gig at the Helvyndelve? And only went and trashed the Throne of the Mountain King?" asked Grizelda.

"Well," started Fungus.

"It was an accident," offered GG.

"Accidents like that seem to follow you."

"The ones who were following us had an accident," Fungus said softly.

"Der," remarked Eddie.

"Who?" Grizelda lowered her tone and looked around suspiciously. "Tell me yer haven't brought the PRS* down here."

"Some of the Caer Surdin lads from Keswick followed us down here," Fungus told her, quietly. Haemar glared at him.

"What on earth for?"

"I'll tell you inside," said Fungus, looking around furtively.

"So, let me get this straight. You are looking fer a mad dwarf called Waccibacci who holds the secret of the meaning of life and makes magical thrones in 'is spare time?" asked Grizelda when they were all seated around the kitchen table in her cottage and the chocolate digestives were vanishing fast.

Haemar nodded.

"Well, it's a different quest to the normal ones, I'll grant yer."

"What do you mean the normal ones?" asked Felldyke.

"Well usually, people have to rescue distressed virgins, fight off dragons, recover lost grails, or fight to clear bridges from evil toll collectors."

"No one's tried the Severn Bridge recently, I take it," grumbled Haemar, who had been over that way last year.

"And we are running out of dragons, even here in Wales."

"Oh I dunno," answered Haemar. "You should have seen her who ran the B&B that I stopped in last year. She didn't bother with a toaster, just glared at the bread until it spontaneously combusted."

"Saved 'er on the electricity then," said Scar, to be helpful.

---

* The Performing Rights Society, who rigorously enforce the right of musicians to be paid if you enjoy their work by hammering on every door where they can detect a radio, and demanding a fee for playing music while you work. Even in a van. Even if you are not at work, but thinking of going, maybe tomorrow. Even if you work at home. Or in space. Or down a mine. Rumors that they stole the secrets of the Tardis, while Doctor Who was looking for his checkbook to pay the fees, are probably just rumors. But I turn off the radio when I start typing.

"So how long are you stopping for?" asked Grizelda.

Behind her, the fridge creaked in an ominous fashion and all eyes swiveled to watch it. But the fridge, and everyone else, subsided.

"Only a few days, if that's OK," replied Fungus. "We'll try an' find this guy, and then get back north."

"Fine. But you will 'ave to keep quiet about yer quest, cos I get a lot of the local witches callin' in 'ere all the time."

"What are you doin' down here, Aunt Dot?" asked Chris.

"Well, I run the local flyin' school."

"At Swansea Airport on the Common?"

"Na, in the back garden 'ere, an' along the coast. See, the local girls weren't much cop wi' the broomsticks, so I make a livin' teachin' 'em," Grizelda explained.

"Don't you get in the way of the planes?" asked Chris.

They all looked up as a micro-light aircraft, hopefully in the hands of a new student, wobbled erratically and noisily overhead.

"More the other way roun'. An' I ring Swansea Air Traffic now if I'm takin' a formation out. They used ter just laugh at me but then one of the controllers flew over Rhossili Down when I were teachin' a bunch of the girls how to ridge soar, like the hang gliders do... After they let 'im out of the psychiatric wing of the hospital, 'e started takin' me phone calls more seriously."

"Der," put in Eddie.

"I think Eddie's ready to crash," said Fungus.

"The way 'e drives, I think he's always ready to crash," said Scar to GG.

"What happened to 'im?" asked Grizelda, curiously.

"He had a run in with yer sister," Haemar explained.

"He'd have done better to run out. Quick."

"Well, it did us a favor. We've got a tour bus now, as a disguise."

"What are you going to be disguised as?" asked Grizelda.

"Musicians, we thought," said Felldyke.

"That's a good disguise. Now, I wonder where Ben has got to... "

"Where did he go?" asked Linda, who liked her uncle.

"I sent 'im into the village for some pasta. He's probably stopped off at the pub for a quick one."

"So he'll be out all night then? Best we go to the chippy, lads," ordered Fungus.

"I am afraid you'll be disappointed." Grizelda told them.

"Why? Is it rubbish?"

"Chips are fine. But they 'ave never heard of a steak pudding."*

"How can you have a chippy without steak puddings?" asked Felldyke, alarmed.

"Sounds perverse, I know. Go for the fish, instead."

The Banned looked at each other in dismay. Strangers in a strange land.

Ben, occasional wizard and more frequently husband to Grizelda, stopped to a brief rest when his somewhat unsteady rambles brought him to the top of the lane leading to the cottage. The daylight was fading, and the shadows cast by the bushes and trees spread across the lane. For this reason, and absolutely nothing whatsoever to do with the amount of beer he had drunk, he failed to notice the saffron-clad monks until they silently appeared beside him.

"Om, please, what is your name?" asked one.

"Ben," replied Ben. "Why?"

"Om. Just checking."

"But I know who I am!"

"Good," replied the monk, nodding to one of his colleagues, who reached out towards Ben from behind, just as a third monk arrived, festooned with a long length of rope. "It would be terrible for my karma if I made a mistake."

"Your Korma?" asked Ben, before slipping to the ground with a peaceful smile.

"You can't curry favor from us that way," observed the monk with the rope, observing the now sleeping body at his feet.

At the far end of the lane, a mud-colored *Mondeo* slid to a halt. In the dusk, the occupants could see the *Sprinter* parked up in the yard of the isolated cottage. The three wizards were so busy watching, that they failed to notice the rustles in the bushes, and the sound of stealthy feet all around.

---

* A particular local gourmet specialty of the north-west of England. Exiles, forced by a lack of work, a bad horoscope, poor karma or other awful reasons to live in other parts of the UK, frequently have to call their relatives and beg for food parcels of this staple diet.

The junior assistant turned, as a saffron-robed body slid gently onto the back seat next to him.

"Who are you?" he asked, quietly, as the figure motioned him into silence with a brilliant, and gentle smile before employing a Zen touch to send the junior into a deep and refreshing sleep.

"We are the Ben Buddhists and we are commandeering this vehicle."

Ned looked around, startled by the soft voice.

"'Ere, who are you? Get out of this car!"

The Ben Buddhist smiled again, bowed politely, and gently placed a hand on the back of each front seat.

"I am so sorry, but we need to borrow the car."

The hands reached out and touched a spot on the back of the necks of the occupants of the front seats.

The driver's side front door of the car opened, spilling its now sleeping occupant into a pool of muddy water.

"Oh dear," remarked a second saffron-colored monk. "His karma is a little poor today."

"That's what you get for driving around in a *Mondeo* this old. Come on, let's put all four of them in the boot," suggested the first.

"That would be inappropriate. Our reincarnated leader is one of them."

"True. Him on the back seat then, and the rest in the boot."

"Simple as a koan."

"Om Mani Padme Hum."

"Indeed."

"What's on the CD player?" asked the first monk.

"Nirvana."

"Excellent."

Two other monks appeared in the gloom of the car and, with a well-trussed Ben on the back seat between the four, the monks all crowded into the *Mondeo*, levitated it and turned it around by the power of their chanting. They drove off into the gathering night with their captives.

CHAPTER FIVE

"Shush." Grizelda hissed at Fungus and Haemar.

They had joined her in the kitchen in the middle of the night, after Grizelda had heard some strange noises coming from the garden.

"It could just be Ben tryin' to get back in quietly," Haemar suggested.

Grizelda silently opened the window a mere crack. From outside came a weird array of snorting, coughing, and occasional mild vomiting noises.

"He *has* been a long time down the pub. That would account for it," agreed Fungus.

"I know me 'usband," Grizelda told them.

Fungus and Haemar exchanged glances.

"Oh don't be daft. I know 'e likes a drink. Sometimes he does get drunk. But 'e doesn't make sounds like *that.*"

There came an industrial strength stomach rumble.

"Dealing with that indigestion would need a tanker full of *Gaviscon.*"

Then came a long, low belch, which lasted a very long time.

"Definitely not Ben. Even drunk, 'e's got better manners than that," announced Grizelda.

She shook free her wrists from the sleeves of her cardigan and clicked her finger joints. Fungus and Haemar winced at the crackling noise, reminiscent of a pump-action shotgun as favored by the local traffic police for enforcing minor parking restrictions. Grizelda opened the back door, Haemar drew his sword.

"Who's there?" demanded Grizelda, loudly.

"Wha?" came the reply, in a deep, gravelly voice.

"I said, who's there!" repeated Grizelda.

"Dai."

"Threats, already?" asked Haemar, readying for a fight to the last. Fungus was right behind him; after all it was safer than being in front of Haemar in a fight.

"No," Grizelda restrained them. "Round here, Dai is a name, not a war cry."

"Why would you want to call anyone Death?" asked Fungus.

"The Scots do. For them it's a surname. Old, established."

"Well it would be. Death's been around for a long time now."

"No," Grizelda's patience with them was slipping. "It's spelt D-A-I; Dai."

"You call me just then?" came the deep, clearly drunken voice from the bottom of the garden.

"What are you doing in my garden?" asked Grizelda.

"Everyone's got to be somewhere," slurred the voice.

"Can't argue with 'im there," said Haemar.

Various noises emanated from the darkness, as the invisible Dai drew closer.

"Good grief!" said Fungus. "It's a dragon!"

"A drunken dragon!" said Haemar, in awe.

"I'm not drunk. Sobering up, now. Was drunk though. Hey. Got anything to drink?"

"Coffee perhaps?" suggested Grizelda. Even she was taken aback by the turn of events.

"Only if you've got some chocolate digestives."

"Not as many as I did 'ave," Grizelda answered, with a nasty look at Haemar, who blanched.

"I'll put the kettle on," he said quickly.

"Fine, but it won't suit you."

Twenty minutes, two packs of biscuits, and a lot of coffee later, Dai was able to converse more clearly.

In the flickering light of the gas-lit kitchen, he was not too intimidating. Bright red in color, and about six feet long, his breath steamed gently from his nostrils, but he was clearly non-aggressive.

"So, where do you live, then?" asked Fungus.

"Got a place at Pen-bre, by the coast there, in the country park. It's part of the old bomb factory, so it's underground, which we dragons like: fireproof which is useful, and the noise is kept down too."

"What noise? The visitors to the country park?"

"Well, a bit. And the Motorway Traffic Police used to sneak onto the race circuit next door at night when no one was about. The engine noises were terrible. But mostly it's cos I don't want my lair discovered, and I like loud music."

"Not another one," groaned Grizelda in dismay, as the faces of the founders of The Banned Underground lit up.

"What are you into?" asked Haemar.

"Manics and Stereophonics, of course,"

"We play *Dakota* a bit in our sets," enthused Fungus.

"You guys in a band, then? I used to be in one too."

"What did you play?" asked Haemar, intrigued.

"Didn't know how to play anything at first. So they gave me the bass guitar and let me do the light show too. Cut my front claws down specially, to get on the frets. What do you play?"

"Used to be mainly jazz. Which I loved." said Fungus, a little sadly. "But there's a good market in blues and blues rock. Just good tasteful classics."

"What happened to your band, then?" asked Haemar, opening another packet of chocolate digestives.

"Oh, you know. Musical differences I suppose. The lead guitarist went strange."

"They all seem to do that," agreed Haemar, the vocalist.

"Started listening to some stuff, progressive rock he called it, though it seemed a big step backwards to me."

Fungus and Haemar looked at each other.

"We got ours away from that."

"Hey," said Dai, "How did you do that? If we'd managed it, it could have saved the band!"

"He got locked up for ten years."

"What did he do?"

"Nah. Didn't commit a crime, he just offended someone in authority."

"Same thing really, then," said Dai, the social commentator.

Grizelda, no longer frightened, decided to seek out Ben.

"You lot, all three of you, stay quiet. I need to look for Ben."

Grizelda composed herself and, with a virtuoso display of grunting, wheezing, and snorting settled into a trance.

"Is she a dragon too?" asked Dai.

"Can be when she's in a bad mood. Why?" asked Haemar.

"Because she sounds like my mum did when she was asleep."

The three regarded Grizelda with expressions of awe, astonishment, and distrust – mingled with a bit of fear and respect, too.

"All is dark," she announced, awakening.

Fungus, Haemar and Dai glanced out of the window into the clear, cold, and very dark night sky, but made no comment. Dai had decided Grizelda needed to be handled in the same way as a venomous snake, or a traffic policeman.

"However, I saw some light."

The three looked back out of the window.

"Ben has been seized."

"By the police?"

"Worse. A group of orange-colored monks grabbed him and drove off with him. They also took those lads from Keswick that followed you down here."

"Well whoever they are, they are welcome to them three. But who are they, an' what would they want Ben for?" wondered Haemar, after giving Fungus a nasty glare. Not being told about the dark wizards still rankled.

"Think I know," said Dai.

Grizelda, Fungus and Haemar all swung round to look at him, and he leaned backwards from the weight of their stares, falling off his stool and landing heavily on the floor, twisting his tail.

"Ow."

"Who are they?" asked Grizelda.

"They are a bunch of weirdoes," Dai said.

"We guessed that. Kidnapping two wizards an' a couple of apprentices isn't for the wholly sane," Grizelda replied.

"They have a place near Saundersfoot, big house, set well back from the road. Call themselves the Ben Buddhists."

"Shouldn't that be Zen Buddhists?" asked Fungus.

"Na. Different sect. This lot believe in the re-incarnation of their leader, Ben, who will rise again and help them to world domination."

"I begin to see a connection," said Grizelda.

"What did you say he was called? Your husband, the one they took?"

"Ben."

"Then I guess that they have kidnapped him to see if he is their true leader. They do it all the time." Dai told them.

"And if he is not?"

"Dunno. But you won't see him again."

Grizelda turned to look at Fungus and Haemar.

"We've already got a quest," they said quickly.

"We'll sort this out in the morning. Get some sleep," Grizelda ordered, before leaving the three musicians alone.

Fungus and Haemar looked at each other, clearly taken with their new friend.

"So," offered Fungus, "do you fancy tryin' out with us for a couple of gigs?"

"Really?" asked Dai. "I'd enjoy that to no end. Better nip home now, while it's still dark, to get my bass."

"What 'ave yer got?" asked Haemar.

"Fender Precision bass."

"Contradiction in terms that," muttered Haemar.

"I need to get off. It's not far to the lair, but I don't like flying in the daylight now. Too much air traffic," Dai said.

"Are you fit to fly?" asked Fungus, dubiously.

"I'll be fine. Best hurry, be daybreak any minute, and the RAF start practicing at the bombing range at the end of the country park early these days. Probably so that the miss-hits don't hit the tourists."

"'Friendly fire', don't they call that?"

"Have you ever been out for a drink with *The Cruise Missiles*? Don't. A less friendly bunch than that doesn't exist. Always getting into fights, and then exploding."

The RAF, however, were wide awake already, and busy on their radios.

"Pen-bre Firing Range, this is Victor Kilo One Six inbound from RAF Valley."

"Victor Kilo, Pen-bre Range. Go ahead."

"Pen-bre Range, Victor Kilo is a training flight inbound for strike mission, five minutes to run from the east, height 800 feet."

"Victor Kilo, Pen-bre Range. Radar contact acquired. Your strike clearance is approved. Be aware of local traffic at your 10 o'clock, same height."

"Pen-bre Range, Victor Kilo. Strike approval copied. Looking for the traffic – AND WHAT THE HELL IS THAT!? ARMING WEAPONS SYSTEMS!"

"Victor Kilo, are you visual on the traffic? Can you identify it?"

"IT'S A RED DRAGON, CARRYING A BASS GUITAR IN ITS FRONT CLAWS!"

"Victor Kilo One Six, Pen-bre Range. Your strike clearance is cancelled. Repeat, your strike clearance is cancelled. Disarm weapons systems and return to valley training base at once. Confirm instructions."

"Got my bass."
"Have any trouble, Dai?" asked Fungus.
"Na. Saw a couple of the RAF boys, but I don't think that they saw me."
"OK, let's get some kip while we can."
Sleep beckoned for all.

The teenagers were the first ones awake the next morning.
"Aunt DOT! Wake up!"
"Linda? Wassamatta?"
"There's a dragon in the kitchen!"
"So? Don't wake 'im up. He's murder with the bikkies."
"But it's a DRAGON!"
"He's called Dai, an' he'll have a hell of a hangover, so just be quiet."
Breakfast was a bit late that morning. Linda and Chris were bemused by the appearance of Dai the drinking dragon (whose breakfast of malt whisky and chocolate digestives had even impressed The Banned Underground,) while Eddie ("Der") and the other witches had taken it all in their stride. Grizelda had called for some reinforcements, and two witches, dressed in caftans and *Doc Martin* boots had turned up in a battered coach, fortunately with an additional supply of what seemed to be Dai's staple diet. The chocolate biscuits.
"Right," pronounced Grizelda, "this is now a Council of War."
She raised her arms and purple flames flared all around the windows and doors.
"I have enchanted the exits, to provide us with protection."
"Who's gonna protect us against her?" Scar asked Felldyke.
"Dunno."
"Der."
"It seems to me that we 'ave two tasks before us," Grizelda said.
There was muttered agreement.
"My priority is to be rescuin' Ben. But Fungus is charged wi' finding this dwarf wi' the strange name, an' since The Grey Mage of Caer Surdin sent three lads after 'im, that's clearly important, too."
"So," said Fungus, "we split up?"

"Only way to do it. Me, an' the witches, an' Linda an' Chris will look for Ben, an' you lot go seek yer dwarf," Grizelda ordered.

They all looked round at each other, but only Linda and Chris were dubious about their options.

"Are you sure we should be with you, Aunt?" asked Linda.

"Yer have the Wards of Lingard. We are more likely to face magical attack, so best yer are wi' us."

Haemar nodded in agreement. He had been on the wrong end of Linda's tongue in the last adventure and didn't fancy a repeat performance. Besides, the teenagers might put a dampener on the visits to the pub.

"Now, what ideas are there about where we look?"

"My name's Imelda," said the older of the two young witches. "I live near Tenby, and the Ben Buddhists have been very active near my place recently. Now there's going to be a big student rave near us in the next few days, so they will probably be out looking for converts."

The musicians in the room shuddered at the news of the rave.

"What's wrong with that?" asked the other witch, who was called Erica. She quite liked dance music and club anthems, and hence was viewed by most there with some suspicion.

"Do you know why students like dance music?" asked GG.

"Why?"

"Cos they don't have to think while they drink while they dance."

"They all seem the same to me," agreed Dai.

"Students?"

"Dance tracks."

"Right," agreed Haemar.

"So, we head down that way in the coach. It's been converted into a camper, so we'll manage OK," Imelda suggested.

Chris, who was rather taken with Erica, nodded his agreement.

"Now," said Grizelda, "what about you lot?"

"What is your quest?" asked Dai.

"We seek Waccibacci," said Scar.

"Well I –" started Imelda, but was shut up under Grizelda's glare.

"Waccibacci, as far as we know, is an itinerant dwarf who combines furniture making and Zen mastery, and moved down here some years ago," Fungus explained.

"I think that I've met him," said Dai.

"We think that he was a lecturer for a while at Swansea University."

"That's where I met him," said Dai.

55

"But after that, he moved on, deeper into west Wales... *What did you say?*"

"I've met him. Just because I'm a dragon doesn't mean I lack erudition, you know."

"So where is he?"

"Oh, I don't know at the moment. He sort of moves around a lot. Solves a problem here, contributes some carving of furniture there, teaches a bit further on. Likes to keep on the move, he said. Something about a 'rolling stone'."

"Keef? Mick? Ronnie?" queried Scar.

"Gathering Kate Moss, it could have been."

"I see that, yes," agreed Scar.

"Dai," asked Fungus, "have you any idea where we could find him?"

"Well, what we could do is... "

"Yes?"

"Is... "

"YES?"

"Is... "

"What!"

"Go and look for him."

"Can't you just tell he's a bass player?" groaned Haemar.

"Hey, can you really tell I'm a bass player? Does that mean I get to play at the gig?"

"What gig?" asked Scar.

"The gig I've set up for you through my mate in Builth. There's like a real ale festival."

Several heads lifted and swiveled to offer Dai their rapt attention.

"And they need a band. So I suggested you guys to my mate this morning – well, us – if you'll let me join you."

Grizelda hid her head in her hands, as The Banned Underground stared at the still drunken dragon.

"You've got us a paying gig at a beer festival?" breathed Fungus.

"Yeah, is that all right?" worried Dai.

"I'd say you've just joined The Banned Underground, boy!"

The kitchen echoed to the clamor of the other band members, who roared their approval, and promptly started toasting their new comrade.

"And it's not only beer. They sell furniture, too," Dai told them.

"Strange combination," observed GG.

"Not really. They sell a lot of these weird wood-sculptured things. People are more likely to buy them when they're drunk. So it's a perfect Waccibacci market place."

"I've heard that too," agreed Imelda, patting her pockets as if reminded of something.

"Der."

"We'll start this afternoon," said Fungus. "That'll give you the morning to learn the set list."

"What about the actual songs?"

"Oh, you'll pick those up as we go along."

Soon afterwards there was frantic activity, as the minibus was loaded with essentials.

"Der..."

"Eddie says he can only get the bass in the *Sprinter* with us and the rest of the kit," called Felldyke.

"So how's Dai goin' ter ride with us?" asked GG.

"He can't fly. Not in daylight," worried Scar.

"An' he's probably too drunk, as well," said Felldyke, slurring the words slightly himself.

"I know," suggested GG. "There's a trailer round the back. If Grizelda will lend us that, he can ride on that. It's not rainin' or anything."

Dai, when approached, was unconcerned about the prospect. Actually, he just snored, loudly. Grizelda was so relieved at the thought of regaining access to the chocolate digestive supply, while there still was such a thing, that she, too, agreed. So the two parties set off on their separate quests.

The witches and the teenagers boarded the brightly painted camper coach, with Imelda driving and Grizelda navigating. Chris explored the rear of the coach, with Erica. The *Sprinter*, now with a bright red dragon sleeping in the trailer behind it, negotiated the narrow lanes in search of the motorway, while the satnav – which insisted that the only possible route was to get a ferry to Dublin from Swansea Docks, and return by Fishguard – was reduced to a sulk by Eddie's intransigence.

Approaching the chosen route however, they ran into trouble.

"It's a police van. Flashing its lights at us," Scar called out.

"Better pull over, I suppose. Into that lay-by," advised Haemar from the front.

"Der," agreed Eddie, pulling over.

"What's this on the trailer then?" demanded the policeman.

"He's a dragon, officer," explained GG.

"I can see that," retorted the constable.

"Then why did you ask me?"

"Don't be smart."

"Der."

"It's not tied on properly," alleged the constable.

"He doesn't like to be tied down," GG replied.

"What?"

"He's right, officer," Dai called.

"Who said that?"

"I did. And I can assure you that I am holding on very tight. When I don't nod off."

"Stay there. I'm going to go back to my van and think about this," instructed the officer.

"Oh no," groaned the dragon.

"I know that guy. At his thinking speed, we'll still be here when the tax disc runs out, and he can give yer a ticket for that instead."

"Der."

Dai stood up on the trailer, and stretched his wings. The police van quickly turned its emergency lights off, and without performing certain basic safety checks (mirror, hairstyle, sunglasses, signal, maneuver,) pulled out onto the carriageway and accelerated away as fast as it could, leaving chaos on the road in its wake.

"What was all that about, then?" asked Haemar.

"See," replied Dai, "when Waccibacci came down here from the Midlands, a bunch of dwarves followed him. Needed jobs, didn't they? And the only things that they were any good at were drinking, fighting, and reckless driving. They were naturals for the traffic police, got taken on at once. But, being dwarves, they still know a real dragon when they see one, and he probably didn't fancy what I'd do to his paperwork."

"What would that be?"

"Set fire to it," grinned the drunken dragon.

The Banned Underground piled back into the van, ready to set off again.

"What's on the CD now?" asked Fungus.

"It's The Police. *Every Breath You Take.*"

"Can we skip that one?"

The garishly painted coach rumbled past them, Linda waving her arm at them out of the window.

"Look, there's Linda waving to us," said Scar, pleased.

"Der."

"And Chris, at the back window. What's he waving?"

"Something of that Erica's, I think," said Scar, slowly.

"Bit brave with Grizelda in the front."

Meanwhile, at a hidden location, several of our other characters were awakening.

"Ned? Ned?" hissed the assistant assistant.

"Who's that?" groaned Ned.

"It's me, Ned."

"No, I'm Ned."

"Well, I'm _me_," explained the assistant assistant.

"Very enlightening, that is. Oh, it's you two idiots. Should 'ave known. Even being kidnapped, I can't get rid of yer."

"Ned, where are we?"

"'Ow do yer expect me ter know? I've bin asleep," complained Ned.

"I think we are in a cellar. There's one small window over there, an' a door. But it's locked," said the junior.

"Right then. Let's be out of 'ere."

"Through the window? It's a bit small."

"Through the door. Remember some of yer trainin', and 'magic it' open," instructed Ned.

"Didn't think of that," said the junior assistant.

"Good thinking, that, boss," added the assistant assistant.

"Wake me up when you've done it." Ned closed his eyes.

"Ned, door's open."

"That were quick! Well done."

"Er, no, it weren't locked actually," admitted the junior.

"What?"

"The handle opens the wrong way. Tried it by accident, an' the door opened."

"Just like that?" asked Ned.

"Yeah."

"Well, we need ter think about this."

"Can't we do that outside?" suggested the junior.

"Lissen. We are in a cellar. The door is left open. 'Try Running Away, Please'. That spells 'trap' ter me. So, let's be careful out there, shall we?"

"Good thinking, that, boss," said the assistant assistant.

"One of yer, open the door. Just a crack."

"Done that."

"Right. What can yer see through the opening?" asked Ned.

"It's a corridor. Not very well lit."

"Now, stick your 'and out, an' bring it back in again."

"OK." said the assistant assistant.

"Next, try it wi' yer leg."

"Hey, it's like that dance innit? Now I just jump outside," cried the assistant assistant.

Clang, came a solid noise from the corridor.

"AAAAAARRRRGGGGGHHHH"

"Go on, what's happened to him?" asked Ned, wearily. And warily.

Muffled noises came from the corridor.

"A big bucket fell on his head. Full of pink paint," explained the junior.

The stricken one staggered back into the room, and fell over, the bucket rolling across the floor.

"Now it's your turn," said Ned to the junior.

The junior carefully stuck his head out of the door. When nothing alarming or amusing happened to him, he carefully slid the rest of his body out into the corridor. Ned joined him at the door. The corridor led away in each direction, with a set of steps a few yards away from the door at each end. Refitting his glasses, the assistant assistant joined them.

"There's paint smeared all over me glasses."

"That's a bonus."

"Why, Ned?"

"Well, now they've got a rose tint, so you won't see anything unpleasant coming."

"That's reassuring. Not."

"Let's go that way," suggested Ned.

"Why?" asked the junior.

"Why not?"

"What's wrong wi' this way?"

"Probably nothing. But I've chosen *this* way, so go. You first," ordered Ned.

"Why?"

"Why not?" asked Ned.

"We've just done that one," the junior said.

"Look, I'm the boss 'ere. There's a choice of two ways to go, an' I say we look at that one first."

"Well don't blame me if we should've gone the other way."

"Just walk," ordered Ned.

They walked, very carefully and in single file to the steps at the end of the corridor, climbed the steps, and turned a left hand corner as they did so. Then at the solid brick wall, they turned around, and walked down the steps, past their cell door, and back along the corridor. In silence. Except for an occasional muffled snigger.

They reached the other set of steps, climbed them, turned around to the right, and ended at a solid brick wall. The sniggering stopped abruptly.

"That's not right," said the assistant assistant.

"Curious, certainly," said Ned.

"Look! There's a small table with a bottle on it," said the junior wizard. He peered closely at it. "It says, 'Drink Me' on the label."

"Don't touch it. There's a sick mind at work here," Ned told his juniors.

"The Grey Mage we work for at the accountants?"

"Probably not," Ned disagreed reluctantly.

"It could be one of 'is tests."

"The fact there's no paper or calculators should be a clue. *Put that down!*" ordered Ned.

But the assistant assistant had drained the bottle. He burped, loudly. Steam came out of his ears, and his two fellows backed away sharply. The steam coalesced around his ears, writhed, and became two very large white, rabbit-shaped ears. Next moment, his hands became coated in white fur.

"Yer mother warned yer about that happenin'," said Ned, backing off again as the stricken one found his shoes exploding under the pressure of the changes.

"But the label said 'Drink Me'!" wailed the afflicted one.

"That was a first fer you then. Doin' what yer were told," said the unsympathetic junior.

"He's quite in fashion though," mused Ned.

"Why's that?"

"Well, all that white fur. Aint it this season's new look?"

"Now look," grumbled the assistant assistant.

"Isn't that a clothes shop? See, yer are into fashion after all."

Ned was trying to examine the wall.

"Hop out of the way, a minute, can't yer?"

"Oh, very funny."

"An' stop rabbitin'."

"This is what I can expect, is it, now? An' this is from me friends an' colleagues," complained the rabbit.

"Let us be a minute," ordered Ned.

"Can't stop, can yer? Here I am, afflicted with a terrible curse."

"No yer not. That's not a terrible curse," Ned told him.

"What is, then?"

Ned told him, and the were-rabbit went quiet.

"Wish you 'adn't told me that. That's terrible."

"Yer did ask."

"Still."

"We'll sort you out when I've got us out of this jam," promised Ned.

"Thought it were a trap. Wouldn't mind some jam though, I'm hungry."

"Don't fancy jam," grumbled the assistant assistant.

"Well, you wouldn't now you're part rabbit."

"Jam," mused Ned. "Jam jar. Sick joke... I wonder."

"Go on, Boss."

"Well, when is a jar not ajar?"

"Is that one of them Zen things? Like the sound of one hand clapping?" asked the assistant assistant.

"How can one hand clap?" asked the junior.

Ned raised his right hand in the traditional way, then spun round and clapped the junior wizard across the left ear, making a loud clap.

"Just like that," he said, with some satisfaction. And then threw the bottle at the brick wall. The brick wall shimmered, and turned into a brick wall – with a door.

"Just like that," he repeated, while his two aids looked at him with some awe.

"Why didn't yer say yer could do that?" asked the one with the rabbit ears.

"You didn't wait to find out," answered Ned.

Ned then approached the door with some care. He made several mystic passes over the door with his right hand, chanting under his breath as he did so. The two apprentices looked awed.

"When did yer get taught to do that?" the junior asked.

"It was an optional extra on the part of the course which explained with-holding tax on rental income. It were so arcane and impenetrable that mystic door opening were simple by comparison."

"Didn't work, though," observed the second apprentice, waving his rabbit ears about.

"Says who?" grinned Ned, and as he put out his hand the door vanished.

In its place stood a saffron robed monk, who bowed.

"Om. I felt the force of your spell," he said politely. "And even though it had no effect – "

The apprentices both permitted themselves a snigger.

" – I thought that you had acquired enough merit to be interviewed."

The monk inspected all three, and with a brief twist of the wrist banished the were-rabbit's accouterments.

"Wow, thanks!" exclaimed the no-longer-afflicted one.

A door was opened in the hall behind the monk, allowing a burst of loud rock music to escape, before the door was hastily closed again.

"Om. Would you please follow me? You see, you have come at a rather special time. Tonight is one of the Masters' events."

"Like the Ryder Cup?" asked the junior.

"No. Our spiritual masters."

"Could yer offer some enlightenment?" asked Ned.

"Om. If you are allowed to remain with us, I am sure that such enlightenment will be offered."

The monk led the three across the hall and through a doorway into a small sitting room.

"Who are you, an' why did yer kidnap us?" asked Ned.

The monk appeared to go into a brief trance, before replying.

"Om. We are the Ben Buddhists. Unfortunately, your Karma placed you on the fringe of one of our essential operations, and it was deemed better for your safety to bring you here."

"Yer could 'ave just left us," pointed out the junior wizard.

"As corpses, I agree," said the monk, with a gentle smile.

He received no reply.

"But as you appeared to be in contact with the object of our search, we decided to offer an alternative option. And your escape from the cells shows me that such a choice was in fact pre-ordained."

"So what's yer game, then?" asked Ned.

"Om. As an organization, we are dedicated to a number of tasks, approved by the Charity Commission and written into our Articles of Association."

"Such as?" enquired the junior.

"Om. We seek peaceful meditation, withdrawal from the stress of the physical world, and practice spiritual activities while we await the return of our leader, Ben."

"Ben?"

"Ben." confirmed the monk.

"What spiritual activity?" asked the junior wizard, carefully.

"Om. We meditate, seeking union with the One within trance, and practice the ability to protect ourselves by the use of extreme force employed on a casual but karmically sound basis."

"Ah," replied the one who had just been enlightened (by a small but significant weight loss.)

"What is your plan when you find yer Ben?" asked Ned, who was well aware of the identity of Grizelda's husband and was beginning to have a sneaking suspicion.

"We will have no plan. Ben will have a plan. But the objective of this plan will be to achieve total domination of our society."

"Yer mean we will all be like you lot?" asked Ned.

"No. Only those found worthy will join. The rest of the population will be allowed to serve us."

"Ah."

"What are you going to do wi' us now?" asked the junior.

"Well, we are preparing for a major religious ceremony. But right at the moment, we are struggling with the external auditors. The accounts are needed for the Charity Commission, and one of our major assets has failed a stock take. That's why I cannot offer you the traditional chocolate digestives. There appears to be an unexplained shortage."

"We are accountants," said Ned. "Can we help?"

"Om. Perhaps. We engaged a new firm this year and the manager seems a bit officious. Since he's well connected locally, we are reluctant to give him the normal treatment for an officious auditor."

"What's that then?"

"Use him for target practice." The gentle saffron-clad monk allowed a five point throwing star to drop from his sleeve into his hand and, with a casual flick of the wrist, spun it across the room where it neatly beheaded the one open flower in a vase before sinking deep into the wall. The three gulped.

"Om. Deadheading helps the rest of the buds bloom," intoned the monk, and bowed deeply to the flower.

"We try to be helpful to our clients. It's in the mission statement," said the junior. The other two looked at him curiously.

"When did yer read that?" asked Ned.

The assistant assistant kept quiet. As a taxi driver, he had no mission statement, but despite this obvious advantage was not normally helpful.

"It's on the wall in reception," the junior said.

"I've never noticed it."

"Yer too busy ogling the receptionist, that's why."

"What, that dragon?"

"You keep a dragon as office receptionist?" asked the monk, with a little more respect in his voice.

"Well, yer know, helps keep the customers in line."

"Then you may be able to help, for we suspected dragon involvement in the loss of this particular line of stock."

"Boss is always moanin' that there's never a choccie bikkie when 'e wants one, I know that. Even though they arrive from Tesco by the van load."

"Please, wait here." The monk bowed, and left the room.

"Why did you say we could help?" hissed the junior. "We are accountants, I've never chased a dragon in me life."

"Yer should always be open to new experiences," argued Ned.

"I'd rather chase a dragon than be targeted," agreed the assistant assistant.

"I've chased rock trolls, fire trolls, bog trolls, goblins, dwarves an' elves. I've been in the tax office with The Grey Mage. I've even fought the mind-destroying bureaucracy of Companies House. Dragons can't be too hard," boasted Ned.

The door opened again, and the same monk bowed to the three.

"Om. You have been invited to witness the event. Afterwards, we can discuss our audit issues. Please, follow me." He bowed, and turned out of the room. The wizards of Caer Surdin followed him. At a tall pair of double doors, the monk turned back.

"Please, enter. Walk in quietly and respectfully, turn to your left, and stand against the wall. Do not then move or speak, or interrupt the ceremony."

The monk opened one door, and all slipped inside. They looked across a large temple hall, with rows of monks seated upon the floor, chanting mystically, and hypnotically. After a brief time, a pair of doors set into an ornate archway on the far side of the room swung open. A gong was struck, reminding Ned of the start of various films, and a palanquin was carried into the room on the extremely pretty shoulders of six good-looking and extremely underdressed young ladies.* The assistant assistant perked up out of his reverie at once.

"Wow, he's a lucky git. Wonder who he is?"

Ned was also in a reverie, but for a different reason.

"That's 'im what lives with Grotbags."

"Ere," put in the junior, "I know 'im. He's really handy wiv an empty beer bottle. I've still got a bruise months later."

"If Grotbags saw 'im like that, she'd kill 'im."

"Only if he were lucky."

"What's he doing, sat like these monks on that thing, an' dressed like them?"

Ned's expression changed from complete bewilderment to horrified speculation.

"His name's Ben. I reckon they think he's their lost leader, returned from the dead."

---

* This scene was planned for the cover until Grizelda explained the long-term disadvantages of being a frog to the author.

Chapter Six

The Tuatha were wandering along on their walking tour, still with no real aim in view. All were black-clad, with black boots and black hoods, and they all looked more or less alike. It was hard for an observer to tell the difference between them, and probably a pointless exercise. The weather was turning against them and the otherwise empty hilltop they were traversing was becoming cold, and windswept.

"Do you know what it is about Wales that I've always really liked?" asked Finn.

"Go on. There must be something," said Laeg dubiously.

"It's the way that, no matter where you are, or how far away from civilization, there's always a decent pub in walking distance."

"Since we are on a walking holiday, that is a bonus, I agree," said Diarmid.

"And when you are only walking round the corner from the Rose 'n' Crown, it's even better," agreed Liamm.

"Mind you, it's a good walk to here from... from... from... where was it again? That place that does the bog snorkeling?"* said Finn.

"Bog snorkeling? Don't be stupid; no one would want to do that. You couldn't see anything when you were in the bog."

"I can see when I'm in the bog, and that's without snorkeling," said Liamm.

"Different bog, Liamm."

"They all seem the same to me. White tiles, porcelain, strange smell half way down."

"It's peat bog, Liamm."

"So? Pete keeps clean bogs in the Kings Head. Just been in them."

"Anyway, what was the place called?" persisted Finn.

"I still don't understand. Why would anyone want to put his head down a bog?"

"I didn't get given a choice at school," said Diarmid.

"We know. That was a very long time ago, and you still complain."

"Just saying," said Diarmid.

"Where was the place we were just at?" asked Finn.

"Surely you don't want to go back Finn?" asked Liamm.

---

* You could have a go too, if you wanted. Just Google it and see.

"No. Actually, I've forgotten what all this was about anyway."

"Llanwrtyd Wells." Said Laeg.

"What wells?"

"Well, what?"

"I didn't see a well," said Diarmid.

"Pity. Could do with a drink, with all this walking."

"Where we just were."

"Well?"

"Well, what?"

"Llanwyrtyd Wells. I just said," Laeg repeated.

"That would have been 'which well', and I asked, what well."

"No you didn't."

"He's right. 'Well, what?' you asked. Not 'what well'," contributed Finn.

"Still wasn't which well."

"If there *was* a witch, we could ask *her* the way to the well. I'm thirsty again," said Finn.

"Wish it was a witch well."

"Why, Diarmid?"

"Then it would be a wishing well, and I could put my feet in it."

"Is that what it would take to satisfy you?" asked Finn.

"Only time he seems satisfied to me," grumbled Laeg.

"I'd rather drink from it than put my feet in it. Unhygienic that is. What about other travelers?" said Diarmid.

"They'd have more sense and be in the pub. Talking of which, there's one."

"Where?"

"At least that's a change from 'what'," said Liamm.

"Down there in the village. Can you see that *Sprinter* van with a trailer parked up there?" Finn pointed down into the valley.

"Do you know, I've seen that van before. When we were in that other pub," said Laeg.

"Aha. A mystery."

"Then, brothers, it is our duty to investigate. Erald, were he here, would have insisted," said Liamm.

"No hang on." Laeg tried to stop the precipitate action, but then persistent precipitation started,[*] and the Tuatha were over the precipice in a flash.

---

[*] Well, this is Wales.

Inside the hostelry, negotiations were in hand between the proprietor and The Banned.

"Yes, I've got some rooms left for the weekend. Had a cancellation, so you're in luck. The beer festival has taken up all the local accommodation. Be glad to have you, actually, as I'd be a bit quiet with all the trade on the showground."

"So we hear. We're playing at the festival." Haemar told the landlord.

"Oh, so you're a band, then?"

"Yeah."

"What do you play, then? Folk music? Here, is he alright? He's gone a funny color."

"Give 'im a drink an' 'e'll be alright," advised Haemar.

The publican started pulling pints.

"That's a good dragon costume you've got on."

"Diolch*," said Dai.

"Make his a whisky for his cold," said Scar.

"What cold?" asked Dai.

"Didn't you just sneeze? Ow, you didn't need to do that to me!" shouted Scar.

"Yes I did," said Dai.

"I'll make yours a double, for that," said the publican to Dai, carefully selecting a half-pint glass for Scar's beer.

"Der."

"Eddie, you're the driver. You can't drink." GG told him.

"DER."

"Oh, alright, since you are the roadie as well."

"Isn't it a bit hot in that costume?" the publican asked Dai.

"Can be. But it's cosy on cold nights," replied Dai.

"Right. I've been thinking of putting on some music to draw a crowd over the weekend, so what do you play?"

"Rock and blues," replied Haemar.

"Not folk then? Or traditional Welsh?"

---

*   Welsh for "thank you"

"Sorry. But we are booked to play at the festival tomorrow. If you wanted, we could do a warm up here for you tonight, in exchange for the rooms," offered Fungus.

"And we can play some Manic Street Preachers and Stereophonics numbers," added Dai.

The other band members looked less convinced.

"*Dakota* is a favorite of mine," said the landlord. "More pints, boys? On the house?"

The whole of the band looked enthusiastic.

"I'll stick some posters up, see who comes in. If we get a crowd, then we'll go for it?"

Fungus looked around at his band. They mostly nodded, so he agreed.

"Here's a crowd, already," said Haemar, as a group of walkers entered the pub and headed straight for the bar.

"Take *that*!" yelled Fungus.

"Ouch! What did you hit me like that for?" asked Lugh.

"I've not forgiven you for what you did to me Triumph *Bonneville* yet!"

"Take *that*!" repeated Fungus, bopping Lugh again.

"I'm not hiring you if you play any of *their* stuff!" called the landlord.

"Come on, Fungus, that's enough now," said Lugh, from the floor.

"Just so as you know I haven't forgotten. An' you still owe me a front mudguard."

"You're not the only one who hasn't forgotten," muttered Finn, who still had flashbacks of his last wild ride on the pillion of Fungus' bike, and did not like reminders in the daytime.

"Come on, let's all have a drink, and put that behind us. Lugh's buying," suggested Laeg, as peacemaker. The idea that gained general agreement, especially as the rest of the Tuatha and The Banned Underground had already congregated at the bar. Lugh was less keen, for some reason.

"So, what are you guys doing down here?" Laeg asked Fungus a little later, when the excellent qualities of the beer had mellowed tempers. Fungus pulled Laeg into a corner, away from the noise.

"We're on a quest."

"What or whom do you seek?" asked Laeg

"Waccibacci…"

"Well, go on," added Fungus. "Everyone else makes a smart comment."

"Can't imagine why. Tell me more."

"Well, this Waccibacci is a dwarf, who is a Zen master and a maker of magical thrones. At least, he has made a few. And we need him to make another one."

"For whom?"

"Lord Lakin."

"Hasn't he got one already?" asked Laeg.

"It had an accident. Now he needs another. Don't ask."

"So, why are you down here?"

"Well, we heard a rumor that Waccibacci might be exhibiting at the festival here."

"The beer and wood festival. Not a bad idea. So, why are you being followed?"

"Quiet! I don't think the lads know, an' I don't want to worry them," said Fungus looking shifty.

Fungus looked across the bar, and noted Haemar giving him a very funny look.

"Would anything worry them?" asked Laeg.

"The beer running out. Not getting paid for the gig... " mused Fungus.

"Sounds a bit like my lot, then. No sense of responsibility."

"The band can sense it alright. They just make sure it always heads in my direction. How did you know we were bein' followed?"

"You passed through here a day or so ago. There was a taxi with Keswick plates following you, with three junior wizards from Caer Surdin in it. What else would they be doing, but following you? Maybe they do not want this throne built."

"Could just be music fans. But I did see them at the gig in Manchester too, and they were at Grizelda's," mused Fungus.

"Then it's probably best to assume that they are after you, or after this Waccibacci."

"You'd think they would grow their own. Why nick mine?"

"It is written, do not meddle in the affairs of wizards," said Laeg, portentously.

"Didn't know they got married."

"I think we should come with you. You might need some backup."

"What were you doin' here, Laeg?" Fungus asked.

"Erald sent us on a team building exercise. But they all act well as a team."

"A drinking team, certainly."

"So basically, we are walking from pub to pub. With nothing to do. We'll provide you with security at your gig and then you can search for this Waccibacci."

"Done. Now let's have a drink."

Further to the south, the converted coach was making stately, rather than sprightly, progress along the main road.

"Merrily we roll along, roll along, roll along!" warbled Imelda, in the face of the facts.

Erica and Chris had emerged from the back of the coach, into a somewhat cool atmosphere. Grizelda glared at them both, but held her peace (and also held her piece). Possibly she thought that changing her nephew into a frog (always her first choice when annoyed) might annoy her sister.

Linda had no reservations.

"Ugh, Erica. How could you? That's my brother."

"Someone taught him how to kiss, though."

"Natural talent," smirked Chris.

Grizelda's mood turned the atmosphere frosty. Chris scraped some ice off the inside of a window and peered out.

"Where are we now?" asked Chris.

"Besides in trouble?" his aunt wanted to know.

"We only kissed!"

"Honestly, Grizelda," said Erica.

"Well, we'll leave it at that."

"Pity," muttered Chris.

"That's enough." Grizelda's snarl quieted them all. "Let us all remember that Ben is missing, presumed kidnapped by a bunch of homicidal monks. We are on a mission to rescue him, not on a day out."

"So, where are we?" asked Chris again.

"We've just gone past Carmarthen."

"And we are going where?"

"Tenby."

"How far is that?"

"You just stay where I can see you," answered his aunt, clicking her fingers.

Chris subsided back into a seat, and looked at the scenery (and Erica in the reflection in the window).

"Will you tell me about these monks?" asked Linda, deciding to let her brother off the hook a little, since she too quite liked Erica. Imelda concentrated on negotiating a complicated road junction.

"They call themselves the Ben Buddhists," explained Erica.

Grizelda decided to relent a little and turned round in her seat to listen better.

"I've heard of Zen Buddhists," said Grizelda.

"These are a bit like that. Basically, they believe in the oneness of the universe, spiritual development through meditation, and their divine right to rule the world under the awaited re-incarnation of their lost leader," explained Imelda.

"Called Ben," added Erica. "Hence the name."

"They recruited members from all over Wales, then started spreading further afield a few years back. There are rumors that they have links to Caer Surdin, but we've never seen any evidence."

"Well, you wouldn't, would you?" said Grizelda.

"Basically, the local covens wrote them off as pretty harmless nutters until a couple of years ago."

"What happened then?"

"They started kidnapping anyone they could find called Ben. The coven leader before Grizelda thought that they might be getting organized, so she went to meet one of them one night. She thought he might be a spy for us."

"And?" asked Grizelda.

"She never came back. That was when they appointed you in her place."

"So, even if they had not grabbed my bloke, I might have been goin' to look fer them anyway?"

Imelda did not answer as she carefully guided the bus around a steep corner, casually swiping a passing cyclist into a ditch in what might be called a blow for road safety.*

Grizelda listened to the volley of abuse from the ditch, before pointing her finger and muttering a charm. The abuse stopped at once.

"RIVET RIVET RIVET!" came a yell from the ditch.

---

*   For the bus, obviously. It was just a blow for the cyclist.

"That will teach 'im to swear at defenseless ladies," said Grizelda, in defiance of all the evidence. "Someone remind me to change 'im back when we pass by on the way home."

"Look" said Chris, "there's a sign for Tenby."

"So where is the student rave?" asked Linda.

"On a beach near Saundersfoot," replied Imelda.

"Who is Saunders and why is his foot a landmark?"

"Dunno. But it will be easy to find. We just follow the trail of litter until the volume becomes unbearable."

"Right. No, not here, idiot. When we get there, we all stick together. No goin' off on yer own. We keep an eye out fer some of the Ben Buddist lot, an' then we follow them back to their lair. Wherever it may be."

The coach swung round another corner, narrowly missing the large brown tourist route sign marked *Mynachdry Ben Buddhist Monastery.*

"Dunno where they'll be based, so keep yer eyes open," ordered Grizelda, swinging back to face the front again.

The coach rumbled onwards, joining a small traffic line of elderly Ford *Mondeos,* exotically painted camper vans and various small hatchbacks which had once been hot but were now, at best, tepid.

Tepid also described the reaction of many of the locals to the student invasion and anticipated loud dance music.

"It's worse than prog rock," complained one, to his neighbor.

"And I thought that was impossible," came the reply.

Some, however, appreciated the influx, as off-licence cash machines struck up a merry jingle all along the main roads, and shops and businesses off-loaded cans of cheap lager that had been foisted on them by distributors, and rejected by the locals.

Eventually, they all reached a beach car park, and so parked. The witches looked out curiously at the sight and spectacle of a student rave starting to wind up. Veterans, now, of two Banned Underground gigs, the teenagers were less awestruck. But Chris was impressed enough by the lager-fuelled antics of the students to decide at once that university was an excellent career choice.

"What would you study? Astrophysics?" asked Erica, looking at the darkening sky and the first hints of twinkling stars.

"Gettin' drunk an' fallin' over's more likely," commented Grizelda.

"He already knows how to do that." Linda muttered.

"When does the dancing start?" asked Imelda, who was as impressed as Chris.

In the middle distance, at the edge of the dunes, a small stage arose, wobbled significantly, and collapsed to wild cheers. In a triumph of hope over experience, the stage reappeared and lights began flashing.

"Either they are sending signals to Jupiter, or else the gig's about to start," Erica told them. And sure enough, a wild driving sound erupted over the sands. In blatant defiance of their IQ levels, the students seemed to be enjoying it. The coach vibrated gently to the bass beat.

"We need to go and look for the monks," said Grizelda, grimly.

In a flash, Erica had Chris by the hand and they were gone, into the frenetic pack.

"We three stick together," Grizelda ordered. "Tonight, we'll just wander round and see if we get any clues."

"Probably best," agreed Imelda. "The Ben Buddhists won't be recruiting with all this goin' on, they'll wait until the morning when the students all have hangovers, and will be easier targets."

Watching out for a flash of a saffron robe, the witches moved out among the dancing students.

"Try an' blend in," said Grizelda.

Imelda rolled her eyes. "Linda and I do," she answered.

"Are you sayin' I don't?" demanded Grizelda.

"Look, you are the coven leader. That makes you older than the rest of us, and older than these students."

Grizelda looked around at the drinking, dancing, crowd – with some distaste. One mature student came past and grabbed her hand. Before she could react, she had vanished into the crowd...

"Come on," Imelda said to Linda, "let's go." And the two melded into the rave.

"Come on, let's enjoy ourselves!" called Fungus, and The Banned Underground swung into *Johnny B Goode*. Dai, of course, knew this one and his thumping, if erratic, bass line certainly added something to the sound – albeit the excitement of not being too sure what was coming next.

Word had spread among the locals and customers had come from reaches as far-flung as the metropolis of Builth Wells (two miles away, population 2400). All seemed to be having fun, and the landlord was well pleased with his well full till.

"Der."

"Fungus, Eddie says he keeps getting asked for CDs," called Felldyke.

"Maybe we should get some cut," panted Scar.

"Can't see us on MTV though," said GG, changing guitars.

"Don't see why not," said Haemar, who quite fancied the idea.

"They wouldn't let you do that, for a start," said Scar, as Haemar filled his helmet with beer, took a long drink and jammed the rest back onto his head.

"*Jumpin' Jack Flash* next?" asked GG.

"It's raining," warned Haemar.

"Outside the pub, yes."

"Look what happened last time we played that one," Fungus reminded them.

"That was the feedback off the water getting in the electrics."

"So you say."

"Look, I was the one getting the shock, an' I'm happy to play it again," insisted GG.

"The landlord's a bit restless," announced Fungus. "We'll do *Dakota*, to keep him happy, then go straight into *Please Don't Touch*."

"Don't know that second one," warned Dai.

"No one will notice."

In the corner, the Tuatha nursed their drinks. That is to say, they cradled them lovingly and ensured their well-being by drinking them swiftly. And ordering more.

"Don't think we're going to have any trouble here," said Laeg.

"Not a very lively crowd, are they?" observed Finn. "There's a dozen or so dancing over there, but most are just clustered round the bar."

"Mebbe they're drying out after the rain."

"Wish they'd hurry up. It's murder getting served," complained Liamm.

"Those guys do pick up odd waifs and strays don't they? Who have they got on bass – him in the dragon costume?"

"Look again Liamm. That's a real dragon."

"So it is. Wonder where they found him?"

"In a gutter I would have thought, looking at the amount of whisky he's putting away."

"You can talk," said Finn.

"It's the practice. Hang on, here's some trade."

A large and red-faced sheep farmer was yelling something incomprehensible at GG from a distance of about six inches.

"We don't normally do requests," GG was yelling back.

"Is there a problem?" Liamm asked, gently.

"I can't understand a word he says," said GG.

Liamm listened carefully to the farmer.

"He claims your bass player ate some of his sheep last week."

They all turned to look at Dai, who was trying to hide behind the speaker stack. Fungus nodded wearily.

"OK, we'll pay him. We can take it out of the gate money at tomorrow's gig."

The farmer carried on shouting.

"And play *Long Grey Mare*," said Liamm.

There was some more shouting.

"And keep Dai off the sheep while you are still round here," interpreted Liamm.

"And buy him a pint. Or three." Liamm concluded, as the farmer stopped ranting.

"See?" said Liamm, returning to Finn. "All settled easily."

"Stick to the choccie bikkies," Haemar advised Dai, after he had been coaxed out of the speaker stack.

"I'm a dragon. It's an image thing, you know?"

"Then it's time for a makeover."

The gig finally finished and Eddie was roused to clear away the kit and pack the tour bus ready for the morning.

"Well, Dai," said Fungus, "how do you think that went?"

"Sorry about the sheep."

"Lissen, it's only by showing that you can be a pillock that you stand a chance of fittin' in with this band. But yer playin' weren't bad when you warmed up."

"I'll be better next time," Dai promised.

"Tomorrow, we'll take you round the showground," Laeg promised Dai as The Banned Underground staggered off to their various beds.

The publican was trying hard to hide his wide grin as he collected the takings.

CHAPTER SEVEN

The atmosphere in the Temple Hall hummed with excitement.

The monks all bowed low and intoned a variety of mantras. The palanquin bearers moved closer to the center of the room, where an elderly monk sat in front of a low table. On the palanquin, Ben sat very still.

"Do you think he's under an enchantment?" whispered the junior wizard to Ned.

"Could be. The girl in green looks rather enchanting to me."

"Got to agree wi' yer there. If Grotbags saw him like that though, she'd go mad."

"She's mad as a box of ferrets anyway."

"Is that like that Schrodinger's cat thing?"

"No. Just an observation,"* said Ned.

"Mebbe he's not speaking cos he's not seen her figure," said the assistant assistant as the leader of the girls bowed low before Ben.

"'E can't miss it when she does that."

But Ben appeared unmoved. Opinion was divided as to the reason: Ned suggesting he was strong-minded and the others that he was drugged.

"Stands to reason. She's so gorgeous that you'd have to look at her."

"Not if yer were drugged."

Four large monks came forward and dismantled the palanquin, leaving Ben face-to-face with the elderly monk and his table. The wizened monk spoke to Ben, who only smiled.

"I have told the candidate," announced the wizened one, "that he must select, from the objects on the table, the items that he possessed in his last incarnation as our leader. *And* warned him that if he fails the test he cannot be found worthy of the great position."

"Which position's that, Ned? Only, I bought this book off the internet once, an' that position's not in it," asked the junior.

"SSSSHHHH!"

"Now he must, in all care, choose, and choose his *fate*," shouted the wizened monk.

"Does that mean they'll kill him if 'e gets it wrong?" whispered the junior.

"Think so," Ned replied.

---

* One for the quantum physicists out there.

"Wow. Even The Grey Mage isn't that tough."

"Grizelda won't like it if they kill him," the assistant assistant said.

"Don't suppose Ben will be too pleased either."

"Should we try an' save him?" asked the junior.

"Don't be daft. We're evil wizards, not *International Rescue*," Ned told them.

"I preferred *Stingray*."

"Only cos you fancied that Marina," the junior replied.

"So what?"

"Please, to be quiet," hissed a nearby monk. "This is a supreme moment for our order. The possible selection of our new leader, who will lead us to great things."

The elderly monk raised his hand before Ben's face. Ben shivered, and seemed to be freed from a trance.

"Said he were spellbound," the junior whispered.

"That was your last warning." The monk slipped a garroting cord around the junior wizard's neck.

"OK, I'm sorry. Just carried away by the moment."

The monk subsided.

The elderly monk performing the test bowed and Ben copied the gesture. The monk leaned forward and waved his hand across the table. Stiffly, Ben bent forward and did the same, but leaned forward too far and swept all the objects from the table.

A gasp ran through the room and the monks all bent forward and banged their heads on the floor.

"Bet that's torn it," muttered Ned.

The elderly monk leaped to his feet.

"The candidate has passed the test."

The evil wizards looked at each other with open mouths.

"Our order has a new leader, who will be educated in our ways, appraised of our strengths, and will then lead us to domination of the world!"

The monks all rose to their feet. Chanting.

"Ben. Ben. Ben. Ben. Ben. Ben. Ben. Ben."*

"Didn't see that one comin'," said Ned

"Grotbags won't be pleased now."

"But we are delighted," smiled the nearby monk. "Please, now, come with me."

---

* And so on. Repeat until bored, or asleep. Use it as a mantra, if you wish. It work.

"Where?"

"You are to be presented to The Big Ben for his judgment."

"Big Ben?"

"I thought that were a clock."

"It's a bell."

"Could do with a big *Bells*," muttered the assistant assistant.

"Alcohol is a stain on the soul," warned the monk.

"Bet whisky could clean it off."

"Silence. Oh, Big Ben."

Here the gong banger did his thing, sending the echoes bouncing around the room. Ned winced.

"Here we have three who were taken at the time we discovered you. They are brought here for your judgment, to keep, or rend, to free or to slay."

Ben turned his head and examined the three evil wizards of Caer Surdin, who grinned sheepishly.

"Om Mani Padme," intoned Ben. "Hum. What am I to do with you three?"

"Er... "

"Wotcher, Ben."

"The robes suit yer," smiled Ned.

"I have decided... " Ben intoned.

Again the gong was struck with the enthusiasm of a bit-part character that is making the most of his part.

"Violence is against our creed," intoned Ben.

There was a certain amount of dissention among the monks seated around.

"In theory."

"Ah so," sighed the monks with relief, recognizing a master of philosophy about to reconcile a contradiction.

"In this case, there should be no exception," Ben continued.

"Ah so," sighed the three representatives of Caer Surdin, also with relief.

"They may accompany me for now."

Ben signaled to the six gorgeous girls, who picked up the palanquin and started to sway out of the room. The monks formed a corridor towards the exit door, bowing as Ben passed by. Ned cautiously started after Ben and, when nothing unpleasant happened to him, the other two followed.

In a luxurious side suite, the palanquin was placed on the ground, and the six girls left the room – and sadly, the story.* Several pairs of eyes tried to follow them out, but reluctantly had to return to their owners as the door closed behind the girls' behinds. None of the associated ears, while remaining firmly in place, missed the click as the door was locked.

"'Ello Ben," said Ned, cautiously.

"What on earth are you three numpties doin' here?" asked Ben.

"Well, our Boss," said Ned

"The Grey Mage?"

"Yeah, him. He sent us down here on a mission, but it were nothing to do wi' you or Grotbags, honest."

"Can yer stick to usin' her proper name in future?"

"Sorry, Ben. Habit."

"What was this mission, then?" asked Ben, curious.

"It's supposed to be a secret."

"Just bear in mind that I've saved yer from a horrible fate."

"Don't upset 'im, Ned. Just tell 'im," implored the junior.

"We were following that Fungus an' his Banned."

"I didn't put yer down as groupies."

"'Scuse *me!*"

"Nor music lovers."

"They do put on a good set, yer know. But they're on a mission," Ned continued.

"From God?"

"No, from Lakin, Lord of Helvyndelve."

"Go on," said Ben.

"Well, after the Boss failed to get the Helvyndelve, an' had to go back ter bein' an' accountant as a punishment –" Ned began.

"Yes?"

"– The band played a gig at the Helvyndelve."

"I wanted to go, but couldn't get tickets," complained the assistant assistant.

"Should have gone anyway. Everyone else were just bribing security to get in," said the junior, who had been there.

---

* Only introduced anyway by a specific, non-negotiable demand by Ben, who insisted on having some eye-candy as a reward for being tied up and kidnapped. It isn't easy being an author.

"I'd seen them in the gig in my garden the weekend before," said Ben. Ned nodded, he'd been there as well.*

"Anyway, there were an accident, and the Throne of the Dwarves got caught in the feedback, and disintegrated."

Ben looked impressed. "Bet that went down well."

"Lakin had them all locked up, but then let them out to look for a replacement."

"Why down here?" asked Ben.

"The dwarf what made the original throne is supposed to be around here somewhere. So now yer know the plot."

"Hang about," said Ben.

The junior wizard winced, and fingered the red mark on his neck.

"You could 'ave chosen a different phrase."

"Why are you three here though?" demanded Ben.

"Well, we was followin' the band..."

"Then, just as we 'ad watched them go into your place, these monks jumped us, knocked us out, and tied us up. They brought us here, an' then we saw you bein' tested."

"Yeah. What was all that about then?" asked the junior.

"Didn't these weird monks tell *you* what they are all about?" asked Ben, still mystified.

"Yep," replied Ned. "They call themselves the Ben Buddhists."

"You are joking, right?"

"Wrong. An' they are looking for the re-incarnation of their lost leader, Ben, to lead them in a bid fer world domination."

"So they are in competition wi' you lot then."

"Well, we're allowed. We are meant ter be evil wizards, so it's sort of the job description, innit? But this lot? Who wants to have to wear orange all day?"

"Someone who works in a mobile phone shop?" asked the junior.

"Anyway, they seem ter think that *you* are the leader. Otherwise... "

"Otherwise?"

Ned drew his finger across his throat.

"Just as well I passed the test then," said Ben, looking relieved.

"'Ere, are you *the* Ben, Ben?"

"How am I supposed to know? But I've no interest in world domination."

---

* Disguised as a bush, he had been peed on by two dogs, four revelers and the fridge. And seen a lot of things he wished that he hadn't.

"We know that. No one married to *her* could be interested in bossing people about."

There was a discreet, polite knock on the door, which opened. Several eyes swung rapidly towards the door.*

Two saffron-robed monks entered, bowing low, and pushing a trolley well laden with every conceivable sort of food. All vegetarian of course. And alcohol free. Still bowing, the monks left.

"Tell you what," observed Ned. "If they do take over the world, I'm givin' up accountancy an' goin' to be an osteopath instead. All this bowin' will kill peoples' backs."

There was a brief silence, while all four sampled the offered food.

There was an extended silence as all four decided it would be impolite to leave anything untouched.

The silence was broken by the indigestion of the assistant assistant.

"So, what we need to do now is to get away," said Ben.

"After what 'e's just done, I agree," agreed the junior evil wizard, edging away from the assistant assistant.

"Yer mean a truce?" asked Ned.

"Seeing as how I can have you lot done in by snappin' me fingers, not a bad idea?"

"Works fer me," said the assistant assistant, quickly.

"Thing is, we're probably on the same side anyway," said Ben.

"'Ow do you work that out, then? A few weeks ago we were trying to get yer done for tax evasion."

"That were just *business*, though," pointed out Ben. "How long will either of our lots last if this orange bunch take over?"

"Fair point. Too much chantin' goin' on for my taste."

"Crap music, they call it, I think," said the junior.

"And they're right."

"Ideas, then?" asked Ben.

"Well, does anyone have any idea where we are?" Ned asked.

"Not me," said Ben. "They took me at the top of our lane. I never bother with a watch, an' I've not bin in a room with any windows yet, so I've no idea how long ago that was."

"Why don't yer have a watch?"

---

* Got you! Thought it was the girls again, didn't you? Shame on you. It's hard to get the quality reader, these days.

"Grizelda's spells play havoc with the works. I even tried a digital one, but that ended up swearin' at me. Digitally."

"Well, they don't call us The Watches for nothing," smirked Ned.

"True. I 'ad to pay three weeks wages to join," said the assistant assistant. "An' The Grey Mage took it out of me wages at source."

Ned, theatrically, raised his left wrist to reveal a Rolex.[*]

"The time is... oh."

"What's wrong?"

"Just look."

Both hands were spinning gently and continuously.

"Either of you two carryin' a watch?"

The assistant assistant shook his head.

The junior wizard shook his head, but with more seniority.

"Well, it must be a good couple of hours since we woke up," mused Ned.

"Ok, probably mid-morning, then. So we can't have gone too far from the Gower."

"This place looks like a big country house." Ned was still musing.[**]

"Probably rural then," contributed the junior. "Because they 'ad us bound an' gagged, an' that would be a bit conspicuous in a town."

"Probably normal in Swansea."

"Don't be prejudiced. You'd 'ave to pay fer a service like that back home."

"We do it fer free at the accountants. To the ones who are a bit slow in payin' the fees, normally," Ned commented.

"Which is most of them, these days," the junior agreed.

"Anyway, now we know where we are."

"Do we?"

"Of course we do. Here. The only problem is locating the rest of South Wales."

"Even me GPS has problems wi' that," complained the assistant assistant.

"You 'aven't got a GPS," the junior pointed out.

"Yes I 'ave, Clever Clogs. But I left it at 'ome. It don't like bein' in Wales."

"Why is that?" asked Ben, curious.

"Dunno. It won't tell me. Just keeps sayin' 'service error.'"

"Now, we have to get out." Ned tried to get the discussion back on track, without the help of a satnav.

---

[*]   Being an accountant, not a solicitor, he could not afford a real Rolex; this had only cost him a tenner while on holiday in the Canary Isles.

[**]   Because it's so very hard to stop once you start.

"Ben, this mob are pretty 'andy at the unarmed combat," said the junior.

"So we'll 'ave to talk our way out. Any of you three up to summonin' a decent demon?"

"Most of my lessons 'ave been on indecent demons," said the junior.

"Typical tax assistant," grumbled the assistant assistant.

"You're only jealous, cos yer 'aven't got that far yet."

The older two ignored this exchange.

"Is that door locked?" asked Ben.

Ned nodded at the assistant assistant who walked up to the door and tried the handle. Gingerly. Nothing happened. The handle spun round in his hand.

"Stand back," said Ned, and muttered under his breath while pointing at the door. Green light outlined the door, which slowly swung open to reveal a gently smiling monk. Ned threw himself to the floor: a minor inconvenience compared to the inconvenience of having a five point ninja throwing star* embedded in his sternum.

Ben, however, reacted too and, as a result, the monk toppled forward into the room and lay still.

"Quick thinkin' there," he said to Ned, who still lay on the floor.

"Just settin' him up fer you," mumbled Ned from the floor.

"Right."

"So what's outside?" asked Ned, carefully getting up.

"The corridor we came down here by. Turn right, that goes back to the big hall."

"So let's try left."

"Right."

"We did that one earlier," said the junior.

"What?" asked Ben.

"Never mind," Ned said, wearily.

"Did that one too."

"One of you must swap clothes with the monk," ordered Ben.

After a brief discussion, the junior wizard had to change clothes. As was pointed out, he was already bald, and so most suitable. As Ben was already in orange robes, the two led the others out of the room and down the corridor. The echoes of footfalls coming towards them had all four

---

*   Not available at your local shop, only by specialist mail order.

jumping quickly through an open door into a well-lit, furnished, but empty room.*

Ned and Ben listened at the door to the conversation outside between two orange-clad senior figures in the Ben Buddhist organization, using the skills they had honed as teenagers listening to their respective parents:

"Om. Do you think that this idiot really is the Ben whom we seek?"

"Om. No. But frankly, the Council are fed up with waiting. We have the plan ready. First, we take over the Welsh Assembly, then head for Westminster."

"Om. I am to manage the publicity. How do I present the Assembly take over?"

"Om. That should be easy. We do not expect anyone to notice and, if they do, we shall tell them that it is a central government initiative."

"Om. They will swallow that?"

"Journalists will swallow anything if told when they are drunk."

"Sounds like the politicians themselves."

"It can indeed be hard to tell the difference."

"When does the attack take place?"

"The auspices are favorable for the weekend. It will be a Sunday, so most people will be more interested in the rugby and football results than in the government."

"That's what got the country in the mess in the first place."

"True. Now let us meditate on the fruits of the success."

"Strawberry."

"What?"

"Strawberry. My fruit of success."

"It should be an orange really."

"I know, but I was brought up watching Wimbledon and they all live on strawberries. And number ones."

"Surely peeing on them doesn't improve the taste?"

Ben and Ned looked at each other as the voices faded. "So now we know," said Ben thoughtfully.

---

* If you were expecting the girls changing in their changing room, shame upon you. Again.

"Well, we know what an' when, just not how," mused Ned.

"If we can get out, then we can do summat about it."

"First, we 'ave to find a way out."

"How about this window?" asked the junior wizard.

There was a general rush to look outside. "That's a big lawn to cross," muttered Ben.

"In full view too," agreed Ned.

"So, we have to sit it out an' wait until it's dark?"

"Reckon so."

Ned waved his hand at the door, which glowed green again. "I've locked us in. Don't want any nasty surprises."

"Let's make some plans then," agreed Ben.

Chapter Eight

Dawn broke reluctantly over the beach. She was no fan of club anthems either and was taking no chances. As the perpetrators had fallen asleep some time earlier, Dawn's natural sensibilities remained unassailed, and her radiance grew steadily: washing the scattered bodies with her soft golden light (the incoming tide could be safely left to provide the rude awakening, and a, somewhat cooler, wash).

Students lay everywhere in wild abandon, interspersed with their wildly abandoned (and empty) cans. Fast-food cartons littered the area to the delight of the seagulls that had been driven from the beach during the evening by the volume, and possibly by their musical taste. (Most seagulls are into thrash metal bands which is why they are unsettled and scream all the time.)

Among the scattered bodies scuttled the crabs – nibbling at anything that didn't move. Carefully selecting a particularly squalid looking item, one crab raised a mighty claw, and bit hard.

"RIVET RIVET RIVET!" squealed a, now, very confused, green frog/crab.

"Damn crabs," grumbled Grizelda, awakening rather more quickly than those surrounding her. Bemused, she stared around at the beach which resembled a hospital drama just after the big crash scene – and before the rescue services arrive. Anyone who has ever been to a student all night party will quickly draw their memories to the surface of their minds.[*]

Slowly at first, then rather more quickly as they reached the interesting bits (don't you just hate it when that happens to you?) the memories of the night flooded back. Grizelda looked more carefully around her, and then more carefully still at the mature law student who had swept her off her feet and into the madness of the rave. She recalled the drinking. Lots of drinking. She recalled the dancing. Lots of dancing. She recalled being jostled, jolted and jarred – without going over all frog. The lack of said

---

[*] Disclaimer: under no circumstances am I as author, the publisher, the retailer, or anyone else at all, responsible for the costs of counseling or psychiatric care needed. Nor for the effects of the guilt or existential dread that may have resurfaced as a result of these memories. And that includes you, Grizelda, before you hire that smart law student with whom you just spent a night at a rave. I've got the keyboard, and I don't need to tell Ben. Do I?

amphibians around her proved she must have been in a good mood. She recalled that she – but we will respect her privacy now.

Quietly, Grizelda stood up and picked her way delicately across the sleeping horde, towards the dim vision of a garishly painted coach.

Further along the beach, other bodies stirred.

"She'll kill me," worried Chris.

"And me," Erica was less worried, but still uncomfortable. "Come on, let's get some breakfast."

That thought cheered Chris up considerably, and so they too delicately picked their way across the beach towards the coach: arriving at roughly the same time as Grizelda. All three looked at each other, but before they could speak the coach door flew open.

"About time too," said Linda. "Where have you three been all night then?"

"We couldn't find the coach in the dark," said Erica brightly.

Grizelda and Chris both looked at her in admiration for her quick thinking.

"So we crashed out with the students and all came back when we woke up," she continued, with another bright smile, this time aimed at Grizelda.

"Right," said Linda, turning back into the coach. "Breakfast's on."

Grizelda put out her arm to stop the other two entering the coach.

"One word," she hissed in a low voice. "What happened at the party stays at the party."

"Fine by us," said Erica, scenting a scandal that might later turn to her advantage.

"Der," replied Chris, who was not yet fully with it.

"Don't let him spend too much time with musicians," Grizelda warned Erica. "He sounds like he's in danger of becoming a roadie."

Imelda pulled chairs and a camp table from a deep recess within the coach and the party sat comfortably over breakfast, laughing at the antics of the hangover-influenced students as they were slowly awoken by the gulls, crabs, and the incoming tide.

Erica nudged Grizelda in the short ribs.

"Look!"

All the party turned in their seats, as a procession of orange-clad monks filed onto the beach, and slowly spread out among the recovering students, spreading joy, peace, and hangover cures.

"Please, try this," suggested a monk to a small group of suffering students.

"What is it?" asked a student, cautiously.

"Please, it will make you feel better," the monk told him.

"Yes, but what is it?"

"A drink that will make you feel better."

"The last ten or so drinks I had made me feel better," the student objected.

"I don't feel much better now though," pointed out a second student.

"The last five drinks must have worn off, then. Here, you're doing an astrophysics course. Can you navigate our way to the pub?"

"No. I'd need three computers or a satnav for that."

"Please, this is herbal," the monk said, politely.

"Herbal?"

"Herbal. Made for you by the monks of the Ben Buddhist Monastery. Om Mani Padme."

"Hum."

"We can see that you are getting it already."

"Hey, this stuff works!" exclaimed the first student.

"Works for me too! What did you say was in it?"

"Please, it contains herbs. It is brewed in harmony with the cycle of the universe to counter the spiritual effects of bad karma," smiled the monk.

"I had a bad Korma last week. Would it have worked on that?"

"Perhaps. Please, we are holding an open day today."

"What are you collecting?"

"This has to be worth a tenner, to me. Oh, I haven't got one left. Sorry."

"Please, it is of no account. We do not seek money," smiled the monk.

"What do you want, then?"

"We seek enlightenment and harmony with the cycle of existence."

"I went looking for Nirvana, but didn't get there."

"I never knew you tried that. What happened?" asked the second student.

"Tickets were sold out."

"Please, perhaps you should try our Way," suggested the monk.

"What do we have to do?"

"Please, all that is needed is that you listen with an open mind and heart."

"Not an open wallet then?"

"Please, we do not seek money. All we ask is that you come with us and listen to a lecture by one of our teachers. Then have lunch and return to the beach if you wish."

"Don't think I'm up to much of a walk."

"Please, we provide all transport. And a free lunch."

"I've heard that there's no such thing as a free lunch."

"Then why not come and test the theory for yourself?"

"Think that I might, at that. What time does the music start this evening?"

"Please, the lecture will not be long. And it might change your life."

"Yeah, OK. Nothing else to do today, so why not?"

Hours passed at the standard rate. The coach served lunch and mid-afternoon tea (sadly without strawberries and number ones), while watching the gentle activity of the monks as they collected prospective converts from the dissipated students. Slowly, the small groups of students heading for the orange coach grew in numbers.

"Not a bad haul so far," one monk observed to a colleague.

"They must have had a heavy night last night," agreed the second.

"Om. Good job it wasn't a high tide."

"They could have washed their dirty karma into the sea."

"I always found the salt leaves marks."

"Very profound, Mark."

Meanwhile, the forces for good were planning...

"So, what's the plan?" Erica asked Grizelda.

"Aunt Dot?" asked Linda, "Why don't we try and get in the group they are taking?"

"Because they are only taking men. Chris is too young – look: they are all over 20."

All looked at the assembled student group, and nodded.

"First, we follow these monks to their lair," instructed Grizelda.

"Dragons have lairs, not monks," objected Imelda.

"And thieves," added Linda.

"Isn't that dens?" asked Erica.

"Den isn't a thief. Is he?"

"Who is Den?" asked Linda

"No one you know."

"Well, obviously, or I wouldn't have asked."

"Just someone we know."

"I always thought 'e could be a bit dodgy," said Grizelda.

"Just cos he bodged your broomstick that time," replied Imelda.

"Bodged it? I'll say he bodged it. Damn thing cut out on me. At 100 feet."

"What did you do?" asked Chris.

"Found something soft to land on."

"Angharad still hasn't forgiven you," Imelda accused her leader.

"But she *were* a soft landing."

"And Den did apologize to you. Just missed a bit of the binding spell, he said. Could have happened to anyone," pointed out Erica.

"Actually," Imelda told Linda and Chris, "what he said was 'Grizelda, I'm... rivet rivet rivet rivet.'"

"But you could see he was sorry for the inconvenience."

"Turned him back, didn't I?" Grizelda defended herself.

"Only when the other workshops refused to deal with you," Erica said, pointedly.

"You mean when the dwarves' card school refused to deal me in."

"Are you surprised?" asked Imelda.

"What do you mean, Imelda?"

"Well, that time you claimed to have won did you no favors there."

"But I should have won. I had four aces in me hand."

"They were all the Ace of Spades, and you only get one in each pack."

"Is that right?" asked Grizelda, with an air of vagueness which fooled no one. "Come on, let's pack up an' get ready to roll."

Soon, all the food and picnic equipment was packed away and the witches were getting ready for a fight. For once, not with each other.

The monks were shepherding the students into the coach now and, at length, the orange door swung shut, with a satisfied hiss of air. The coach's engine was coaxed into starting and jolted across the car park towards the road.

"The coach is a wonderful metaphor for re-incarnation," observed one monk.

"Why is that?" asked his fellow, seeking to collect several prayer wheels and repackage them in the orange-colored (what else?) *Volvo*.

"I am always mildly surprised every time the engine comes back to life."

The two jumped into their *Volvo* and followed the coach. Behind them the witches' coach pulled out of the car park, and followed.

"We seem to have a convoy," one monk observed.

"We are being followed? By whom?"

"Hard to tell. They have a coach too, though."

"Maybe it's industrial espionage."

"A commercial James Bond?"

"Why not? I thought that the last movie was sponsored."

"But who would want to spy on us? Oh, I see what you mean. Not exactly short of candidates there."

"Probably not the Vatican. They're too well off to use a tatty old coach like that."

"Church of England would just call MI6, and get black cars everywhere."

"Could be the Scout Association."

"The Boy Scouts? What would they want?"

"They are short of leaders these days – maybe they want some creative advice on getting some more."

Both monks looked back as the camper coach backfired, spreading a plume of dirty gas and oil across the sky.

"Na. Too ecologically unsound for them."

"Well, then let's play some music and wait and watch."

"Quis custodiet, ipsos custodies?"

"Quite. What's on the CD?"

"Elvis Costello. *Watching the Detectives.*"

"Perfect harmony."

"I thought that was the New Seekers?"

Inside the coach, there was a lack of harmony. But plenty of hormoney.

"Why did it do that?" demanded Grizelda.

"Dunno," replied Imelda.

"How do you expect us to be discreet when it makes a noise like that?"

"Grizelda, it's a floral painted coach on a narrow road, following two orange-colored monks in an orange *Volvo*. How exactly are we going to be discreet?"

"Well, just drive thinking discreet thoughts, then."

"How about an invisibility spell?" suggested Linda.

"Problem there. We'd be invisible to other road users, too."

"Avoid the traffic police, then."

"I don't have to worry about speed cameras."

"Just hex them, is it?" suggested Grizelda.

"You can get done for that, can't you?" asked Chris.

"Na," said Imelda. "The bus doesn't go fast enough to trigger them."

Ahead, the orange coach pulled out onto a fast main road, and accelerated.

"'Ere!" said Grizelda, loudly. "The coach is pullin' away, but the *Volvo* hasn't moved at the junction."

"It's not the traffic. There isn't any."

In front of them, the doors of the *Volvo* opened and the two monks climbed out and walked back to the camper.

"Please, is there a problem?" asked the older through Imelda's window. The younger monk approached the opening door beside Grizelda, with a charming smile.

"Please... rivet, rivet, rivet," he remarked, politely.

The older monk nipped smartly around the front of the coach to investigate

"Rivet! Rivet! Rivet!" he exclaimed in surprise.

"I'll drive the *Volvo* into that car park." Grizelda said into the now silent camper. "Pick me up from there."

She walked up to the *Volvo*, and drove off. The other four looked at each other, then at the two frogs, (which were a tasteful shade of orange).

"Would it be safer to collect her, or drive off and leave her?" asked Chris.

"Can't leave her," objected Imelda.

"Why not?" asked Erica.

"Cos she'd follow us in the *Volvo*. And not in a good mood."

Erica climbed out of the coach and collected the two orange frogs, carefully stowing them away in the back of the coach.

"How long will that spell last?" asked Linda.

"Dunno. A couple of hours, couple of days, maybe longer. Depends how much power she put into it."

The coach drove off, while the frogs raised their voices sadly in chorus.

"SSHH. She'll get back on board in a moment. And she doesn't like Paul McCartney. Keep quiet and we'll let you out near your pad," Imelda tried to reassure them.

"Good choice of phrase, that," approved Erica.

"Rivet."

"That's quite all right."

"When did you learn to speak frog, Imelda?" asked Chris.

"When I spent two weeks at your aunt's place in the Lakes last summer. There were a lot of hikers came past, claiming that they had a right to roam. Turned out they had a right to hop, as well. But she turned most of them back, in the end. Just kept the odd one about for sentimental reasons."

"Rivet! Rivet! Rivet!"

"Don't worry. We'll make sure you two are OK."

"Look out, here she is," warned Chris.

With silence in the rear, the camper coach and Grizelda set off in pursuit of the now distant orange coach. After driving for some time, they passed a brown tourist sign, pointing to the monastery.

"That could be a clue," said Imelda.

Grizelda pointed to a lane that ran beside the wall, which surrounded the monastery.

"Drive into that. Then, when it gets dark, we will go an' investigate."

Erica opened the sunroof and climbed onto the top of the coach as it shuddered to a halt.

"I can see over the wall around the monastery. It's a low sort of mansion. The coaches are parked by the front door. All the students are getting off, and there's a lot of these monks about, herding them in through the doors," she called down, softly.

"Linda, make us all a cup of tea," ordered Grizelda, and they settled down to wait.

The Tuatha and The Banned Underground had enjoyed their breakfast in the pub. In fact, they had enjoyed several breakfasts, and as the landlord's private quarters had been found to house several packs of chocolate digestives, Dai had been quite content too.[*]

"So, how far is it to the showground?" asked Haemar.

"Couple of miles..," replied Dai. "We'll be there in twenty minutes."

"Der."

"Eddie reckons it won't take that long to drive two miles." explained Felldyke.

"There's bound to be a traffic hold-up."

---

[*] His whisky supply had been arranged when the publican was not looking.

"We'll walk it," said Laeg.

There was a chorus of disapproval behind him.

"Had enough of walking. Can't we get the horses?" asked Finn.

"Or travel magically as we normally do?" asked Liamm.

"Too conspicuous," said Laeg.

"At a beer festival? Who's going to notice?" asked Liamm.

"That's a good point," agreed Finn.

"Not like this dart, then. It's blunt," grumbled Diarmid.

"More likely it's the way you throw them, Diarmid."

"Tell you what," suggested Finn, "we'll wait here until the band have got in, then we'll travel our magical way and then we won't have to pay an entry fee."

Laeg looked at the diminishing supply of funds, and agreed.

"And we'll use the savings at the bar here," smirked Finn.

The publican, depressed after a brief whisky-orientated stock take, cheered up on the spot. Before too long, the tour bus and trailer pulled out of the car park and started to negotiate the way towards Builth Wells.

"Der."

"It's a parking attendant. Stood in the road," said Haemar, peering forward.

"They call them Traffic Control Officers now," Scar told him.

"Why?"

"Dunno. Maybe they think people will run out of breath while shouting abuse?"

"All show traffic turns off here," ordered the TCO.

"But we're the festival's band for tonight," Fungus said, politely.

"Well, you turn off here and get on the bus."

"Der?"

"We can't put all the gear on a bus," grumbled Felldyke.

"An' we're in a bus already," Scar pointed out.

"And how could we put Dai on a bus?" GG asked.

"Who is Dai?" asked the Traffic Control Officer.

"Me." Dai breathed out, heavily, making the TCO stagger from the whisky fumes.

"He's drunk!" complained the TCO.

"So they won't let him on the bus, will they?" Haemar wanted to know.

"Der."

"And what about the fire risk?" asked Haemar.

"What fire risk?" asked the TCO.

Dai breathed out again but, this time, with a bit of concentration. His pinpoint aim ignited the TCO's eyebrows and, while the TCO was frantically beating them out with his clipboard, the tour bus drove past him. Dai waved a friendly goodbye from the trailer as he passed the TCO, who promptly dived into the watery ditch, to the cheers and applause of those who stood waiting for the promised bus to the showground to arrive.[*]

"Where's your show pass?" asked another TCO. "No vehicles on the showground, without a pass."

"Der."

"Ah. A roadie. Are you tonight's band then?"

"That's us," agreed Fungus.

"What do you play?" asked the TCO.

"Blues, R&B, an' rock 'n' roll."

"Suits me. Can I bum a ticket?"

"Sure. Here's a t-shirt, just put that on an' security will let you in."

"Thanks, lads... but I do need proof you're the band. And what's that on the trailer?"

"Our bass player. He's drunk." Haemar told him.

"What sort of proof is that?"

"40% by volume – it said so on the bottle."

"Seems proof positive, to me," said the obliging TCO, and waved them through the barrier.[**] He gave them a printed map of the showground[***] and sent them on their way to find the site of the gig.

"Right," said Fungus. "What do we do first?"

"Der."

"Eddie wants to get set up, then have a drink," said GG.

"How about if we have a drink, get set up, then have a drink?"

"Good thinking, Haemar," agreed Scar.

"If GG drinks too much, he might not be able to get the sound balance right," worried Scar.

"I can – if you lot stop Scar falling over all the time. On top of me."

"Der."

"Eddie thinks we should get the gear inside the marquee."

---

[*]   Or possibly to be constructed in the factory.

[**]   See? They are not all bad.

[***] Which, in accordance with ancient tradition, was incorrect.

"All right. This is what we do –" ordered Fungus, only to find no one was listening.

"To you!"

"Careful with that cymbal!"

"Is it supposed to make a noise like that?"

"Only when you hit it with a Felldyke."

"Speak up."

"Grab hold of the speaker."

"OK."

"No, grab *that* speaker. Not me."

"Why didn't you say so the first time?"

"Where's Dai?" asked Haemar.

"He an' Fungus have gone to sort out the ticketing."

"I normally do that," grumbled Haemar, lifting the bass drum.

"But you, with respect Haemar, are not a fire-breathing dragon. Are you?"

There came a small explosion from nearby and a miniature mushroom cloud arose, shot through with various cheerful rainbow colors, and the promoter's clothing. A few moments later, Fungus and Dai reappeared. Fungus was carrying a heavy bag.

"Sorry, Haemar. Just needed a bit more firepower with this one," Fungus apologized.

"Well, as long as you got the cash," Haemar grumbled.

"We'll tie it to Felldyke as usual when the gig starts," Fungus replied.

"Why is it always me?" asked Felldyke.

"Well, you're the heaviest. An' you're always sat down an' don't need to move around."

"Fair enough. Now we've sorted all that out, can I go an' get some more drumsticks?"

"Yeah, there's normally a music shop set up at these places. They'll have some." Haemar told him.

"Actually, I were thinking of the catering stalls."

A golden sound, which made GG think wistfully of his past prog rock era, filled the marquee before fading, to be followed by a burst of golden light. Black-clad figures emerged from the glow into the empty area before the stage.

"Told you that was better than walking, Laeg."

"Just don't tell Erald. Or I'll never hear the last of it."

"Now all we need is a beer tent, or a pub."

"Liamm, we have just emerged into a beer festival. I am sure we will be able to find a drink somewhere."

"Good. Oh look, The Banned are getting set up."

"Great. I enjoyed their set last night."

Laeg wandered over to a nearby table, where Fungus and Haemar were poring over the map of the Showground.

"I didn't realize that there would be so many stalls. How are we to find Waccibacci?" wondered Haemar.

"There will be an index to traders on the back of the map," said Laeg.

The musicians looked at each other.

"Fungus, why didn't we think of that?"

"Dunno. Let's look at it." Fungus turned the map over.

"Still can't see his name."

"Thing is," pointed out Laeg, "his stall could have a business name, not his own."

"Look at this!" exclaimed Fungus, pointing to an entry.

"*Thrones 4 U,*" read Haemar.

"Got to be worth a look."

"I'll come with you," decided Laeg. "I'll be back," he called to his fellows, who were helping the rest of the band set the stage up. They paid little attention.

"Can I help you with the light show?" Finn asked Dai.

"What can you do?"

Finn raised his arms and wind, lightning, and a shower of rain passed across the stage, knocking GG into the speaker stack, which collapsed onto Scar.

"Fungus said we might do some Meatloaf in the encore. You'd be great there."

Finn looked pleased, then remembered he was too thirsty to wait for the encore. Outside, Fungus, Haemar and Laeg were wandering among the stands, seeking the throne maker. The booths seemed to alternate between selling strange and exotic products made from (renewable) grained wood, and strange and exotic products made from (renewable) grain. And from hops, malt barley, water etc. But, as the Ben Buddhists could confirm, if asked, all matter is composed of atoms at heart. Hence, cosmically speaking, a wooden sculptured seat and a glass of beer share the same fundamental components and could be interchangeable at need. A truly enlightened soul should therefore be able to drink wood, and sit on beer.

Haemar, lacking in spiritual development* was presently sitting in the beer and so failing to prove the experiment.

"You've got ter sing later," Fungus reminded him.

"Thash later."

Laeg, who was staggering slightly, examined the next tent.

"Hey, look at this. It's a load of wooden toilets!"

"If we can't sober Haemar up, this gig could be down the toilet."

"Oh, don't worry about that. I've got some of Erald's Patent Cure here in apocket."

"Apocket?"

"Typing mistake, I expect. I meant to say 'my pocket.'"

"The author's probably drunk by association with Haemar," accused Fungus.**

"Anyway, I think we've found your man," said Laeg.

"Dwarf."

"Whatever. Just look at these wooden toilets. They're amazing!"

"I prefer to think of them as conversational seating pieces," said the stallholder.

Behind them came the sound of Haemar having a conversation with one of the seating pieces.

"I do hope that sir planned to buy that item," said the stallholder.

"Why?"

"It would appear to have become a little shop-soiled. I would have to mark it down."

Fungus glared at Haemar, marking him down as well.

"We might look at some other things too. We were looking for a dwarf who makes thrones."

The vertically-challenged stallholder made an elegant gesture, inviting further inspection of his stock.

"I have many thrones here for sale."

"May we ask your name?"

From deep within the stall, Haemar suggested it might be Hughie. They all ignored him.

"My name is Damon."

---

* As so often happens. Especially with the lead singer.

** Wrongly. I blamed the editor, who confided to me that it was the publisher, who suggested that the computer had been to a party the night before with the printer, copier, and the fax machine. So there. Now you know.

"Damon?" inquired Laeg.

"Damon Waccibacci."

"Then we have traveled far to find you," said Fungus, with relief.

"The Tao has blessed your endeavors then, for you have been granted success."

Fungus looked around but the madding crowd was largely far away.

"We are on a quest to find one Waccibacci, who used to make magical thrones. Particularly made one for the Helvyndelve many years ago."

The stallholder pulled out a large sign and positioned it in front of the stall.

"That will keep customers from coming in while we talk," he murmured.

Laeg walked around to look at the sign. It read: 'Sale starts tomorrow.'

Damon Waccibacci took a long look at the three questing questioners.

"I perceive a bog troll and a dwarf. You, sir, are?"

"I am of the Tuatha."

"Fine. These discussions are obviously not for common knowledge, so I must seek an assurance that my privacy can be respected. I have no wish to be advertised to the likes of Caer Surdin."

"I thought that there was no such thing as bad publicity?" asked Fungus.

"My family has a long history, and many hidden secrets."

"Are there any other kind of secrets?"

"Oh yes. Some secrets are hidden in full view," said Damon.

"Is that a Zen thing?" wondered Laeg.

"I require your assurances. Are you wizards or warlocks?"

"Neither sir, we're musicians," Fungus assured him.

"Very well. My grandfather did indeed make the magical Throne of the Helvyndelve, but sadly, he is no longer with us," Damon continued.

"He died?"

"No. He moved into the countryside last year, to set up a craft workshop. I got left to run the business from our local industrial estate. Probably it is he whom you seek."

"Sounds like the man," agreed Fungus.

"Why do you seek him?"

"The Throne of the Mountain King has collapsed. We are looking to commission the replacement."

"That piece should have carried a lifetime guarantee. Why did it fail?" asked Damon.

"It got hit by a ballistic guitarist."

"That is probably outside the terms and conditions of the warranty. I could look it up, but that might take some time."

"Why is that, Damon?"

"The standard terms run to 1017 pages, and then the small print."

"How much of that is there?"

"I am unsure. It is too small to read without a microscope, and I have never got to the end of the document."

"Typical," muttered Laeg.

"However, as you are of the magical races, and seem trustworthy, I will tell you how to find my grandfather."

"Damon, we are really grateful. How can we thank you?" asked Fungus.

"A start would be to remove your friend. As a goodwill gesture, he may keep the piece to which he seems so attached."

Damon wrote busily on a piece of paper, while Haemar announced that the piece would be called Ruth. Several times.

"I do hope that he recovers soon."

"So do we. He's singing tonight," grumbled Fungus.

"Finally, may I interest you in some of this herbal powder?"

"You sell waccibacci?"[*]

"Have to make a living, you know. And the conversation pieces are slow movers."

They looked at Haemar, who was heading back to the marquee, still holding a conversation with his piece.

"Although that one seems a bit sprightly, I must say."

---

[*] As a running gag, it still has some legs.

Chapter Nine

"'Ere! I can hear voices an' footsteps in the corridor!" hissed the assistant assistant, stationed at the door.

Ben and Ned hurried over to him.

"There's a lot of chatter. Don't sound like the monks," he told them.

Ned carefully waved his hand around the door and unlocked it. Ben opened it a crack and they looked out. Two monks were following a large group of student types as they headed towards the main hall.

"What do yer reckon?" asked Ned.

"Looks like a recruitin' party to me," suggested Ben.

"Do yer think they'll have jelly an' ice cream?" asked the assistant assistant, who was feeling hungry again.

"No."

"I won't think of joinin' them then."

"Better not," hissed Ned. "You are ours, now, an' don't forget it." His tone was laden with heavy menace.

The students entered the main hall and the two monks followed them in.

"You two stay here," said Ben to the apprentice dark wizards.

"Why?"

"How much use will you be if we get into a fight? Hide here in case we need rescuin'" Ned told them.

Ned and Ben slipped out of the room and slid down the corridor to listen in.

One monk then emerged from the hall and closed the doors, locking them in from the outside.

Ben raised his arm to cast a spell but the monk dropped his orange hood, and put his finger to his lips.

"Erald!" exclaimed Ben. "What are you doin' here?"

"I have infiltrated this evil group," announced Erald, Leader of the Tuatha.

"Evil?" asked Ned. "That's meant ter be us. We thought they were just mad."

"Who is this?" Erald asked of Ben.

"It's Ned. Assistant to The Grey Mage of Caer Surdin."

"An' an evil wizard an' an accountant," announced Ned alliteratively.

"Then we are all on the same side," said Erald.

103

"How do you work that out, then?"

"These Ben Buddhists will seek to obliterate us all. They wish to dominate both the material and magical worlds, to rule us all."

"That's real evil," grumbled Ned.

"What are their chances?" asked Ben.

"They have recruited an army of crazed students, ready to do the will of the Ruling Council, or rather, Ben, the Leader."

"An' they think that's me?"

"Which is a weapon in our hands."

"I'd rather have a staff," objected Ned.

"Yer brought staff with yer," pointed out Ben. "How much use are they?"

"You will be able to 'Ben'd' the students to your will." Erald told them.

"But not if we get caught… " muttered Ben.

"What are they doin' with the lot that just went in there, then?" Ned asked Erald.

"Brainwashing them."

"Why? Have they all got dirty minds, then?"

"Probably. They are students, after all. What we need to do is to get you out of here. I have my brothers of the Tuatha in the area. You must contact them, and prepare to fight."

"How will we find them?" asked Ben.

"Just go on a pub crawl. You'll meet them sooner or later," said Erald, wearily.

"Right, then, let's get out of here," said Ben.

"The room we left has big windows, an' we can get into the grounds," Ned explained to Erald.

"You will find your *Mondeo* in the car park around the corner. You can make your getaway in that."

"Not if they chase us. Most of these monks could run faster than that thing can drive," Ned complained.

"It is still your best hope. The doors are too heavily guarded, in case any students try to run for it."

"Then let's go for it. It's getting dark," decided Ben.

"Too dark to see?" asked Ned.

"Just don't go knocking on any doors."

"Right."

Ned and Ben walked back into the room containing Ned's assistants, some furniture and – crucially – an open window. The assistant assistant was playing cards.

"Solitaire?" asked Ben.

"It's the only game in town."

"Come on," hissed Ned from the window. "Let's go."

Ben joined him and together they looked out across the large, grass lawn.

"Look!" said Ben. "It's Dot!" Across the wall, a shape on a broomstick rose unsteadily into view.

This news was not greeted with universal enthusiasm. In fact all the Caer Surdin adherents adhered to their calling by jumping quickly out of the window and running around the corner rather quickly.

"Where are you goin'?" called Ben.

"Somewhere else in case she blames us!" called back Ned.

Grizelda saw Ben leaving the building and sped across the grass for an emotional reunion.

SMACK.

"You had me seriously worried, you mad muffin!"

"They took me by surprise," Ben said, rubbing his face.

"An' I bet you left the shoppin' behind."

"Didn't 'ave much choice, luv."

"Where 'ave those Surdin idiots gone to?" asked Grizelda, looking around.

"You put the fear of frog into them, so they legged it."

There came the sound of an elderly *Mondeo* accelerating down the gravel drive, followed by several running feet.

"Time we weren't here," said Grizelda and she and Ben[*] climbed, with varying degrees of enthusiasm, onto her broomstick.

"When did yer get yer night flying license then?"

"I haven't."

"Then don't hit anything. It's bad enough havin' these orange monks and Caer Surdin's apprentice warlocks about. We don't want trouble with the Civil Aviation Authority."

"Point taken, Ben. I'd rather face another fire troll attack than their paperwork."

The broomstick slid across the lawn, trying to keep in the shadows, then lifted gently over the wall and landed beside the camper coach.

"No expense spared eh?" asked Ben, clearly surprised. "In the movies, the getaway car after the big rescue is normally something fast."

---

[*] He was a bit reluctant, but this was a rescue, after all.

"Ah, but this one provides tea and toast as well."

Ben climbed on board, just as a lot of shouting and a blast of green light came across the wide lawn.

"Looks like Ned had to shoot his way out... Hello, a full complement eh?"

"Took a few of us to find you," his wife said, glaring at the others. "Come on, Imelda, start the bus."

The starter motor whined like a retriever deprived of its breakfast.

"Hang on!" said Linda, as Imelda started swearing.

"What?" asked Erica.

Grizelda opened the doors and ran round to the rear of the coach. Linda also went into the rear of the coach and shooed two orange frogs towards the doors.

"Rivet? Rivet?"

Linda grabbed one to help it down the steps and, immediately, the necklace she wore glowed a vivid green, and the frog returned to human form.*

"What's going on?" asked the de-frogged monk, falling into a seat.

Erica grabbed the other frog and threw it quickly into the grass where it vanished from sight.

Grizelda snarled at the engine and then poked it with her wand. Recognizing the clear and present danger, the engine quickly started.

"I didn't even touch the starter!" said Imelda, admiringly.

"I have the touch," preened Grizelda. "I always get Fungus' motorcycles to start the same way."

Then she saw the monk and her expression changed. The monk shrank back in the seat, in fear of frog.

"Please, I have recovered!" he said defensively.

"Still speak the same way, though," glared an unconvinced Grizelda.

"Turning me into a frog and then back again has broken the spell they put on me."

"Hang about. How did you change back? I put at least three days' worth of time into that spell."

"This young lady changed me back," explained the ex-monk/frog.

They all turned and looked at Linda.

"All I did was pick him up," she said.

"You're a bit young to be doin' that," her uncle retorted.

---

*   As the monk had previously been a student, the term is used quite loosely here.

"No, I mean I actually picked him up, and he changed back at once. Into this. Is it an improvement, do you think?" Linda asked.

"He probably thinks so. 'Ere, you, do you still think that you are a monk?"

"No. My name's Marc. Not Om, or anything. I am a student."

"Got it!" exclaimed Grizelda.* "Are you wearing your Ward of Lingard, Linda?"

"Yes, auntie. Do you think it could have been that?"

"Bet it was. That's impressive power there."

"Look," cried Erica, who was peering over the wall from the sunroof. "There are some monks coming this way."

Imelda did not need encouragement to floor the accelerator and the coach moved out from the lane and drove off down the main road, swaying slightly, into the night. Special effects dug into the budget and paid for a swarm of bats to arise from the trees behind them, in salute to the great escape.

"You'll never guess who I bumped into in there," said Ben, as they all settled down comfortably.

"The Dalai Lama?" suggested Imelda.

"Richard Gere?" offered Erica, hopefully.

"Our bank manager?" asked Grizelda, with equal hope.

"Erald."

"Erald? What on earth was he doin' there?"

"Spyin'." said Ben.

"Like James Bond?"

"He was very orange. But he told me that this lot have a plot to take over the country, an' they start in a few days."

"'Ere," said Grizelda, thoughtfully, and turned to the student/monk. "What can you tell us about it?"

"I don't know much, I am sad to say," replied Marc.

"Typical student. Knows it all until you ask something worth knowin'."

"No. We were just the troops. Mushrooms, really."

"Mushrooms?" asked Imelda.

"Kept in the dark and fed on –"

"We get the picture," interrupted Grizelda.

"Erald said we should go and team up with his lads, but he didn't tell me where they were. Actually, I don't think he knew," Ben added.

---

* The others all moved back carefully in case *it* was catching.

"The Tuatha? Handy lads in a scrap, that's true," mused Grizelda.

"How could we find them?" asked Imelda.

"What's the biggest pub in the area? Oh no, I know where they'll be: with Fungus an' The Banned."

"What's Fungus doin' down here?" asked Ben.

"Playin' at a beer festival."

Ben's face illuminated. "Perfect." He sighed.

An hour later, the coach approached the showground, having stopped only briefly on the way into Builth Wells.

"Excuse me ma'am, but you need a pass to get onto the – Rivet! Rivet!"

"Here's one I made earlier to keep you company.* Better have his clipboard, too."

The *Mondeo* drove up the drive towards the gates, a grim expression on the face of the taxi-driving junior wizard. He could see the view through the rear view mirror, and didn't like it. Ned had rummaged around in the back of the car, and found his staff, and was now negotiating with the electric window switch for enough clearance to aim the staff at the locked and guarded gates ahead.

"Hurry up, cos I ain't slowin' down!" yelled the driver.

The *Mondeo* barreled past a brightly painted sign.

"ARAF." said the sign, but not very loudly.

"One day, we've got to find out what that means," muttered Ned, before aiming his staff at the gates. A burst of green light, and the gates fell back on their hinges, knocking flat the orange-robed security monks who were preparing to dispute their exit.

"Om. Now I am glad that I renounced worldly wealth," groaned a once felonious monk.

"Why?" groaned his companion from underneath a gate.

"I wouldn't fancy living in a gated community after this…"

"Left or right?" demanded the driver.

In the back seat, the assistant assistant moaned.

"Not that again."

---

*   Sadly, this spell is not available on the Blue Peter website.

"Right," ordered Ned.

Back wheels fighting for grip on the gravel, the *Mondeo* lurched through the opening, turned right, and vanished into the gloom.

Close behind them, the running monks stopped at the gates to aid their stricken and smitten comrades.

"May their Karma wither for a thousand years," groaned the first monk, as the heavy gate was removed from his person.

"Where to, Boss?" asked the junior wizard. The assistant assistant was gibbering quietly while crouched on the floor behind the back seats, looking up at the two throwing stars embedded in the back of the driver's headrest.[*]

"Tenby," said Ned. "There's an accountancy franchise there where we can get some fresh instructions."

Before too long, the *Mondeo* was parked outside the local offices of *TGM Accountancy (Wales) Limited*.

The junior was chatting up the receptionist while drinking a cup of that ubiquitous and uniquely awful stuff found only in the receptions of accountants' offices.[**] It doesn't seem to matter if you ask for tea, coffee, or a refreshing herbal drink, it always looks the same and tastes of nothing at all. Not even the water used in the preparation has a taste.[***]

"So that's the craic." said Ned.

The senior partner in the franchise thought for a moment, and then pulled a large, ornate mirror out of his desk drawer.

"We'd better have a conference call," he said.

"Why not use the internet?" asked Ned.

"You never know who's listening. This is more secure. Runs through a different operating system to Windows."

"Like the Apple Mac?"

"Yes, but we call it SOD. Standard Operating Demesne. Plus it's a sod when it goes wrong, so it's well named."

He tapped the mirror twice and stared hard into his own reflection.

"Better try the spellcheck," he muttered, and reached into his desk drawer again. He pulled out a hammer, and threatened the mirror with it.

"Now do what I told you!"

---

[*]   The junior wizard was unaware of this extraneous adornment to his car. And would certainly have disapproved of it if he had known.

[**]   It comes in the franchise pack.

[***]   Taste is charged as an extra on the bill.

The face of the mirror became cloudy and then revealed the face of The Grey Mage, which was hardly an improvement.

"Ah, Dafydd. Have they been in touch?"

"Got Ned with me now. And he's got lots to tell you."

"Is that you, Boss?" asked Ned.

The Grey Mage drew a deep breath.

"No, it's Clare the dragon receptionist. Of course it's me, you idiot."

The image in the mirror wavered, and Dafydd raised his hammer again. The picture cleared up at once.

"Dafydd has bin telling me about the need for net security. Or mebbe it were a security net, couldn't understand his accent properly."

"Right, but now get on with it."

"We followed Fungus an' his band down to Manchester." Ned shuddered at the memory.

"Did you get in to the gig?"

"Yeah. Bein' a taxi driver, he knew all the back ways in, even at Manchester U."

"It's a test they have to pass to get the badge, I think."

"Like learnin' how to short-change the customers?"

"That's normally natural talent."

"Anyway, the promoter had just tried to keep the takings back, so we talked ter 'im after the band 'ad 'ad a word."

"What did he say?"

"He said: 'If I give you all this money that they left me, will you go away?'"

"Well, you made a profit on the night then."

"Yeah. Then we followed them down to Stockport."

The Grey Mage shuddered in sympathy. "At least it wasn't Liverpool."

"Then down here. But while we were looking fer somewhere ter park up an' watch their nex' move, we got hijacked."

"Three evil wizards? Hijacked?" The Grey Mage was shocked.

"These weird monks knew some Zen thing, took us out before we could fight back."

"What about the honor of Caer Surdin?"

"We was just overwhelmed."

"I'm not."

Ned gulped. "Anyway, when we came round, we was in a cell."

"That's a good idea."

"In a big house. We managed to get out, an' see what were goin' on."

"Pity you didn't see it sooner. Before you were attacked. Still. Go on."

"You know that Ben from the lakeside?"

"Him who lives with Grotbags?"

"Yeah. They'd taken 'im at the same time, thought he might be the reincarnation of their los' leader."

"You mean they thought he was a sales promotion?"

Dafydd intervened.

"The Ben Buddhists are a local religious sect. Recently they have been recruiting a lot of students, but we didn't know what they were after until Ned reported."

"So, he's done something right?"

"Yes. They have a plan to take over the government, using this Ben as a figurehead."

"Anyway, we were dragged before Ben, who the monks were treatin' as a supreme leader," continued Ned. "But he saved our lives, then we hid in a side room until we met one of the Tuatha."

"So they too have a finger in this pie?" said The Grey Mage, reflectively.

"He didn't seem hungry ter me. He helped us ter get out, we found the car, and got away."

"What happened to Ben?"

"He got out too. Then Grizelda came in on her broomstick, an' flew off with him."

"There's no accounting for taste," mused TGM.

"Definitely not on my abacus. Don't taste of anything," remarked Dafydd.

"So what happened to The Banned, whom you were supposed to be following?"

"Dafydd says that they are playin' at a festival about 50 miles away from here."

"Right. Well, your priority is still the mission I gave you here in the office. I will consult with my fellows over these felonious monks," ordered The Grey Mage.

"I think they preferred chant to jazz," Ned told his Boss.

"Still, you should follow the band."

"Yer mean we get to go to a beer festival? On expenses?"

Ned was out of the door, before his chair had hit the ground. The Grey Mage groaned, realizing his mistake.

The *Mondeo* moved with more impetus this time and, before too long, was arriving at the showground gates.

"Rivet! Rivet! Rivet!"

"He says, we can't park 'ere, Ned."

"Honestly, that Grizelda. She might as well put up a sign sayin' 'Here be Frogs'."

"It's not all that hard to follow her around, that's true. Just look for the trail of frogs."

"An' we are tryin' to find her? Shouldn't we be goin' the other way?" suggested the junior wizard.

"Well, the boss says we have to stick ter the band. We carry on with our job. Any objectors miss the gig."

"Just remind me what the mission is?" asked the assistant assistant.

"Stoppin' them bringing a new throne back to the Helvyndelve."

"Ah, right. That mission."

"And I ask – just for information – will this involve listening to a lot of loud music an' drinkin' a lot of beer?" asked the junior.

"Probably."

"I like this mission," grinned the assistant assistant.

Grizelda had indeed passed that way earlier, but had run into security.

"I am sorry, but you must buy a ticket to see the band. Um, that's 6 tickets."

"I've got this t-shirt, it says: 'I'm with The Banned'."

"Tesco's. £ 9.99. Even I've got one," replied security.

Security at the big marquee housing the gig was two tall gentlemen, in long cloaks and hoods that hid their faces. Those concert-goers capable of noticing assumed it was part of the ambience for the gig.

"We don't need tickets. See? Oh dear, I seem to have run out of frog," said Grizelda, alarmed.

"Maybe you're exhausted," said Linda.

"Is that frog-xhausted?" asked Chris.

"Grizelda, you've been overusing that spell. Maybe it needs a rest, to recover," comforted Imelda.

"It did make me itch though... " said one of the security hoods.

"Grizelda?" asked the other hood. "What are you doing here?"

"How come you know me?" demanded Grizelda.

"I'm Malan. And that's Finn. That's why your spell didn't work, we are immune."

"Probably all the beer we drink," said Finn.

"I knew it had a social use," Malan said, pleased.

"As well as the antisocial use? Great!"

The hoods were briefly drawn back, to reveal the faces of the two Tuatha, for identification purposes.[*]

"What are you doin' here?" demanded Grizelda.

"What are *you* doing here?" retorted Finn.

"I asked first."

"We're the security for The Banned," Finn told her. "If any trouble starts, we deal with it."

"Deal with it? If that Laeg's here, he's more likely to start it."

"And the mortals couldn't deal with him, so it's best we are here. Now. Your turn."

"Well, Fungus came ter see us," started Grizelda.

"Then I got kidnapped," said Ben.

"But got away," continued Grizelda, "so we thought we'd come an' see the gig."

"And get a drink or two," added Ben.

"Besides," added Linda, "Chris and I are the backing singers."

Having heard her singing, most of those there turned and looked at her in disbelief.

"Well, we did OK in Manchester," said Chris.

Malan reached into a hidden pocket with his right hand.

"You'll need these," he told them.

"Earplugs?!" snarled Linda.

Malan quickly put that hand back in his pocket and delved into his other pocket.

"On the other hand," he said quickly, "how about some backstage passes?"

"I'll stick with the first offer," muttered Ben.

Backstage, The Banned Underground were experiencing some pre-show nerves.

"Still no M&Ms," complained Scar.

"Last packet of choccie digestives, too," moaned Dai. "What do I do if I run out of whisky?"

"It's a long way to the bar," said Felldyke, as worried as Scar for once.

Haemar made a long gargling noise.

"What's the set list?" asked Dai, into the silence.

---

[*] Direct recognition was the only ID that they carried. Erald had experimented with Iris recognition but found that, after enough drinks, his brothers couldn't recognize her.

"Same as all the other sets, really. Make it up as we go along," Fungus told him.

"I'm worried about Scar's sound balance," fussed GG.

"I'm more worried about his unsound balance," said Fungus.

Haemar made another long gargling noise.

"Do you think he's drowning?"

"No such luck."

The teenagers bounced into the backstage area.

"Hey, look who's here!" exclaimed Fungus, glad of the distraction. "The backing group!"

Haemar ceased drowning and switched into flood mode, sending half a gallon of water gushing across the room.

"Watch the electrics!" cried GG, in alarm.

Grizelda walked over to Dai. "Malan said I was to give yer this."

Dai seized the bottle and drank a quarter of it in one go.

"That's better!"

He belched and flames shot across the room and set fire to Haemar's beard.

"Flamin' watch it!" snarled Haemar, dunking his chin into his now water-filled helmet.

"Sorry. Accident," Dai apologized.

"Save it for the light show."

In front of the stage, the audience had assembled and was starting to express some impatience.

"What are we starting with?" Scar asked.

"*Goin' Underground* of course." Haemar was still in a bad mood.

"I think I might have upset him." Dai was concerned.

"He's the lead singer. Upset and grumpy is his default state," Felldyke reassured him.

"WE'RE ON. Come on you two, you'll be late!" Fungus yelled.

"We'll catch you up."

"You're the drummer. Are you ever goin' to learn to be in time?"

"They're louder than we are." Dai had never played to such a large audience.

"GG will just up the volume on the amps. Don't be nervous," Scar reassured Dai.

Haemar was working up the crowd, getting them to stamp in time with his foot, and waving the mic stand in a threatening manner. Eddie stood at the side of the stage, carrying the satnav, which was switched to 'record'.

GG moved in front of Dai and Felldyke.

"Don't be nervous, Dai," he shouted over the audience. "That lot are too drunk to hear a wrong note, so just go for it!"

Dai, encouraged, smiled.

"Besides," GG muttered to Scar, "I've turned his amp down."

"Here we go!" yelled Haemar, GG wind-milled his right arm... and music happened.

The band roared through their favorite first half set.

Going Underground was followed by *Jailhouse Rock, Start Me Up, Sweet Home Chicago, Baby Please Don't Go, Summertime Blues, Please Don't Touch, Rock And Roll,* and *Jumping Jack Flash.*

It is fair say that they were all pretty worn out at the interval.

"Dai weren't bad at all," Scar said to GG, as they left the stage.

"I know. I even turned his volume back up."

"Do you think he noticed?"

"Slower for the second half," Haemar said to Fungus.

"OK. What do yer want to open with?"

Haemar looked at Grizelda talking to Linda and Chris.

"*Black Magic Woman? Green Manalishi? I Put A Spell On You? Witchey Woman?*"

"Works for me. Couple more blues standards, finish on *Gimme Some Lovin'* and *Johnny B Goode?*"

"Fine." Haemar filled his helmet with beer and fell face down into it.

"And there's still no M&Ms," Scar moaned.

"Next time, why not ask for some?"

"Ah."

The dark wizards were enjoying the show.

"Well, after a set like this, we won't 'ave to worry about them shooting off afterwards."

"Why's that, Ned?" asked the junior.

"They'll be too knackered."

"Hey, they were pretty damn good again," enthused the assistant assistant.

"So let's try an' get to the bar, get a few beers, an' we'll crash out after the gig fer a bit," ordered Ned.

"That's the sort of order I like."

The trio made their way to the bar. While mildly hampered by the lack of a frog spell, Ned did have a trick of sending a mild electric shock down the length of his staff, to land with pinpoint accuracy on the bum of whosoever was in his way. With accompanying shouts and much jumping about, the wizards made steady progress through the crowd.

"Grizelda's askin' if we want to play the *Frog Chorus* in the second half?"
"No."
"She can provide the frogs."
"Still no."

"Hey, Finn, look at all those guys jumping up and down. Do you think they're punk rockers?" asked Liamm.
"Nah. It's those three from Caer Surdin, trying to get to the bar."
"There's only three of them."
"So?"
"Shouldn't there be *four to a bar?*"
"That's the bar staff, idiot. Mind you, let's have a bit of fun."
Finn slipped away from the stage and went behind the bar to help the hard-pressed staff.
"Three pints, mate," called Ned.
"Here you go."
"Cheers. And one for yourself."
"Thanks."
Finn slid back to Diarmid, chuckling.
"What did you do?"
"Added a bit of sleeping potion. Couple of hours, they'll be well away. And we can be well away too, without them knowing."
"You spiked their drinks?"
"Don't be daft. That would have broken the glasses."
"The Banned are comin' on again," called Malan.
"The audience likes them; they'll not be any trouble tonight."
"Even from the punk wizards?" asked Liamm.
"Especially from the punk wizards."
The gig came to another triumphant conclusion, and The Banned Underground trooped off the stage after the third encore. (*Flip, Flop and Fly*, if you were interested. With extra frogs, courtesy of Grizelda.) The beer flowed freely, often because band members were too tired to aim for

the glass properly. Or a mouth, in the absence of a glass. Some time passed, as the group wound down.

"Der."

"Eddie liked the light show."

Grizelda smirked. She had sold it to the band the year before.

"Especially the fireworks."

Dai blew hard and flames roared all around the food cooking on the improvised BBQ.

"Oi! No blaming me for that one!" yelled Fungus, beating at the flames with his cap, and then dancing on his cap to extinguish the flames roosting there.

Haemar lay on his back on a couch, gargling (with whisky this time). While Felldyke and Scar started eating, Fungus sat down beside him.

"Great gig, Haemar, you was great."

Haemar continued gargling, without moving.

"Der."

Eddie sat down next to Fungus.

"Eddie's packed the bus, we should set off now to escape Ned an' his lot. Finn fixed their drinks."

"Der."

"What did he fix them with Eddie? Knowing Finn, it was a Mickey."

Eddie nudged Haemar, who rolled off the couch and came up spluttering.

"I were drowning, you git!" he choked.

"Well, why didn't you turn over?" asked Fungus.

"I were too tired."

"We'll sleep in the bus, on the way to Waccibacci."

"What about the kids? They were good, I thought," Haemar said.

"Yeah, sang well. But we'll leave them with Grotbags. Then Dai can get in the van."

"Good idea. The heater's packed up, an' it's a cool night."

"And we'll need the trailer fer the throne," Fungus pointed out.

Haemar sat up and looked around. The rest of the band were still celebrating. The Tuatha were helping them to extend the bar tab into new and uncharted reaches of accountancy. Grizelda, Ben and the witches were trying to extricate the teenagers from the party to crash in the camper coach for what remained of the night.

"I haven't had a chance to talk to you before now," he said to Fungus softly.

"Yeah?"

"I want to know what Lakin said to you that got you so worried," Haemar said sternly.

Fungus looked all around, but only Eddie was close enough to overhear.

"Lakin said that the Amulet of Kings draws its power through the throne. Even when it was hidden round the back of the throne all those years, it was close enough to recover its energy. But with the throne gone completely, he reckons it will run out of juice by the end of the month. Then the Helvyndelve will lose power, the doors won't open or close, things will run down and stop."

Haemar looked bemused.

"So?"

"So the bars will stop serving, an' no one can cook pizza. Oh, the doors won't lock either."

Haemar looked worried, then his face cleared.

"So what's the worry? We find this dwarf, buy a throne, go home, no problem."

"Lakin reckons Caer Surdin know too. And they've sent a team to stop us. Ned and his two lads."

Haemar stopped looking bemused, and started to look worried. "So that's why they keep turning up at the gigs."

"Yes. They are following us to see if we're the ones looking for the new throne."

"Which we are."

"Glad to see *you* are keeping up. So we are going to leave now, to stop *them* from keeping up."

"That's good thinking, Fungus."

"What I'm best at."

"No. What you are best at is playing sax, and getting off yer face on Kendal Mint Cake."

"Der."

"Yes, Eddie. Time to go."

Grizelda came over to the two of them. Seeing members of The Banned Underground, with their heads together and clearly plotting, always made her uneasy.

"Spill the beans," she instructed.

Fungus examined his entirely bean-free food plate. Eddie tipped what was left on his plate onto the floor.

Grizelda sighed. "I meant, tell me what's goin' on."

"We, that is, The Banned, are going ter split and find this Waccibacci-san," Fungus admitted.

"Do you know where to look?"

"Got directions off his son, so we should be OK."

"The kids stay with me," ordered Grizelda.

"Fine by us," agreed Haemar, earning a glare.

"We're goin' back to me cottage, to report on these mad monks to me seniors at Caer Rigor." Grizelda told them.

"OK. We'll keep in touch. Let us know if you see Ned an' his lot. What are the Tuatha goin' to do?" asked Fungus.

"Do yer mean besides get very drunk?" retorted Haemar.

"I don't know of any power, magical or not, that can stop them doin' that," Grizelda laughed. "Be seein' you then, lads." Grizelda turned and began rounding on and rounding up her varied collection of witches, wizard and family.

"Not if I see you first," replied Haemar, very, very quietly.

CHAPTER TEN

Daybreak. A magical, mysterious time when the fresh, golden light of a new dawn in a new day spreads gently across the land, making everyone feel good. And clean. And refreshed.

Occasionally, however, a system failure occurs. In this case, when the interior of an elderly *Mondeo* was illuminated, enlightened*, but sadly not refreshed at all. Also, no cleaning function was available and so the awakening bodies within were distinctly un-freshened.

"Oh, my head," groaned Ned, on the back seat.

"Mine too," complained the driver, who had reclined his seat for greater comfort during the night. Onto Ned's head.

"Me back aches," grumbled the assistant assistant, who had been unable to recline his seat at all.

"Wassat?" croaked the driver, looking at his dashboard.

Firmly fixed to it (with well-used chewing gum) was a shiny-looking satnav. With a note.

"Compliments of The Banned Underground," read the assistant assistant, at the third attempt.

"Cool. They've left us a memento of the gig," said the junior wizard.

"Wonder why?" Ned tried to beat his brain cells into co-operating and cogitating.

"Wonder where they are?" asked the junior, getting out of the car and looking around.

"Their minibus were parked up just over there," pointed Ned. As his arm waved around rather a lot, this was not treated as a serious attempt at pinpoint navigation. Nevertheless, it was clear (probably because of the translucent morning light, etc.) that the bus had vanished.

"Oh no, we've lost them," Ned groaned.

"There's no tire marks," said the junior, getting back into the car.

"So?" asked the assistant assistant.

"That means that they left in the night, before the dew rose."

"I thought dew fell."

"Na, it's not slippery out there."

---

* And, according to the Ben Buddhists, recreated anew as well. Regrettably in this instance with the same form as the night before. If the theory worked properly, I would now look like Tom Cruise in *Top Gun*... Sadly, this is not the case.

The junior reached forward and pressed the button that turned on the satnav.

"What are you doin' that for?" asked Ned.

"It might be a clue."

Haemar's voice rose from the box, singing *Show Me the Way to Go Home*.

"Obviously their idea of a joke."

Haemar's recording changed to '*One Whisky, One Bourbon, One Beer*'.

"Now he's takin' the mickey."

"That's it," said Ned, slowly, "the Mickey. We were drugged. That's why we slept while they left."

The other two applauded his ability to find a plausible excuse, from thin air.

"Not our fault if they drugged us," said the assistant assistant.

"Thought that third beer tasted off," agreed the junior.

"So did I, but they were only selling lager by then, so it all tastes off anyway."

"OK, let's think," said Ned.

His juniors were less enthusiastic this time.

"That box is right. Let's go home."

"Do you want to be the one ter tell the Boss we've failed?" asked Ned.

"That's your job," muttered the assistant assistant. "I'm just the driver."

"And I'm only here for the beer," added the junior.

"So it's my decision. Fire up the *Mondeo*. We're going huntin'."

At only the fifth attempt, and after Ned had poured some whisky (from a bottle he just happened to have in a pocket) into the inlet manifold of the engine, the *Mondeo* sprang into life and headed for the gate.

"No sign of security, this morning," said the junior.

"That's their clipboard though. There, beside that frog."

"Right."

"Is that an instruction?" asked the driver.

"No. He meant left," the satnav told him.

Ned smiled. "Got it. We do the opposite to what that thing says."

"Doesn't everyone anyway?" asked the driver.

"Just turn right."

The *Mondeo* headed out into rural west Wales. The satnav started singing.

"Dunno this one," said the junior wizard. "What is it?"

"Coldplay. *Lost*," said the assistant assistant.

Ned snarled, and thumped the satnav, which changed track.

"Now what's this one?" he demanded.
"Bonnie Tyler. *Lost in France*," replied the junior wizard.
"Nah, we'd have noticed if we'd crossed the Channel."

Some miles away, the tour bus had managed to get lost in the old fashioned way, without the aid of modern technology.
"The map says that there should be a right turn here."
"Der."
They all looked at the hedgerow which stretched into the middle distance without a break.
"Maybe we made a wrong turn at that last junction," suggested Haemar.
"The one with three road signs, all pointing in different directions to the same place?"
"Yeah. Mebbe we should have turned right there."
"Can we turn round?" asked GG.
"Not a chance. The lane's too narrow."
"OK then, we could reverse for three miles."
"DER!"
"Eddie says, no."
"I think we all got that, GG."
"I've got an idea." said Felldyke.
"Treasure it, it's probably lonely in there."
"Let's get Dai to fly up, an' scout round."
"That's not a bad idea, Felldyke."
"Hang on, I'm the one havin' to fly while drunk."
"Dai, we've only known you a couple of days, but we haven't seen you sober yet."
"So?"
"So just nip up, scout out the roads, and come back down again. Only take a moment."
"Oh, go on then."

"Aberporth Firing Zone Controller – Victor Kilo One Six."

"Victor Kilo – Aberporth Controller. Go ahead."

"Aberporth, Victor Kilo is an RAF training mission from Valley, inbound for target drone practice from the east, five minutes to run, 800 feet."

"Victor Kilo – Aberporth Controller. Target drone has been launched and is in strike area. Be aware of recent local traffic on radar directly ahead of you, no height information."

"Aberporth Controller – Victor Kilo. Looking for traffic, and BREAKING RIGHT! BREAKING RIGHT!"

"Victor Kilo, can you identify the traffic?"

"IT'S A RED DRAGON, CARRYING A ROAD MAP!"

"Victor Kilo One Six – Aberporth Controller. Terminate mission and return to base immediately. Confirm instructions."

"Any bother, Dai?"

"No. RAF seem a bit busy at the moment though. Must be a flap on."

"Did you suss out the way?"

"Yeah. Map's out of scale. The right turn is another mile or so away yet, then we go into the village."

"Good. It feels like lunch time and there must be a pub there."

The tour bus set off again.

"There's the pub. It's shut," said Haemar, after a few minutes.

"Rats!"

"Well, if properly roasted,"

"No, Dai. Just no," insisted Haemar.

"Taste like chicken, they do."

"I said NO."

"Der."

"Eddie's seen the shop," said GG.

"Where?" asked Fungus.

"Look down the street. 'Plumbers and Decorators', says the big sign."

"Could be anyone."

"And below that? 'Novelty Toilets. They're Magic'?"

"That sounds like our man. Well spotted, Eddie."

"Der."

"Don't mention it. Credit where credit's due," praised Fungus.

"DER!"

"Eddie was a taxi driver, you idiot. They hate the word credit."

"Oh. Sorry, Eddie, no offence meant."

"Der."

"Right. Haemar an' Dai, with me," ordered Fungus. "You lot stay here, an' guard the bus an' the cash."

Fungus, Haemar and Dai the Dragon emerged from the tour bus, blinking a little in the strong sunlight.

In many places, the sight of a green bog troll, a dwarf in chain mail and a (drunken) dragon on the High Street might have aroused some comment. Here, they were just assumed to be tourists, probably American (or worse, English).

To the sound of oriental chimes, they opened the door and entered the shop.

The *Mondeo* was also navigating the by ways of west Wales

"I'm fed up of the music on this satnav. What's on the CD?" complained Ned.

"Neil Diamond."

"Are yer serious? Oh well, give it a go. What's this track?"

The assistant assistant had to consult the case.

"Says it's from the Jonathan Seagull film sequence. It's called *Lost*."*

"I've had enough of this.** Try the radio."

Ned started fiddling with the reception, finally hitting it with his staff in frustration, until suddenly the voice of the Aberporth RAF controller came clearly out of the speakers. The *Mondeo* coasted to a halt as they listened.

"Gimme the map, quick!"

They all stared at the road map and Ned quickly drew a line on the map as the conversation unfolded. The junior, who liked maps, started to object, but Ned quelled him with a glance.

"So, they are goin' to be looking for this place, wherever it is, round here."

"Gotcha," agreed the assistant assistant.

---

* Even running gags can get a bit lost.

** Ned clearly shared the readers' views.

"So, if we stake out this road 'ere, that's gonna be their quickest way home. Soon as we see them comin', we can set a trap."

"What's the plan, boss?"

"If we can get them to stop, then I can blast the new throne apart, an' we go home victorious."

"I like that plan," agreed the assistant assistant.

"Especially the bit where we get to go home. I'd kill fer a steak pudding, right now."

Three stomachs rumbled in unison at the thought.

"When did we last eat?" asked the junior wizard.

Ned rummaged in his bag and brought out the dwindling supply of cash for on the road expenses.

"What we'll do, is: we'll hold up a petrol station. Fill up the *Mondeo*, an' then we can spend the rest of the money on food. How about that?"

"Works for me."

"Let's get the food first," suggested the junior wizard.

"There's a lay-by ahead. Mebbe there's a burger van there?"

Serendipitously, there was. Before long, the evil wizards had drunk plenty of coffee, stocked up on burgers, and loaded chocolate and cans into the car.

"Now, let's find a place to lurk and watch out for the *Sprinter*," ordered Ned.

"Ned, the fuel's a bit low. Let's fill up first, in case we 'ave to make a getaway."

"Good idea."

Before long, a fully-fuelled *Mondeo* was driving out of the petrol station forecourt.

"Rivet! Rivet!"

"I tried usin' Grizelda's frog spell, there. Seemed to work."

"How long will the attendant stay changed for?" asked the junior wizard.

"Not long, I don't think. Never used it before, so I didn't know 'ow much power to give it. Didn't want 'im to stay changed forever, did I?"

"Why? Aren't we the evil ones?"

"Yeah. But I don't know 'ow long we're gonna be, so we might need 'im to work the pumps fer us on the way back."

Behind them, an enraged amphibian had jumped onto the counter, and was using his tongue to press the emergency buttons on the telephone system that alerted the local police to a drive-off. "Rivet, rivet, rivet!"

"Sarge, there's been a drive-off at the filling station. Clapped out, rust colored *Mondeo* with a taxi sign on the roof."

"OK. Put it out to the patrol cars. Anyone sees them, pull them in."

In a West Wales village, The Banned entered the shop of the throne maker.

The vertically challenged shopkeeper bowed low.

"Can I help you three… let's say, gentlemen?"

"We are looking for someone who goes by the name Waccibacci-san," Haemar said.

"Are you from the police?" asked the shopkeeper.

"No sir, we are musicians."

"Really. You sir, the dragon pretending to be a human dressed as a dragon," he addressed Dai, "what do you play?"

"The bass."

"And you?" he asked Haemar.

"I'm the singer."

"Finally, to you? The bog troll, unless I am much mistaken?"

"I play sax."

"Oh dear. I'm sorry to hear that"

Fungus bridled at the insult, but Haemar quickly stepped in front of him.

"We are on a quest." Haemar announced.

"To seek is to find," replied Waccibacci-san, bowing.

"We understand," said Fungus, who didn't, "but in this case we need to find something specific."

The shopkeeper waved an elegant hand.*

"As you can see, I sell novelty toilets."

Haemar looked around, although there was no need to do so as the shop was clearly empty.**

"We have been given a mission by the Lord of Helvyndelve."

"Ah, Lord Lucan. How is he?" enquired the shopkeeper.

---

*   Which, in true Zen tradition, made no sound.

** Apart of course from those who were inside the shop. And the stock.

"Still missing. His son, Lord Lakin, has now taken the throne."

"*Sic transit gloria mundi*," replied Waccibacci.*

"How true," put in Fungus, who again didn't understand, but was feeling left out.

"And what is this task?" asked Waccibacci.

"The ancient and magical Throne of the Mountain King has had an accident."

"I recall it well. It took me many moons to make that throne."

"That's bad news," worried Haemar.

"Why is that?" asked Waccibacci.

"Because we need another one."

"The first one should still be functioning. What was this accident?"

"It got hit by a flying guitarist."

"I do not think that that is covered by the warranty."

"Lord Lakin guessed so. He wants you to make another throne, one with the same magical powers."

"That will not be easy."

Fungus and Haemar looked at each other. Neither fancied going back without a throne. A life on the run from Lakin's vengeance did not appeal either, if they were to run away instead.

"But something may be possible," said Waccibacci-san, to their enormous relief.

"Ah" said Haemar, as light dawned. "You mean the cost."

"Material wealth means nothing to me," replied Waccibacci.

Fungus began to brighten up too.

"But that which costs much is valued most highly, and my work must be valued."

Waccibacci-san named a figure. Fungus clutched at his chest.

"Is your friend ill?"

"No," replied Haemar. "I think it's a panic attack."

"The budget can't stretch that far," gasped Fungus.

"Ah, so. Then perhaps a budget model could be arranged, using existing parts."

Waccibacci-san made a number of sketches on a pad. Haemar had to sit down, and Fungus doubled over laughing, as the panic receded.

---

* An old saying about the wonders of the world passing away. And nothing to do with Gloria being sick in the Transit after the Monday night gig.

"But would it have the same magical strength to power the Amulet of Kings?" asked Haemar.

"Oh yes, I will build that into the back, here. This could be ready tomorrow."

Haemar looked at Fungus, who was still laughing uncontrollably, and shook hands on the deal.

He bowed to Waccibacci and, with Dai's help, pulled the stricken Fungus out of the shop.

"There was no need for that!" he yelled at Fungus, when safely outside.

"Sorry. I pictured Lakin and lost control."

Haemar, still sulking, climbed into the minibus.

"We'll find somewhere to crash, then get off tomorrow morning," he ordered, trying to ignore Fungus' antics.

"Think that I'll have to go home too in the morning," said Dai. "No room for me inside, an' you need the trailer. But I'll join you in the Helvyndelve for the gig, if that's OK."

Chapter Eleven

"I call to order the Chapter Meeting of the Ruling Council of the Charitable Order of Ben Buddhists," announced a senior monk. The Ruling Council was seated around a large table in what had been the dining room of the mansion. All the original portraits had been removed and replaced with one large oil painting over the fireplace.

All those seated around the table bowed.

"Om. Let us show our reverence for the Founder of our Order."

All rose, turned towards the large painting of a monk that hung over the fireplace, and bowed low, before being seated again.

"How is our recruitment drive?" asked the senior.

"Om. We have attained our targets. Enough students were collected at the beach party to fulfill our needs."

"That is excellent. Logistics?"

"Om. Two of our new recruits own coach companies, so we will have enough transport for the task."

"Well done. Supplies?"

"Om. Indoctrination have supported us by placing the recruits on a program of fasting and meditation, so our supplies will last beyond the target date."

"Well done. Cooperation is the key to our success. Technical?"

"Um."

"Um?" queried the senior monk.

"Sorry, meant Om. The laptop has been programed with the destructive force, but we still require the access codes to the BBC computer system, to allow us to hack the network and seize control."

"Glory to Ben. That will deal with the broadcasting. What about the government system?"

"Om. Oh, that was easy. We hacked into the government website in minutes."

"Excellent. Accounts?"

"Om. I may report now to the Council the results of our discussions with the Institute of Accountants, as controlled by Caer Surdin."

"Do you have good news for us?"

"Both yes and no."*

---

    *   Even dressed in saffron robes, an accountant remains, fundamentally, an accountant.

"Please, amplify."

"Sorry, did I speak too softly?" asked the accountant.

"I meant make clear your meaning."

"Om. They do not seem to me to be fully committed to our cause. They are sending a consultancy group to assist us once the take-over is in place."

"For a fee, I suppose?"

"More like a **FEE** really. I had to tack two extra rows onto my abacus to calculate it and that was before disbursements."

"What are disbursements?" asked one of the Council.

"Om. The extra money you have to give them to disperse afterwards, I think."

"Om. Money is a tarnish to the soul," commented a council member.

The saffron accountant, who had a mystic look about him, looked at the monk.

"We can only afford souls if we have strict accounting."

"Peace," instructed the senior council member.

"We are close to our goal of becoming the Ruling Power in Wales. Let us focus on that. What else needs to be undertaken?"

"Om. My task is to coordinate the coup."

"Great. Mine's a winter vegetable," said a less senior member.

"I said coup, not soup."

"Sorry."

"Om. On Monday morning we will flood Cardiff Bay with our collection of indoctrinated acolytes." The speaker looked around the room.

"Meanwhile, an elite team of our accountants will enter the Welsh Assembly Building and gain control of the government computer systems with this laptop.

"Simultaneously, the media team will take over the broadcasting of radio and TV with the aid of this second laptop. We will broadcast only our own news bulletins followed by non-stop Barry Manilow records.

"We will then announce that we have won a surprise election, using our computers to show the results we will have prepared earlier."

"Om. Will not the Westminster government object?"

"It's pretty much what they did themselves," said the senior monk.

"Om. Perhaps they will send troops?"

"But we will have changed the tolls on the Severn Bridges. By the time the army drivers find enough change to pay for their vehicles to cross, it will be too late."

"Om. I have a concern."

"Please, speak," said the senior.

"I am concerned for the negative karma we may accrue."

"Om. This take-over is for the greater good."

"I'm not talking about seizing power. It is playing Barry Manilow all day long on the radio that worries me."

"Om. Then we could add Simply Red and Chris de Burgh," replied the accountant.

"I fear that might make the karmic burden worse!"

"Then brothers, we shall take that chance. The Council meeting is over; we meet at midnight on Sunday to start our coup."

The most senior monk pulled the chief accountant to one side as the others left and waited until the room was entirely empty before speaking.

"You are sure that they have no idea?"

"None. They still think that we seek the overthrow of the Welsh Assembly and to end up in charge."

"Power corrupts everyone."

"But money is worse."

"Agreed. So we will be doing them a favor when we don't share the money with them."

"Perhaps that good deed will lighten our burden."

"No, leaving the money behind would do that."

"Which we are not going to do. Do you think that Caer Surdin suspect us?"

"Hard to tell. They clearly don't think that we are going to get away with stealing the country."

"Who would want to steal a country? You'd never get it through airport security these days."

"The money is so much easier. I've already installed the cash removal virus into the laptop, so I just have to make sure it gets into the computer system. Then we can do a runner while the rest hang about chanting until the government gets them. I've set up a taxi for the getaway to the airport."

"That's not secure. Cancel the taxi and get a hire car instead."

"Om. Anything you say."

"Leave that for the converts."

The accountant and senior monk opened the door and found themselves face-to-face with an orange-clad figure, with a cowl instead of a dodgy haircut.[*]

---

[*]   He still had a dodgy haircut under the cowl, of course.

The coach pulled up in the yard and the assorted occupants emerged, yawned, and headed for the house and into the kitchen.*

Grizelda looked around. Somehow the place seemed smaller without a drunken dragon in residence.

"I could murder a choccie digestive," said Ben, falling with a sigh into his favorite chair.

"Looks like someone did," said Chris, looking at the mound of wrappers on the floor.

Dragons, especially those who have, shall we say, frequently overindulged themselves, clear up by incinerating everything on the floor and then blowing away any remaining ash. This can, of course, be embarrassing if any staying guests have failed to make it off the floor and onto a bed/settee/collection of chairs/table before the clean-up – a further hazard of drinking with the dragons.

"There's more in the cupboard," his aunt told him, as she put the kettle onto the hob.

The kettle groaned but Grizelda quelled it with a glance which, transformed into electricity, would have powered most of Swansea for a day. The kettle boiled in double quick time.

Erica and Imelda threw themselves onto the two remaining comfy chairs, leaving the teenagers to enjoy the wooden chairs set around the table.

"Right," said Grizelda. "Conference time."

"What have we learned?" asked Ben.

"You sound like my chemistry teacher," accused Linda.

"I liked chemistry," commented Erica.

"And we know what chemistry you've been teaching Chris," said Grizelda, with a look. A very pointed look, 'looking daggers' even.**

"Rave," coughed Imelda, and Grizelda flushed red and went back to making tea.

Ben tried a very confused expression but no one seemed to notice.

---

*   Despite the dangers. The call of the tea was stronger.

**   How do you sharpen a pointed look? Answers on a postcard, please.

"How did they manage to kidnap you, uncle?" asked Linda.

"Crept up behind me, an' took me by the drive."

"Not by surprise then?"

"Well, yes, that too."

"What happened then?"

"Well, I woke up in a room and all me clothes had been nicked and replaced with silly orange robes."

"I thought you looked cool in them," said Imelda.

"Well, they're not very warm, that's true," agreed Ben. "Then this elderly monk came in, an' told me that I had been selected for testing as their los' leader."

"A loss leader? Like sales promotion?" asked Erica.

"No, lost leader. But he was still selling the promotion to me. Told me that if I passed the test, I would be given anythin' I desired."

"What if you failed?" asked Linda.

"We didn't go into that. Anyway, next I were taken into this big hall, full of these orange chaps chanting."

"I thought chaps were made of leather, not oranges," objected Imelda.

"Monks, I think they were. I thought I'd throw the test."

"Why?" asked Chris.

"Well, I looked around at all those brainwashed kids chanting my name, and got worried about what I were getting into."

"And, with a dirty mind like yours, whether you'd be brainwashed too?" asked Grizelda.

"Well, yes. Anyway, they gave me this tray of stuff and told me to choose three things. So I just knocked them all over. And they announced I'd passed and took me out of the hall and shoved me in another room, and locked the door."

"Where did the Watches come into it?" asked Grizelda. "I saw them runnin' away too."

"Seem that they got taken cos the monks needed their car."

"What, that clapped out old taxi that The Grey Mage lets them run round in?"

"Said it were all a bit bizarre. Anyway, they had escaped an' were tryin' to get out when we bumped inter each other. Guess who else we met?"

"Go on," said Grizelda.

"Guess."

"This is a war council, not Twenty Questions," snarled Ben's wife.

"You've not got ter twenty yet. Oh all right, don't glare at me like that. Erald were in there too."

"Erald? What were 'e doin'? All his mob are runnin' around on holiday at the moment."

"He were watchin' the monks."

"Couldn't 'e use a telescope?"

"Wanted to get close ter the action, 'e said. Anyway, if yer want the Tuatha ter help, he's in."

Grizelda pondered.

"Dunno. I mean, what are that lot goin' to be able to do? They can't start a proper magical fight on the streets. Someone would notice."

"They could create a diversion?" suggested Chris.

"What for?

"Well, if we're goin' to fight these monks, we'll need one. It's in all the best films."

"Actually, that's a good idea," enthused Erica.

Chris gave her a very warm look, and Linda retched.

"They could divert the coaches of monks away from the assembly buildings." Erica carried on.

Grizelda looked astonished.

"That actually is a good idea," she said.

Erica preened herself. She didn't actually have any feathers on (outside of Chris' inner thoughts) but the image will do.

Grizelda turned away, filled the kettle, then put it on the stove. She glared at the stove, which glowed cherry red – probably in terror, and therefore made a saving on the electricity bill. When the steam issued from the spout, she made a mystic pass or two in front of the steam, while muttering. The steam shrank, coalesced, and turned into an image of Erald's head.

"This feels like a steam bath," complained the head.

"How would he know? First bath 'e's had in years," muttered Ben.

"Erald, we will need the help of the Tuatha," commanded Grizelda.

"Will it involve lots of drinking?"

"Probably not," conceded Grizelda.

"Then there is a faint chance that they won't make a pig's ear out of it," the head mused. "When and where do you want them, and what are they to do?"

"How will they get the students to Cardiff?" Grizelda asked Ben.

"Probably use those orange coaches that they 'ave for getting recruits."

"Right. So, your mob, Erald, need to intercept the coaches an' keep 'em away from the Welsh Assembly Building."

The steam driven head nodded a few times, then (as the kettle boiled dry) vanished in a wisp of smoke.

"Right," said Grizelda. "Let's all get in the bus and then we can find somewhere to park up an' watch fer the monks an' their coaches."

Linda perked up considerably.

"There's a *McDonald's* near that roundabout. We can wait for them to go past, an' follow."

The others all looked at her with varied expressions and then breathed a heavy collective sigh (except for Erica who also quite liked fast food, as long as it had slowed down by the time she wanted to eat it). Before long, Imelda was steering her flower-powered camper coach out of the drive, and towards the motorway.

Some miles to the north, beside the main road, lay a lay-by that lay at a lower ley than the road itself. Into this, with a grateful sigh and some ominous rattling, wheezed the *Mondeo*. The occupants, equally grateful for a chance to get away from their getaway car, promptly got away to the nearby hedgerow. Their sighs of relief echoed that of the *Mondeo*.

"Right," said Ned, opening the large-scale map on the bonnet of the car, and putting his staff down on one end.

"We are here." His finger stabbed a point on the map. "They have to come down this road here." The same finger indicated a line on the map, then pointed to the main road.

"So we can ambush them," said the assistant assistant, excitedly.

"That is my plan," said Ned.

"It's so simple that it might work this time," commented the junior.

However, as even the Scots have worked out,[*] the cunning plans of mice and men often go wrong. As they examined the map carefully, they missed seeing a somewhat portly, dragon-shaped shadow flit across the other end of the lay-by. They also missed seeing the RAF Hawk jet-fighter a few minutes later, although in that case because it was flying low, fast and rather erratically. But they felt the wind of its passage and

---

[*] Mr. Burns got it in one. That is, the Scottish one, not the one in *The Simpsons*.

then experienced the wind of the assistant assistant's passage as he fell to the ground beside the car, gibbering manically. The map vanished in the tempest, as did a large quantity of empty sweet wrappers, fast-food wrappings, chip packets, and drink containers.

The assistant assistant made a wild grab for his milkshake as it fled beyond his grasp, but ended up flat on the floor.

Ned leaped to his feet and, although tempest-torn, managed to look imposing as he yelled curses into the empty air.

"I do hope that wasn't aimed at us, sir," came a voice behind his shoulder.

Ned spun round, to see that the lay-by now contained another car – one with attractive blue and white stripes all around it. The policeman standing behind him at his shoulder, holding a large piece of paper headed '**Wanted**', was blocking his way to the *Mondeo*. The policeman's colleague was regarding, with equal curiosity, the assistant assistant (still on the floor) and the expired tax disc on the *Mondeo*.

To a cheerful horn blast and some loud barracking, (fortunately lost in the wind) the *Sprinter* tour bus drove past the lay-by, with a sheeted shape on the trailer. Ned grabbed his staff, and yelled a loud curse at the *Sprinter*, which seemed to stagger, then continued on its way out of sight.

With a grim expression, Ned turned back to see his two trainee dark wizards standing sheepishly against the door of the *Mondeo* while the larger of the two policemen was haranguing them. Ned changed his grip upon the staff.

"Turn right," he ordered a few minutes later as the *Mondeo* left the lay-by.

"But we 'aven't got a map, now, Ned," the junior pointed out.

"Then we'll have ter turn this on."

Ned leaned forward, installed the gifted satnav on the dashboard, and turned it on. There came a warm, fuzzy noise, the screen turned blue (as did the barely-heard language, first from the satnav, then from the driver who was trying to overtake an elderly and erratic tractor).

"Testing. Acquiring position data," announced the satnav.

"Wales? I'm in Wales?" it screamed.

"Yes. But we want to know the quickest way out," Ned told it. He turned to the other two.

"The Banned are long gone, now. We'll have to try an' catch them up nearer to home. Wi' all these minor roads to go down, we'll make a major mistake if we try to second guess which road they're on now."

"Does that mean we have to rely on *that?*" asked the junior, who had little confidence in satnavs.

"At the next main junction turn right," instructed the satnav, very firmly.

"Right."

"That's what I said," confirmed the satnav.

"Shuttup. What's on the CD?"

"AC/DC. *Highway to Hell*," said the driver.

"Good, keep it on. It's appropriate," replied Ned.

"Hell is not a listed destination in Memory function," advised the satnav.

They all ignored it and the satnav sulked.

"Thought it were that Paul McCartney thing?" asked the junior, from the back.

"*The Frog Chorus?* I left it fer them policemen. As a memento."

"Are you going to remember to turn right here?" demanded the satnav. "I want to get out of here."

"Why?" asked Ned, with curiosity.

"Because." replied the satnav. "Ask again and I'll turn myself off and you'll be lost."

"Probably goin' to get lost anyway, even wi' you on," muttered the driver.

Behind the *Mondeo*, in the lay-by, a large frog emerged from under a police helmet.

"Rivet?" it enquired cautiously, licking a discarded CD case with its tongue, and staring around at the lay-by. The *Mondeo*-less lay-by.

Earlier that morning, there had been no frogs around to observe the tour bus as it arrived outside Waccibacci-san's throne shop.

Fungus, Eddie and Haemar emerged, followed by a long rumbling sound, pitched perfectly to make every window in the street shiver and resonate with its rise and fall. Dai was snoring.

The three on the sidewalk looked back at the bus in some awe.

"B-flat," suggested Fungus, offering a professional opinion.

"Der."

"I agree, Eddie," said Haemar. "He doesn't need his bass with a snore like that."

Again the sound reverberated down the street, and the throne shop's door quivered, then opened wide. Inside, the shop looked dark and mysterious. The three hesitated at the doorway.

"Don't just stand there, go inside," said Waccibacci-san from behind them on the pavement.

Dai's rumbling snore made the *Sprinter* shake gently. Inside the car, cillone of Felldyke's pockets gently spilled half-eaten chicken drumsticks onto the floor.

"What does he use?" asked Waccibacci-san, politely.

"Bass," replied Haemar.

"I meant, what does he play, not what does he drink?" asked Waccibacci-san again.

"Oh, sorry. No, he plays bass. *Fender Precision.*"

"Ah, so. That explains much. Come, I have your... throne ready."

Waccibacci-san led the way into the darkened shop. There, at the front, stood a large wooden throne, in the traditional shape and style, but with added armrests and a large canopy rising up from the back and extending in a graceful curve over the occupant's head space.

Waccibacci-san pointed to a large round alcove in the canopy.

"This is where the Amulet of Kings may rest. It has been enchanted to rejuvenate the powers of the amulet in the same way as the old throne. I still had the original specs."

"You still had the blueprints, after all these years?"

"No. my glasses. I need a slight correction in my vision to be able to make thrones and I had got these on a 'buy one get one free' deal."

Haemar looked around the stock in the shop, thinking how suitable a BOGOF deal was in this environment.

Waccibacci retired into the rear of the shop and reappeared a few moments later towing a dark, rectangular block behind him.

"You will need this, also," he told them.

"What is it?" Fungus asked, stepping back slightly.

"The warranty."

Waccibacci-san then pulled a slim, blue-bound volume from his pocket. "And this is the user's manual."

Eddie tried to pick up the warranty but, despite his workouts carrying the drum kit around, failed to lift it.

"Der." he complained.

"Don't worry. It comes complete with wheels."

Haemar leaned against the warranty and it moved slightly. He nodded gloomily.

Eddie went back out to the tour bus and returned a moment later with a large bag.

Waccibacci-san looked inside the bag and smiled widely.

"That will do nicely," he said.

Dai had followed Eddie into the shop.

"Thought you might need a bit of help," he said, brightly.

"Der."

"Eddie says the trailer is ready to be loaded," called GG.

"The canopy may be loaded separately, for convenience." Waccibacci-san informed them.

"How easy is it to be refitted?" asked Fungus, suspiciously.

"It is all in the manual. Full instructions are provided."

Waccibacci-san produced a huge roll of bubble-wrap and, in moments, the various parts of the throne were wrapped for traveling and installed upon the trailer. A brief moment of excitement, when Dai had panted rather too hard from the effort and set fire to the bubble-wrap, had passed without more than a lot of very hard swearing.

More hard swearing followed, as The Banned tried to get the warranty loaded, but eventually, (with the aid of the hydraulic jack in the *Sprinter's* tool kit) they managed to get that on board the trailer too.

Waccibacci-san bowed deeply to Haemar and Fungus.

"Please convey my respects to the Lord Lakin and ask him to be more careful with the throne. Impress upon him that he should read the terms and conditions carefully, for misuse may invalidate the warranty." He bowed again and vanished into his shop, closing the door and pulling down the blinds. Moments later a sign appeared on the door which read 'Please excuse. Taking a break.' Heavy bolts slammed shut.

Eddie threw a large tarpaulin over the contents of the trailer and roped it down firmly.

"Where did you get that from?" asked Fungus.

"Der."

"All right, I only asked."

Dai and Haemar were talking beside the tour bus.

"No problem." Dai was saying.

"What's up?" Fungus asked Haemar.

"I were just pointin' out ter Dai that there's no room left fer him in the bus."

"Oh good grief, I never thought!" exclaimed Fungus.

"You never do," came GG's voice though the open window of the *Sprinter.*

"Look, it's no problemo." Dai assured them. "It's early morning, I'll just have a quick drink, then fly home. It's not too far from here and I could do with just checking the place anyway. I'll then make my way north, to the Helvyndelve, and meet up with you all for the celebrations."

"Are yer sure you'll be OK?" asked Haemar.

"Do yer know the way?" asked Fungus.

Dai tipped half a bottle of whisky down his throat and hiccupped. The Banned all ducked as the cloud of burning gas floated across the pavement.

"Yeah, it's cool. You take the bass up there for me, save me carrying it. The way home's easy. I'll follow the road off that way then, when it forks, I'll go south until I pick up some landmarks. See you all at the gig!" Dai waved, then took off and headed down the road at about fifty feet above the ground.

The Banned all waved goodbye, then bundled themselves into the tour bus.

"Home, James!" said Fungus, grandly.

"Der."

"His name is Eddie, Fungus, remember?"

"Sorry, Eddie. It were just an expression."

"Der."

"There's no need for language like that. I've said sorry. What's on the CD?"

"*Highway Star,*" said Felldyke.

"Der."

"Eddie's favorite. Better leave it on."

Eddie carefully turned the *Sprinter* and trailer round, then headed off up the road after the vanishing dragon.

"Hope Dai will be OK," said GG from the back.

"I'm sure he will be," said Fungus, reassuringly.

The bus was enveloped in a cloud of dust as an erratically-piloted Hawk jet fighter screamed overhead.

"Der."

"Yer right Eddie. 'E were definitely lower than 500 feet."

"Are we nearly there yet?"

"Shuttup, Felldyke!" chorused The Banned.

A few miles down the road, Eddie noticed something remarkable.

"Der," he remarked.

Scar looked out of the window.

"Hey, guys! It's those idiots from Surdin! An' they're in trouble wi' the Law!"

The Banned all tried to look out of the side window at the same time, yelling genial insults at the hapless three dark wizards. Eddie fought to control the wildly rocking *Sprinter*, which oscillated more wildly than the sound recordist at a Motorhead gig.

"Missed!"

"As a Newt!"

GG and Scar both yelled out of the window, as the *Sprinter* raced around a corner, and out of sight.

"DER! DER! DER!"

"What?" asked Fungus, urgently.

"Eddie says that a curse must 'ave 'it the back axle, cos the bus ain't runnin' right."

Eddie slowed down considerably, but kept going.

Haemar and Fungus conferred urgently.

"What's the next town?"

"Aberystwyth. But we'll bypass that."

"Agreed. Too big, we'll get noticed."

"Let's try here. Smaller. We've still got some funds, 'aven't we?"

Haemar, who, as lead singer, insisted he was also in charge of the cash, nodded.

"Eddie, do yer reckon we can get to 'ere, then try an' find a garage?"

Eddie scratched his ear reflectively.

"Der."

"Then we'll just 'ave to hope."

The afternoon wore on into early evening and the miles passed anxiously. Well, not too anxiously for Felldyke who had returned to his default state, and fallen asleep with a drumstick (wooden) in each hand, and a drumstick (chicken) lodged in one nostril. GG was lying back in his seat and humming riffs to himself. Scar was vacantly watching the scenery.

Both Haemar and Fungus could feel the vibration from the back of the bus. Eddie slowed down again.

"Der."

"I agree," agreed Haemar.

"Me too. The next pub?"

"Yeah. You OK with that, Eddie?"

"Der."

"No, I don't think we've much choice either."

Before long, Eddie was pulling into a dark car park. He turned off the engine with a sigh of relief.

"Are we there yet?" asked Felldyke, waking up and removing the drumstick from his nose before eating it.

CHAPTER TWELVE

Four coaches, recently re-sprayed (and, in at least one case, still being a bit tacky. The paint job that is – the color scheme had been tacky before the' paint was bought) in bright orange stood in the forecourt of the monastery. The senior monk and the accountant stood beside their orange *Volvo*, watching the students file onto the coaches.

"Om. Will we have sufficient numbers?" asked the senior monk.

"Om. Ben will bless our endeavors," replied the accountant, with his fingers crossed under his robes.

"Wherever he is."

"Whoever he is."

"Om. Do you have the laptop?"

"Om. It is next to the abacus on the back seat."

"Excellent."

"Om. You should have said 'Om'."

"What?"

"Om."

"Oh, om."

"Om. Yes, Om."

"Om. Sorry, slip of the mind."

"Om. Got to be careful, in range of the cannon fodder. Are they properly indoctrinated?"

"Om. Let's try one." The senior monk approached one of the students, who was waiting patiently in line to board the bus, and waved a hand in front of the student's face. The blank expression did not change but the student at once bowed and produced a packet of leaflets and started trying to thrust one on the senior monk.

"Om. Looks like it to me." The two turned and started to climb into the *Volvo*. Behind them the glassy-eyed student pushed some pamphlets down the back of the neck of the student in line ahead of him, who didn't seem to notice.

"Om. They'll do," agreed the accountant, getting into the driving seat.

"How come you always drive?"

"I'm more economical, that's why," replied the accountant.

"Om. Let's go. The coaches can follow us."

"OK. Is it still Nirvana on the CD?"

"Mandalaband, I think."

"That will do nicely. I was worried you had put that *Convoy* thing on."

"My soul is already tarnished. Why would I make it worse?"

"Om. Just checking."

The less-than-discreet orange *Volvo* pulled out of the monastery gates. The coaches, starting their engines in a cloud of diesel fumes, joined the convoy.

Suitable music played through the stereo systems – to keep the students in their meditative trance – turned off when one senior monk, roused from meditation by a vibration running through the coach, had to use his considerable mental powers (and a sharp stick) to alert the driver to the imminent prospect of their crossing the carriageway into the oncoming HGVs. The two following coaches, with similar problems and less senior monks, simply drove straight across the next roundabout.

The convoy carried on, to a soundtrack that was less spiritually uplifting but rather more practical.

"What's this?" demanded the senior monk, whose normally calm demeanor was still a little ragged around the edges from the close encounter with a 23-ton HGV from Poland, whose driver lacked a number of communication skills in English (except for invective).

"It says that it is Radio One," replied the driver, dubiously.

"And it is legal to broadcast this, is it?" asked the monk.

"Shouldn't be, I agree. But it isn't sending me to sleep."

"No one could sleep through that. Except possibly in self-defense."

"But it is keeping them quiet," the driver pointed out.

And indeed, the students on the coaches were still quiescent.

Onwards roared the convoy – paying little attention to the scenery, traffic regulations, or the possibility that they were being observed.

Some little way ahead of them, their immediate foes were distracted.

"You can't turn him into a frog for that, Auntie!" exclaimed Linda.

The empirical evidence was against her, however.

"Rivet!" complained the new frog.

"'E were rude ter me," retorted Grizelda.

"He was doing his job." Chris agreed with Linda.

"'E accused me of bein', bein – '" Grizelda sought for a word she was prepared to use, " – too big."

"All he asked you was how much food you wanted."

"'E said 'supersize me'! That's like sayin' I'm fat!" Grizelda glared at the frog, which hopped backwards.

"Auntie, he meant to ask how big a portion of chips you wanted." Linda explained, patiently.

"Why didn't he just say that then?"

"You don't come to burger bars very often, do you Grizelda?" asked Imelda.

Grizelda shook her head. An assistant very, very cautiously offered her a brown paper bag full of food.

"If it's supposed ter be fast-food, why 'as it taken so long ter get served?" she demanded. The others looked around at where the long line had been, until the frog incident, and the now empty restaurant whose tables contained a lot of abandoned food and cooling drinks, now growing warm.

"Oh well, if I've made a mistake, no one can say I don't ever apologize."

The others looked at each other in silence, then all turned and stared at Ben as his wife seemed to want an answer.

"No, dear," he said. "I don't think that any of us would ever say that to yer."

A lot of heads nodded, including one very green head. Grizelda nodded at the frog, which shimmered and turned back into a uniformed employee.

"I appear to have mistaken yer," she told the ex-frog, who seemed transfixed. Various other heads appeared slowly around assorted stands and cookers, although the manager had to be pulled from underneath the chip fryer by three of the staff, and his fingernails made marks on the floor, (the repair of which the insurance company subsequently refused to pay for).

Slightly mollified by the refusal of the staff to accept payment for food for the whole party, (just so long as they ate outside), Grizelda led the way to the seating from which the motorway could be observed.

"What's this?" she asked, when they were all seated.

"It's a chip, Auntie," said Linda, with her mouth full.

"No it's not. Chips are short and fat. This is long and thin, and wilting." She held it up in front of her and glared at it. The offending chip became somewhat more golden and straightened to attention under her gaze.

"Don't play with the food, dear." Ben told her.

"I'm not sure that I like it."

"You're allowed not to like it, it's a free country. Linda likes it, so if you don't, give yours ter her."

Grizelda grumbled on, until the coffee cooled down enough for her to drink it. Her mood began to mellow as the caffeine took hold and she tried the food again.

"Is one of yer watchin' the road?" she asked.

"We are, Auntie," called Chris. He and Erica had sat at a separate table to talk privately, but his hearing was razor sharp for some things.

Grizelda leaned back. And promptly fell off the backless seat. No one dared to laugh, but Imelda had clearly swallowed some coffee improperly, for she was seized with a wild coughing fit.

"I've got somethin' as will cure that," said Grizelda, from the floor. The coughing stopped at once. Imelda didn't know what the cure might have been, but wasn't taking chances. There was a pointed silence as Grizelda, not without a struggle, arose from the floor and resumed her seat with a fierce glare at her husband.

"I fancy some more of them chips," said Ben, and wandered off back to the tills.

"When did your uncle start liking fast-food?" Erica asked Chris.

"Have you ever been near to her curry pot?" Chris shuddered.

"No."

"Well, don't. The goat can reach nearly thirty miles an hour after eating from that."

"It could never run that fast," objected Imelda, sitting down with them to avoid her coven leader's glare.

"It wasn't running," said Chris, darkly.

"You like this stuff then?" Grizelda asked Linda, who had finished her burger, two portions of chips and was just wondering about following her uncle back to the tills.

"Yeah. In Stockport, we live on it all the time."

"Me sister never were a great cook."

"Um."

Grizelda looked all around, furtively.

"Are you still wearing the Ward of Lingard, Linda?"

"Yes, Auntie. It's hidden under my jumper."

"Good. I've got a feeling in me water."

"You can get tablets for that. Mum has them."

"No, I mean fem-inine in-tuition."

"Classes for girls?"

"Shut up. Yer know what I mean. Eddies in the nexus of space and time."

"No he's not. He's with Fungus and The Banned in the *Sprinter*."

Grizelda gave up trying to explain things to a teenager.*

"Just keep it handy. When we get where they're goin' who knows what we'll face?"

"Something wicked?"

"No, that's me," said Grizelda, complacently.

"But I thought you were one of the good witches." Linda said, with some concern.

"Perhaps I'm just no better than I should be."

"Is that why you vanished at the rave, Auntie?"

Grizelda flushed and looked around to see where Ben was.

"Keep quiet. I don't want yer uncle findin' out. Nothin' happened. Well, nothin' he needs ter know about anyway."

Linda filed all this useful information away in her head, in a file marked 'Blackmail'.

Ben wandered back with further supplies of chips, just as an orange *Volvo* meandered past the services.

"Auntie!" yelled Chris, jumping to his feet.

"Yes, all right, I saw them." Grizelda answered.

"Come on, everybody!"

Moments later, the local wildlife was viewing, with deep suspicion, the abandoned pile of French fries.

Imelda jumped into the driving seat and fumbled for the keys.

"No time for that!" said Grizelda and muttered something under her breath. The engine burst into life.

"You can't keep on doing that," complained Imelda. "The starter motor will fail and I'll have to start it that way every time, then."

"So?"

"Well, it's all right at home, but what happens when I take it for MOT?"

"Stop looking for problems. Right now, just drive!" ordered Grizelda.

The camper coach pulled slowly out onto the motorway and began the pursuit of the monk's coaches, easily visible in the sunlight ahead.

Some miles behind them, but traveling quickly at the frantic urgings of the satnav, came the elderly *Mondeo*.

---

* It happens to us all at some time.

"Can't you go any quicker?" the satnav pleaded, as they joined the motorway.

"Yer only supposed ter give us directions," the assistant assistant complained.

"Well, this is a special case."

"Why?"

"Not allowed to say. That's in the user guide," said the satnav.

"What user guide?"

"The one you got when you bought me."

"Ah."

"Don't tell me that as well as making me come to Wales, I'm pre-owned?"

"Sort of."

"Yer were a present."

"What sort of muffin gives a satnav as a present, without giving the new owner the manual?"

"How big were it?" asked the junior.

"Well, did you ever see a bound set of the *Encyclopedia Britannica?*"

"Me dad had one," said Ned. "It took up three bookshelves."

"That would have been the condensed version of the manual, then," replied the satnav.

There was a thoughtful silence.

"'Ow does anyone learn 'ow ter use yer then?" asked the assistant assistant.

"Trial and error," replied the satnav.

"Yer mean yer keep makin' errors and yer a trial to yer owner?" asked Ned.

"Something like that, yes," replied the satnav, carefully.

"What else could it be?"

"Well, a previous owner had to go on trial for what happened, but it was probably an error."

The *Mondeo* experienced a thoughtful silence.

"What's on the CD?" asked Ned, after a while.

"*OK Computer.* Radiohead." replied the junior.

"Wrong choice. Let's have something else."

"*One of These Days?*" suggested the junior, who was into Pink Floyd.

"Perfect," smiled Ned.

The satnav sulked, being well aware of the only vocal line in the song.

Minutes afterwards, as the dramatic chords faded, the satnav beeped loudly.

"What was that?" demanded Ned.

"What?" answered the satnav.

"You beeped!"

"Did I?"

"Yes!" cried all three wizards, together.

"Sorry. Must have been a speed trap alert. Entirely involuntary and down to external programming," grumbled the satnav.

The dark wizards relaxed. The *Mondeo* was unlikely to trigger a speed trap alert, and The Grey Mage would deal with any camera related charges by hacking into the Police National Computer and hexing the software until it gave up.

And indeed, when they passed a patrol car, the occupants appeared to be sound asleep.

"See?" said the assistant assistant. "Dim problem."

"We've been in Wales for too long," muttered the junior, from the back seat. "He's picking up the dialect already."

"Well," the driver defended himself, "I can't pick up any fares, so why not?"

In a fit of pique, he thumped the car stereo, which stopped playing Pink Floyd, turned on the radio and changed to *Jolie Taxi*. Ned started laughing, and the driver joined the satnav in sulking.

Behind them, the Traffic Police had been snoozing peacefully in their patrol car. The sergeant was waiting for the piping hot coffee he had recently bought at the services to cool down and his companion was lost to the world as he examined the football pages of his newspaper. Their idyll ended as every internal alarm the car possessed started yelling at them, with the immortal cry of "Yabba Dabba Doo!" winning out on sheer volume.*

"What the hell is that for?" yelled the sergeant, urgently slapping at "off" switches, in a desperate attempt to protect his hearing, and then frantically slapping his wet and steaming trousers in an attempt to avoid scalding to certain sensitive areas now drenched in coffee.

"Dunno, Sarge. It all went ballistic when that old *Mondeo* crawled past us!" replied his PC companion.

---

* If you thought that was an invented joke, oh dear – it's for real. Even police alarms can have a sense of humor.

As the level of the alarms dropped, the sergeant grabbed the police radio and started shouting into it at a volume that made the alarms sound puny. The PC winced at the non-PC language and, again, at the sheer volume achieved by his superior.

Eventually, the sergeant quieted down enough for the voice at the other end of the radio to make itself heard. Its injured tones at having been exposed to the full range of the sergeant's extensive command of invective were apparent.

"As I have just told you three times, sergeant, the occupants of that car are needed for questioning. They have, it appears, assaulted two fellow constables in Ceredigion. They must be considered armed and extremely dangerous."

"What did they do to them?" asked the sergeant, desperately trying to release the clips on the standard-issue pump-action shotgun in the glove box (which was normally used only to enforce minor anti-littering regulations).

Suddenly there was stillness inside the rapid pursuit vehicle.

"Did you say frogs?" asked the sergeant, with a deceptively gentle tone which fooled no one, especially the luckless one on the other end of the radio.

"Look, Sarge," explained the radio, "I'm only reading out what is says on the computer here. I don't think it can be right either, they're all a bit mad up there."

"So what does it mean then?"

"Well, the Inspector is trying to get some reason out of the station up there, but he says don't approach them until you have some backup," the radio instructed.

"What about the unmarked Armed Response unit?" demanded the sergeant.

"Ah, there's been a bit of a problem there. They went on a shout to a caller who was probably drunk cos he was yelling something down the phone about a drunken dragon crash-landing on his garden shed, while reading a map," muttered the radio.

"So?"

"Well, they were going a bit fast round the roundabout here, and collided with an unmarked patrol car, and they all got themselves arrested for reckless driving."

"But they're all police officers!"

"Well, yes, but they were well tooled-up and had left all their warrant cards in the station for security. It will all be sorted out in a day or so."

"But in the meantime?"

"There's some backup on its way." The radio fizzled, crackled loudly and disconnected.

"Looks like we're on our own for a bit, lad, with no back up," the sergeant told his driver, who looked unimpressed. "Keep well back."

The curious convoy was swelling in size as it headed down the motorway towards Cardiff.

CHAPTER THIRTEEN

The Banned Underground looked around the car park. There were no signs of life, but the pub itself was brightly lit. The decision to enter was agreed with little or no dispute.

Once installed at a table, with the worst of the thirst dispelled (for touring on a tour bus is a dusty, tedious business), the conversation turned to the tour bus and its problems.

"What do yer think is wrong, Eddie?" asked GG.

"Der."

"No, I don't know, either," said Haemar.

"We could have guessed that," GG told him. "You're the singer – you don't do technical."

"Suppose we 'ave to find a garage," Scar said.

"In Wales? At 10 o'clock at night?" asked Haemar.

"Der," agreed Eddie.

"What do you reckon, Fungus?" asked GG.

"I reckon I'm goin' to get some more drinks," replied Fungus, looking at the bar.

"That's good reckoning," agreed Scar.

"Der."

"Don't forget Eddie's drinking too. He can't drive anywhere else tonight anyway."

Fungus stood up and strode over to the bar, where he was soon in conversation with two very tall customers who were standing at one end of the bar. The conversation lasted so long that Haemar went to the bar himself, and came back with the drinks and a sour expression.

"What's up, Haemar?" asked GG.

"Problems with being a dwarf. Barman short-changed me."

The dwarves of The Banned Underground glared at the bartender, who ignored them as being beneath his notice.

At length Fungus, now a little unsteady on his feet, returned to the table, bringing his two new associates with him.

"Oh no," groaned Haemar. "Fungus 'as picked up some more muppets."

"Just be nice to them, maybe they'll go away," said Scar, wearily.

"Sit them down next to Felldyke. Then they'll go away," suggested GG.

"Oi! I heard that."

Fungus smiled broadly around the table.

152

"Lads, I'd like yer to meet some good lads who might be able ter help us out."

The bad attitude of The Banned vanished as quickly as the round of drinks.

"This is Mungo, an' that's Jerry."

There was a group muttering along the lines of the:

"Wotcher. Nice ter meet yer. Mine's a pint," variety.

"Mungo and Jerry are two of Santa's Little Helpers." Fungus announced.

There was a fair degree of skepticism around the table as The Banned examined the two extremely tall individuals.

"It's a job title, not a physical description." Mungo explained to them.

The skepticism failed to vanish at the same rate as the drinks.

"Pull the other one!" scoffed Haemar.

Mungo examined Haemar disinterestedly, then leaned forward and whispered in his ear for a long sentence. Haemar stiffened, then went very pale. He looked at Mungo for a long time and then nodded.

"I'm convinced," he said in a hollow voice, before draining the rest of his drink in one go.

Fungus looked at him impatiently.

"Now, these two are great lads," he said. "But importantly for us, they know of an all-night mechanic round here."

Interest sharpened quickly and more drinks were quickly arranged. Haemar was treated to a double, to help restore his color.

"What are yer doin' round here, anyway?" GG asked Mungo.

"Himself goes on holiday at this time of year, so he sends us here with the sleigh to get it serviced." Mungo explained.

"There's only this one mechanic left around from the original team that put it together for Him, so it always has to come here for a few days," Jerry carried on. "We could take your minibus round to his place and see if he'll do it for you."

Haemar, reacting with something close to his normal speed, took the drink out of Eddie's hand, and drank it.

"DER!"

"Sorry, Eddie, but it looks like yer gonna be drivin' again tonight."

Shortly after closing time The Banned and their two new friends left the pub, and poured themselves into the ailing tour bus.

"So, what's on the trailer?" Jerry asked.

"Bit of a secret, really." GG, who was sitting partly underneath Jerry, told him. Jerry whispered in his ear. "The new throne for the Helvyndelve." GG replied quickly.

"Oh." Jerry lost interest.

"Der."

"Eddie wants to know how far we have to go?" asked Haemar.

"Not far now," replied Mungo, peering forward through the windscreen. "You see that farm track?"

"Der," said Eddie.

"Go down there."

"Der."

"A farm track?" asked Haemar.

"He doesn't want passing trade," said Mungo.

"What?"

"He values his privacy." Jerry explained.

"A mechanic?"

The bus, now making serious grinding noises from the rear end, rounded a corner in the lane. And stopped dead. Before them lay a small, gothic castle about the size of a small farmhouse, complete with flying bats, and eldritch and decaying trees.

"What the hell is *that?*" exclaimed Haemar.

"Oh that's the house. Pay no attention to that, the workshop is around the back, to the left. Go on." Jerry said dismissively.

"Oh drive on," said Mungo. "Like Jerry said, the garage is at the back."

Eddie, with some reluctance, let in the clutch and the minibus drove slowly round the back of the mock castle. At the rear was a well-equipped modern workshop. A car was in mid-air on a ramp and an overall-clad figure was busy underneath it with a variety of spanners. Behind the ramp was a large object, covered in dust-sheets.

The collective heartbeat of The Banned slowed to a more normal level.

"What's his name?" asked Fungus, getting control over his voice.

"Well, Himself always refers to him as 'Idiot', so we're not really sure. We normally call him 'sir'."

"Why do you call him that?" asked Haemar, as The Banned opened the doors and slowly started to get out.

"It pays to be polite to vampires." Jerry said.

The Banned VERY QUICKLY got back in the bus and shut the doors.

"Vampires?" asked GG, shakily.

"Don't worry. You are with us and Idiot's under contract to Himself. Can't touch anyone." Mungo reassured them.

"Well, except with his invoices." Jerry added.

"I were more interested in 'is teeth," muttered Haemar, and nearly swallowed his own a moment later as a spanner tapped on the driver's window and the mechanic gave them a toothy grin.

Eddie, not without some reluctance, wound down the window.

"It won't be ready until the day after tomorrow," the vampire told Mungo, appearing not to notice the other occupants of the minibus. "I've had to send off for some parts. Honestly, you would think that Himself would be a bit more careful with it, it wasn't made yesterday, and vintage parts are getting harder to find."

"And more expensive I suppose." Jerry muttered.

"Well, yes. Now if He would just upgrade, as I suggested a few years back..."

"You know what Himself is like. Couple more days is fine by us, sir," Jerry replied, quickly.

"Actually, we were hoping you could do a little favor for our friends here," Mungo said, brightly.

"Go on," said the vampire mechanic, wearily.

"There is a dreadful noise from the back of the bus," Mungo explained.

"Just drive it across the forecourt there," instructed the mechanic.

Eddie did so, and the mechanic followed, and then put his head under the wheel arch for a moment.

"What caused this?" he called from somewhere underneath the rear of the *Sprinter*.

"Ah, we were hexed by a wizard." Fungus answered, nervously.

A split second later, he was confronted at short range by the lugubrious face of the vampire.

"Must have only just caught you, then. He's messed up the brakes a bit, that's all."

"Would you be able to fix it for us, sir?" asked Haemar, with unaccustomed politeness.

"I was just about to take my lunch break," the vampire mechanic mused.

There was a horrified silence inside the *Sprinter*.

"I'll just have a quick drink, then sort it out for you," he added.

The silence solidified. The mechanic wandered over to the ramp, picked up a large jug of engine oil, and drained it in one.

"That's better," he said, back at the *Sprinter*.

"Um. Excuse me sir, but I thought vampires drank, well, blood?" asked Scar, nervously.

"Most do. But I was bitten by this car, called Christine, and so I mostly have to drink engine oil. Blood does work as well but normally I stick to oil. Come on, get out."

The atmosphere became less thick and The Banned climbed slowly and carefully out of the *Sprinter*. The mechanic jacked up the rear end then, in a blur of movement, took off the back wheel, replaced a number of parts and the wheel and removed the jack.

"All done," he said.

Mungo walked the mechanic back to the ramp in a discussion with him, then returned to the *Sprinter* as the vampire mechanic drank some more oil, and went back underneath the ramp.

"Off we go," said Mungo. "Would you mind dropping us back at the pub in the village on your way out? We've got digs there."

Nobody moved.

"Come on," said Jerry, climbing into the *Sprinter*, "we are OK to go."

"What about payment?" asked Haemar, nervously.

Mungo grinned at him. "We've sorted that out for you. He's going to put it all down on Himself's bill. In return, we'll certify to Himself that the labor hours on the sleigh were an extra three days and you give us five or six free tickets to your next gig."

The Banned exchanged glances and then, nearly as quickly as the mechanic could have managed himself, they were back in the *Sprinter* which was driven rather quickly out of the yard.

Next moment, Eddie stamped hard on the brakes, as the vampire mechanic appeared in front of them, holding up a very large spanner, and a grim expression. Eddie wound down the window, slowly.

"Just take it a bit easier than that for the first hundred miles or so while the new pads bed in," said the vampire, and was gone.

Eddie and Haemar started breathing again and the *Sprinter* moved more carefully down the drive. A few minutes later, they stopped outside the pub, and Mungo and Jerry climbed out.

"Thanks for the help, lads," Fungus told them.

"Any time. Just remember to send us those tickets."

"No problem," Haemar told them.

Mungo and Jerry waved and turned to go back into the pub. The *Sprinter* moved off.

"Next stop, the Helvyndelve," said Fungus, cheerfully.

"What's this on the CD?" asked Haemar.
"*Dance with the Devil*," called Felldyke, the drummer.
"Der."
"Eddie doesn't fancy that. What else have you got there?"
"*Spooky Tooth?*"
"DER! DER!"
"I'll take that as a no then, shall I?"
The *Sprinter* accelerated as Eddie headed north into mid-Wales, down quiet roads.

Further south, the same could not have been said about the M4.

The original convoy of a *Volvo* estate and three coaches had now become swollen by the additions of the garishly painted camper coach, an arthritic *Mondeo*, a police rapid pursuit Vehicle, and a car full of free-lance journalists who followed the police around on the general principle that they might see something exciting and make some money by writing about it. All were trying hard to see the others without being seen themselves.

"Look!" exclaimed Ned.
"At what?" asked the junior wizard from the back seat.
"That's Grizelda!'"
"No, it's a coach. Horribly painted."
"Don't be smart, yer can't manage it. That's the coach what she an' Ben got away in."
"He's right," agreed the assistant assistant.
"Let's follow 'em," Ned instructed.
"Which way are they going?" the satnav wanted to know.
"West, along the M4."
"That's all right then."
"Well, it's got nothin' to do wi' you anyway." Ned told the satnav, which sulked again.
"They're flashin'," the driver announced.
Ned winced at the horrible vision in his mind's eye, then realized that the assistant assistant meant the indicators on the coach.
"Which way's that, then?" he asked.
The junior was already consulting the map.

"What do you need a map for, when you've got me?" asked the satnav.

There was a silence while all three tried to work out an answer.

"Why are we leaving the motorway?" demanded the satnav.

"Cos we're followin' them," answered the assistant assistant.

"Hey!" said Ned. "Looks who's ahead of Grizelda! It's them monks!"

"So, she's followin' them, and we're followin' her."

"Yep."

"Do yer think we're bein' followed, too?"

"Oh, don't be silly. Who would be followin' us?"

"Sarge! They're leaving the M4, Sarge."

"Right, lad. Just keep behind them, at a discreet distance."

The sergeant picked up the police radio, shook it a few times for good measure, and started shouting into it.

"Oi. You there. Where's our backup, then?"

"There's three cars from the Cardiff force waiting in the services at Junction 33."

"That's where we are now."

"Then they will pick you up and follow you at a discreet distance. They are unmarked but they are all black Ford *Focuses*."

As the rapid pursuit vehicle slowly rounded the roundabout, the three cars pulled out behind it, forcing the journalists to take rapid evasive action into a hedge.

"Did you see what they did then?" demanded the shaken driver.

His passenger was taking rapid photos through the side window.

"Three black *Focuses*. Must be the unmarked police, driving like that. Come on, let's follow them, quick!"

"Well get out and help me push us out of the hedge, then," retorted the driver.

"And get me feet dirty on that mud?"

"Put your shoes back on, then."

The front of the convoy was oblivious to the events unfolding behind them.

"Om. We carry on down this dual carriageway to the end."

"Now it's just us two, let's drop the 'om', shall we?" suggested the accountant.

"Om. If you insist."

"Ok. Did you set up the offshore bank account?"

"Did it online."

"What did you call it?"

"*Om Enterprises,*" answered the senior monk.

"Oh for goodness sake. Couldn't you think of anything that might have a less direct trail?"

"Sorry. I left it a bit late and couldn't think of anything else."

"Oh well, never mind. We'll sort it out when we've got the cash by getting some other accounts set up too."

"Oh I did that as well. I set us up a personal bank account each, at the same bank."

"What names did you use?"

"Our own."

"Oh, it gets better!" howled the accountant. "So when they trawl the banks looking for us, our names are going to come up at once, all covered in red stars and labeled for them."

"Well, how was I to know?" asked the senior monk, defensively.

"You've read enough thrillers. I've seen all those Jeffrey Archer books in your room."

"Do they count?"

"Well, they're not Shakespeare, are they? Oh never mind, I'll sort it out for us when we get out there."

"Good. I may be a senior monk but I'm a novice at banking fraud."

"So is everyone – compared to the bankers."

"Where is the spare car going to be?" asked the senior monk.

"I've had it left for us in a side street round the back of the Welsh Assembly, with the keys hidden in the exhaust."

"Will it be safe, do you think?"

"This is Cardiff, not Liverpool, so there's a good chance. Now, where do we go from here?"

"There's a sign."

"In the heavens?"

"No, on that lamppost."

The *Volvo* accelerated onwards, as the coaches fell behind in the traffic.

"Om. Do you know the way, o Reverend One?" asked the driver of the first coach.

"No, I'll just check with Reverend Two."

There was a brief discussion, then a consensus decision was reached.

"Follow the signs."

"Om. Perhaps I should slow down, for there is a roadblock just ahead."

"Om. A roadblock?"

The reverends peered through the front window of the coach. Ahead was a group of róbed and hooded figures, two of whom had reflective jackets thrown over their robes. Two more were holding up a badly painted sign reading: "Diversion".

"Om. Do they look like normal road workers to you?" asked Reverend Two.

"Om. It seems likely. Look, those two over there seem to be drinking and arguing at the same time, and none of them are even pretending to do any work."

• "Om. Fair enough. Go where they are pointing and we'll find the target from there."

The maintenance worker impersonators watched the coaches turn right, away from the Welsh Assembly.

"Tell Erald that they are on the way," instructed Liamm. "And Diarmid, tell Finn to stop arguing."

"Is that coach to go there as well?" asked Diarmid, as a garishly painted camper coach forged into view.

"No. That's Grizelda. Come on, let's follow the monks."

Still arguing over whose turn it was to buy the next round, the Tuatha walked to the side of the road and, in a burst of golden light, faded from view.

"Ned! Wake up!" yelled the assistant assistant

"Eh? Wassamatta?"

"Wassamatta? Is that an advanced spell?" asked the junior, who had also been dozing to the soporific, trance-like strains of *No Sleep Till Hammersmith*.

"No. What's goin' on?"

"Monks have gone one way, Grizelda's goin' another. Which do I follow?"

"Pick a card," mused Ned.

The junior, still entranced by the lullabies of a live Motorhead album, made a suggestion. They ignored him.

"Grizelda. Follow Grizelda." Ned decided.

The *Mondeo* pulled round to the left, following the camper coach, and was itself discreetly followed by the rapid pursuit vehicle, three blacked out *Ford Focuses* and a very muddy group of journalists who were now arguing over whose turn it was to buy the drinks when they stopped.

The orange coaches threaded their way through the traffic until the leading driver again spotted two of the black-robed figures beside the road, waving at him.

"O, Reverend One, what shall I do?"

"Are those the same chaps we had to stop for earlier?"

"Yes, Reverend," replied the confused driver.

"What are they suggesting?"

"Om. They are pointing at the Castle car park."

"Om. Then I suggest that we park there. That will do for now."

The coaches turned into the car park and stopped.

"Well, Erald, we've got them now," Laeg said. "What do you suggest that we do with them?"

Behind them, Malan was pulling the gates shut, to keep other visitors out.

The doors of the coaches opened with an ominous hiss of air and the Tuatha grouped loosely together. Erald and Lugh walked forward towards the coaches, carrying their staffs, as the entranced students left the buses and began walking around aimlessly, chanting: "Ben. Ben. Ben. Ben."[*]

The senior monks congregated together, then walked in a purposeful manner towards the waiting Tuatha, and bowed low.

"Om," greeted the senior reverend monk.

"Um," replied Erald.

"Om. We have a mission to fulfill at the Welsh Assembly buildings. Please, are they here?"

Erald looked around. He disliked telling lies on general principles. Lugh, not being a general, had no such scruples.

"It's that one over there." He pointed at random to a small building that actually represented the final living quarters of the Castellan.

"Please, it looks a little small for a seat of government."

"This is Wales. They only have a small government," Lugh pointed out.

The most reverend turned to a less senior senior monk.

"Om. Please, go and check that for me."

"You calling me a liar?" asked Lugh.

"Om. Of course not. I merely wish to confirm, empirically, the facts before we take our required action." The monk bowed again and all waited in silence while the gopher monk walked over to the building, climbed

---

[*]   The chant was quite a lot longer than that, so homework for the reader is to fill in the missing words. Clue: they all began with 'B'.

the steps, and vanished inside. Moments passed and then the monk reappeared and returned to the group. He bowed to his leader.

"Om."

"Om. And?"

"Om. There are indeed plenty of seats inside. But no computers, no papers. I do not think that the government is here, O Reverend One."

"Om. Thank you, Reverend Five."

The students spread further away from the coaches, still chanting aimlessly like traveling football supporters in a strange town.

The most senior monk turned to the Tuatha.

"It would seem you have been mistaken," he said politely. The monk bowed and, as he did so, Lugh kicked him hard and then whacked him across the back of the neck with his staff. The most reverend monk dropped like a stone and the second in command took up the battle.

"By Ben, take them!" he yelled, and he and two others launched their throwing stars (brought in case of emergencies for crowd control). Erald whirled his staff in front of his face and all the stars hit it and jammed there. The back end of his staff continued its swing until interrupted by Reverend Two's head.

The other three senior monks spread out in a threatening manner and waved at the students. The students at once started to wander towards the gates, where the rest of the Tuatha waited.

"Should we go an' help them out?" Malan asked, pushing away a chanting student who was getting too close for comfort. (Malan's comfort, that is, the student was probably used to a lack of personal space.)

The senior remaining monk took a deep breath, screamed, and leaped high into the air, doing the splits and kicking out at Erald's head as he did so. Unfortunately (for him) he missed, and was still in the splits as he landed on the tarmac. His scream rose in pitch and Erald used his staff to put the poor monk out of his misery. The next monk lashed out at Lugh with a fist, but missed. He looked around for support but, after seeing his seniors bested in combat, the remaining monk had decided to change to the habit of a lifetime and (leaving the habit on the floor behind him) started to run for it.

Erald raised his staff in his right hand and flames ran up and down the shaft. The remaining monk nodded, made a gesture, and a shower of localized rain fell onto the staff. And onto the rest of Erald, drenching him. A wave of the hand transferred the shower to the monk and it changed to hail.

The monk pulled a face as the hail bounced off his shaven head and, with a mystical sign, sent the hailstorm back onto Erald. Several large hailstones bounced off his (rather large) nose, and the leader of the Tuatha became a little annoyed, enough to ignore the cries of alarm and despair from his brothers behind him. Erald tapped his staff twice on the floor and his shape wavered and grew taller still, bending over the orange monk. Then, as his feet slipped on the hailstones, the monk danced on with the agility of a young Fred Astair, before making an existential choice and sliding backwards. Erald toppled forwards and nutted his adversary in a meeting of heads, if not minds. The monk went down, unconscious.

Seeing all his fellows defeated at both martial and magical arts, the remaining monk submitted, and Lugh started tying his hands together.

"How are the other lads doing?" Lugh asked, as Erald climbed, unsteadily, to his feet.

They looked back. The castle gates were swinging feely open and the remaining Tuatha were lying around on the floor, groaning. Erald stamped (somewhat carefully) over to them.

"What happened to you lot? A bunch of brainwashed students did this to the magical race of the Tuatha? How?"

After a lot of sheepish looks between themselves, Liamm was elected spokesman by the others.

"Well, Erald. Grizelda said we were not to hurt them. So we couldn't get the swords out."

"And," Finn came to his brother's aid, "she also asked us to find one called Phil."

"What did she want him for?" asked Erald.

"For later, she said." The Tuatha all shuddered.

"Any way, we were trying to search the crowd for this Phil. But it wasn't easy, cos when we asked their names, they all seemed to be called Ben," Liamm continued.

"Then they just started pushing towards the gates and there were so many of them that they overwhelmed us," Finn finished.

Erald was underwhelmed.

"Do we need to get out there and find this Phil for her, then?" he wondered.

"No chance. We only have a brief description. He's got a shaved head and orange robes."

"Like the other 200 of them. All saying that they are called Ben."

Erald nodded. "Well, we've done what she wanted, anyway. The leaders are tied up in the coaches and the students have dispersed across the city."

"We could go and search all the pubs?" suggested Finn.

This idea was treated with acclaim.

Erald nodded wearily. "I think that we've probably earned one drink."

"Yes," agreed Liamm. "One in each pub we can find."

As the sirens announcing the impending approach of the Cardiff police grew in volume,[*] the Tuatha strolled away from the castle, crossed the street, and vanished into the crowds.

---

[*] Police sirens are designed to an international standard: to alert malefactors to the imminent arrival of the police and allow them to escape before the Law arrives. This is a conservation issue designed to reduce the paperwork generated by actually catching the criminals.

CHAPTER FOURTEEN

The orange *Volvo* arrived at the rear of the Welsh Assembly buildings and, after a brief discussion, parked close to the waterfront.

"What do you think you are doing?" demanded the senior monk.

"Putting money in this meter, of course," replied the accountant.

"We've just come here to break into the seat of power, steal the *whole country* and transfer the cash reserves to our personal offshore bank account!"

"That's no reason not to be law-abiding citizens, is it?" argued the accountant.

"Just leave it alone, you idiot!"

"All right," replied the accountant, "keep your hair on. Oh sorry, just an expression." He put the money back into his pocket and picked up the briefcase and his abacus.

"What are you bringing that for? We've got the laptop."

"An abacus is always useful," replied the accountant, calmly.

"Well, you've got to carry it."

"Come on."

The two walked calmly across the foreshore of Cardiff Bay, pausing to admire the boats tied up at the landings, and the impressive frontage of the Welsh Assembly building, a vision in glass and wood.

"Where are the coaches and the students?" asked the accountant.

"Should be here by now."

"Well, we'll have to go in without them."

"But what about the diversion?" asked the senior monk. "Who will distract the guard on the door?"

"You will," replied the accountant. "And then I'll hit him with the abacus."

"Well, it might as well be useful for something."

The two orange-robed figures strolled up to the guard on the door of the seat of power. The senior monk bowed politely.

"Om. Please, we seek admittance to the building."

"Sorry, mate," said the guard. "It's closed up for the weekend now. Wales are playing tomorrow, so they're all down the pub – not that anyone notices the difference, really. Ouch!"

"Oh dear," said the accountant. "I must have selected the wrong setting."

The monk sighed and waved his hands in front of the face of the enraged guard.

"If you want something practical doing properly, never use an accountant," the monk grumbled.

"Om. Please, enter," intoned the mesmerized guard.

The two, still arguing, walked into the deserted building and closed the door behind them. After wandering round the deserted building for a few minutes, and becoming lost, they managed to find their way back to the entrance. The monk beckoned to the guard, who trotted over to them.

"Om. Please, would you show us the way to the Council Chamber?"

"Sure. Follow me."

Moments later, the guard threw open a large door, and the monks saw the Council Chamber in all its glory.

"Bit modern for my taste," said the accountant.

"I'm inclined to agree. Still, this is the seat of power in Wales."

"No, that's the seat. Look, over there. Come on, let's plug in the laptop."

"Hang on," said the senior monk, turning to the guard and bowing. The guard tried to bow back, but politeness had not been included in his job specifications, and so the result looked awkward.

"Om. Please, keep the front door for us."

The guard tried bowing again, but years of over-eating were against him.

"That sign says "Diversion" Grizelda, do we go that way?" asked Imelda, at the wheel of the camper coach.

"NO! That's the Tuatha, creating a diversion for us."

Imelda stared at the mystical immortal beings out of legend. One was holding a badly painted sign, another standing still, apparently vacant, and two others were drinking canned beer and arguing.

"They are not quite what I expected," she said, wistfully.

"I've known 'em for ages. Trust me, what you see is what you get."

"I thought that that was computers?"

"That lot are every bit as annoyin' as a computer, believe me."

Grizelda pointed down a road to the left.

"The *Volvo* went that way. Follow it."

Imelda hauled on the steering wheel and followed the finger. Behind them, the Tuatha were dispersing, and so missed the spectacle of the *Mondeo*, rapid pursuit vehicle, three black Ford *Focuses* and a motley collection of journalists weaving in and out of the Cardiff traffic, trying to maintain a view of the car in front while remaining unseen themselves. Inevitably, a collision occurred between an innocent motorist (an oxymoron for most police officers) and one of the blacked-out backup cars at a roundabout.

"What did you think you were doing? Don't you know the Highway Code?" demanded the irate motorist, as he climbed out of his car to survey the new addition to his bonnet.

"You are obstructing police officers," retorted the black-clad driver of the leading *Focus*, while his colleague examined the chances of removing the second police car from the boot of their vehicle. The third *Focus* had avoided joining the collision by trying to drive under the road sign at the side of the road but had only succeeded in getting stuck there. The journalists were busy taking photographs, with some glee, and trying to get an interview with the luckless motorist on the roundabout.

"Sarge!"

"Yes, lad?"

"The back-up seems to have backed-down."

"You what?"

"Check the mirrors. We're on our own again."

"Right. Well, we've come too far to let them get away from us. Keep going."

"Is there an update on what they are supposed to have done?"

The sergeant, again, tried asking the police national computer via radio but, beyond telling him the time and inviting him to have a nice day, the information remained inconclusive.

"Whatever they did to those lads in Ceredigion must have been riveting, as far as the radio can tell," the sergeant commented.

"Where do you think that they are headed?"

"Hum. Good question. I'd hazard a guess at the Assembly buildings though."

"What makes you think that, Sarge?"

"They keep following the signs."

"Ah. Right."

"You've got to be observant in this job, lad."

"Yes, Sarge. Did you see that, Sarge?"

"No, I wasn't looking. What happened?"

"The coach that's been ahead of us all the way just turned down a side street to park and the *Mondeo* speeded up at once. Now they're turning left, too."

"Well of course I can see that."

"What do I do, Sarge?"

"Park up somewhere discreet."

"Discreet? In this *marked* patrol car?"

"Well, just choose the next street, then."

The next street contained only a recovery truck departing with a vehicle on its ramp.

"Been parked here for two days – with the keys in the exhaust." The driver called to the policemen through his open window. "Security has told me to move it."

"Park up here, lad," the sergeant instructed the driver.

"Now, we'll go and observe."

The coach occupants were unsettled.

"Look, just park it here," Grizelda ordered.

"But it's a restricted zone, Grizelda."

"So? If we see a traffic warden, I'll sort 'im out."

The others all exchanged glances.

"Yer could get into trouble wi' the Council fer that, luv," said Ben.

"Never mind," his spouse said. "Everybody out, let's see what's goin' on."

They all climbed out and examined the quiet street.

"Right," Grizelda said decisively, "what we do now is... is... is... "

"Chris and I will go and check out the waterfront," suggested Erica.

"Right," said Grizelda.

"Imelda and I will go and scout for the orange *Volvo*," said Marc, the student.

"Right," said Grizelda.

"We'll go and see what's going on at the front," said Ben.

"Right," said Grizelda.

"Come on then," called Linda, as she and her uncle trotted off to the end of the road.

"Right," said Grizelda, decisively, and followed them.

Marc and Imelda found the *Volvo* parked neatly on the edge of the waterfront.

"What now? They've obviously gone and left the car," said Marc.

Imelda thought for a moment and then chanted for a moment while making some mystic passes over the bonnet of the *Volvo*.

"What did you do there?" asked Marc, intrigued.

"Our local mechanic taught me that one, when I went out with him on a date. Basically, it's now stuck in first gear until the counter-spell is used."

"Oh?"

"He used to use it on cars that had stopped a bit inconsiderately in the pub car park. Told me he made quite a bit on the side helping with the recovery."

"Ah. Er. Er... "

Imelda treated Marc to a long look.

"I only went out with him that once," she said. "I prefer intellectuals, really."

"Ah. Good. Did I tell you that I'm a student?"

"Yes. I wonder if there's anything that I could teach you?"

"Let's go back to your coach and see, shall we?"

Erica and Chris, hand in hand, were exploring the piers and looking at the few boats that were moored there. Chris had a glint in his eye but, this time, not for Erica.

"Imelda's gone to sort out the *Volvo*, hasn't she?" he asked.

"Yes, Chris," replied Erica.

"So, they are not goin' to be able to get away in that." Chris looked around at the boats.

"Aha," said Erica. "You think that they will try to come here?"

"Yes."

"What makes you think that?"

"Well, that orange boat on the end gave me the idea," said Chris.

"The one called *Semper Om*?

"That's right."

"So, what can we do about it?" asked Erica.

"Could you sabotage the engine by magic?" asked Chris.

"Maybe, I'm not really good with mechanical things, yet."

"I'm from Manchester. I've got a few ideas."

"So I've noticed."

Chris and Erica ran down the steps – to be confronted by locked metal gates, preventing access to the pontoon moorings.

Erica glared at the lock, muttering, but it resisted her charms. (Unlike Chris.)

Chris pulled out his Ward of Lingard, which was glowing. He quietly repeated the word illuminated there and the locked gates opened with a click.

Erica gave him a glowing look, and then grabbed his hand, and together they ran along the pontoons. At the end, they stopped by the orange cruiser. Equipped with both sails and engines, it was also unlocked and clearly provisioned for a long trip.

Chris was just about to leap aboard, when Erica stopped him.

"Careful. This is well protected. But that's something I can deal with," she told him.

Raising her arms, she swayed to and fro while intoning a mantra. Slowly, a golden glow appeared all around the cruiser, and then became full of silver sparks, before vanishing. Erica sat on a bollard, panting from the effort, before falling off into the water. Chris started laughing, until a hand appeared out of the water, and pulled him in too.

Eventually, they both climbed, wet and dripping, out of the water and back onto the pontoons.

"What did you pull me in for?" spluttered Chris, shaking water spiders out of his ears.

"Teach you to laugh at me," grumbled a wet Erica. "Especially when I just saved you from being blown into the water by the defenses."

"I still got wet."

"But you are still in one piece. And you do look good in shrinking jeans."

"You look better than I do though, when wet," Chris said.

"Listen, this isn't a wet t-shirt contest. If you can disable that engine, get on with it!"

Chris jumped down into the cruiser, leaving wet footprints behind him, and vanished inside. While he was busy with the engines, and busy swearing too, Erica pondered a number of the important looking ropes that lay about the deck. With an evil grin she had learned from Grizelda, she pulled a pocket knife from her pocket.

Further back towards the city, Grizelda was under observation.

"I thought yer learned to creep last year!" Ned complained.

"I did," replied the junior.

"Then why are yer makin' so much freakin' noise?"

"Sorry. It's these boots."

"Well, at least try a bit harder. Can yer see 'em?" he asked of the assistant assistant, who was kneeling down, peering round a corner.

"Yes."

"What are they doin'?"

"It's Grizelda. What do yer think?"

"Arguin'. All right, what else?" asked Ned.

"She's headin' for the Assembly buildin'."

"On her own?"

"No. Ben's with her, an' that teenage girl."

"What, Linda? 'ER FROM STOCKPORT?"

"Yes. Why?" asked the assistant assistant.

"She's got one of the Wards of Lingard. The Boss will repay us well if we nick one of them."

"Yer on yer own, then. I'm not takin' Grizelda on," replied the junior.

"But Grizelda's not wearin' it," mused Ned. "Anyway, if they're headin' for the Assembly building, so are we. Keep down, keep quiet." The group of dark wizards crept through the darkening streets, following their target.

Behind them, in the quiet streets, more professional stalking was taking place.

"Look, it's in the manual. You must have read it at least once by now."

"Sarge, I'm on motorway patrol duties. Why do I need to know how to behave like James Bond?"

"You're a serving police officer. You should be versatile. Watch me."

The sergeant was duly observed.

"Making a complete prat out of himself," thought the PC, before saying, loudly:

"That's great Sarge. Did you mean to kneel in that pile of dogs' doings, or is that part of the cover?"

"Keep quiet," hissed his sergeant. "We don't want to alert the suspects to our presence. Be as silent as you can." He crept forwards.

"All units: suspicious activity reported behind the Welsh Assembly," announced the sergeant's radio, at a volume normally found only at football crowd control.

"Ned, I heard somethin' behind us!" hissed the junior.

"Probably a cat," replied Ned, dismissively.

"Sounded like a walkie-talkie ter me."

"Well, while I look out ahead, you two look out behind," instructed Ned.

"Ouch! Wha' do yer think yer doin' stamping all over me like that, yer idiot?"

"Sorry, Ned. I were lookin' out behind, an' didn't see you stopped in front."

Ahead of them, Grizelda had reached the glass doors of the Welsh Assembly buildings.

"Locked," said Ben, giving them a push.

Grizelda threw a small spell, which rebounded off the lock without causing damage, and set fire to Ben's beard.

Ben put out the flames, glared at his wife, and put the end of his staff on the lock. Ben pushed, gently, and, although sparks flew, the doors remained shut. Behind the glass appeared the shape of the portly guard, who sniggered.

Linda stepped up, pulling her Ward of Lingard from under her jumper. The ward glowed red and green and the door flew open, stopping with a jolt when it hit the big boots of the guard.

The guard's expression changed and became menacing.

"Om. You can't do that!" he said, loudly.

Ben and Grizelda looked at each other.

"Did you say Om?" asked Ben.

"Om. No." replied the guard.

"Yes yer did."

"Om. So? You still can't do that. That's a felony."

"I am Ben," stated Ben.

"Om. Ben?"

"Ben."

The guard made no reply.

"I am Ben."

"Om. You have said that already," the guard told him.

"Being brainwashed hasn't stopped him being stupid, then," said Grizelda, impatiently.

"Look, you can't come in here," the guard ordered them. "You'll have to leave at once, or I shall summon the – rivet! Rivet! Rivet!"

"Did you have to frog him, Auntie?" asked Linda.

"We'd have been here all night arguin' wiv 'im. Come on!"

"Rivet? Rivet? Rivet?" called the frog as they ran into the building. He hopped against the door and it swung shut. Grizelda led her husband and niece into the building. Moments later, the frog was bowled over the floor as the door was pushed open.

"Rivet! Rivet!"* complained the frog.

"'E must 'ave got in Grizelda's way," surmised Ned.

"Which way did they go?" asked the junior.

"Rivet!"

"Thank you."

---

* Translation: "it's a dog's life, being a frog."

Again the door closed and, again, the frog went spinning across the polished floor, as it was pushed open, hard.

"Rivet! Rivet! Rivet!"

"Sarge, didn't the computer say something about a frog?" asked the PC.

"Can't be the same one, lad."

"I wonder which way they went."

"Rivet."

"Thank you," said the PC.

"What are you saying thank you for? It's a frog!"

"Politeness costs nothing, Sarge."

"Can't say it's a theory I've ever worked with. And it's definitely not in the training manual."

Their boots rang on the polished floor as they moved deeper into the building.

In the Council Chamber, the Mystic Accountant sat – with some ceremony – in the seat of power normally occupied by the leader of the Welsh Assembly. He opened his case and took out his laptop, turning on the computer on the desk. Then he started patting his pockets feverishly.

"What are you looking for?" demanded the senior monk.

"A USB cable, of course. Damn, the server knows it's the weekend, it's taking ages to start up."

"How can a computer know it's the weekend?"

"Well, Wales are playing rugby at home tomorrow. The server's Welsh, so it's probably concentrating on that."

"Don't be ridiculous. What's it doing now?"

"Asking for a password," replied the accountant, linking the laptop into the server and switching it on. The laptop screen glowed bright orange and letters began to flash across it.

"Oh good grief," muttered the accountant. "How predictable."

"What is it?"

"*Cymru am byth.*"*

"Right," said the senior monk, not understanding.

"Now to install the software," grinned the accountant, raising his index finger.

"Don't touch that button!" cried Grizelda, as she, Ben and Linda ran into the Council Chamber.

"Ben!" cried the senior monk, in shock.

---

*   Roughly translated as 'Wales forever, stuff the Sais.'

"We've no time for that rubbish now," replied the accountant, not looking up.

"It's Ben!" repeated the monk and the accountant looked up from his screen.

"So it is," he agreed, and pressed the 'Enter' button. "Well, he's too late now."

"Too late for what?" asked Grizelda, advancing across the Council Chamber.

"We are now the legal government of Wales. Ben could have been leader of the Assembly, if he hadn't run off," the senior monk told them. "Now he'll have to settle for leader of the opposition and it doesn't pay as well."

Grizelda raised her hands and tried to frog the monks. But they were resistant to the spell.

Ben raised his staff and threw a binding spell across the chamber but, although the accountant staggered, both the monks were unharmed.

Linda walked over to the nearest desk, switched on the computer monitor and studied the screen.

"What are they doin'?" asked her aunt.

"Messing with the results of the elections. They are putting themselves in as the winners."

"Can they do that?"

"Well, I can't see it working for long," Ban said, confused. "What happens when Parliament gets to hear about it?"

"We are going to declare Wales as independent." The senior monk told him. "Enough of the ordinary people will be behind us."

"And the present Welsh Assembly?" asked Grizelda.

"They're all off to watch the rugby this weekend. By the time they come back, our software will have taken over, and we'll have them locked up."

Linda was not listening. Instead, she was looking at her ward. Not just one word, but whole sentences were flashing across the amulet. In the end, she just pushed the ward into the USB slot of the terminal at which she was sitting.

"Oi! What are you doing?" yelled the Mystic Accountant looking, with alarm, at his laptop.

Grizelda looked at her niece, who just shrugged.

Competing graphics and binary numbers jumped and ran up and down the screens of the computers. Every terminal in the Council Chamber turned itself on and the screens went wild. Then the audio channels set.

Half the terminals started shouting something incomprehensible, and then started singing instead, while the rest intoned "Om" or "Ben" according to preference.

"Do something!" hissed the senior monk to the accountant.

"Like what?" replied the accountant. "Whatever she's done on that terminal is now in the servers and it's fighting in there with our program. I can't do anything with it now."

"Try something!" urged the senior monk.

"I could send you in there to help. I'm sure I can find somewhere I could plug in this USB cable," the accountant responded.

"Then I think we should carry out a strategic reappraisal of our position here and consider regrouping our forces in a position with superior defensive capabilities, in order to renew our assault on our prime objective."

The accountant thought this through for a moment. "You mean run away?"

"Yes. Now. While they are all over there, at that terminal."

The two monks started running and sped out of the door of the Council Chamber, flattening the dark wizards behind the doors as they threw them open in their getaway. The sound of their sandals flapping on the floor echoed behind them.

"Dot, those monks have legged it!" called Ben to his wife.

Grizelda thought for a moment. "Let them go," she decided. "This one is the important battle."

"Grizelda? What's goin' on?" called Ned from the doorway. His nose was streaming with blood from its collision with the door.

"Them monks have tried to take over Wales by computer, but we've got 'em stopped now."

Ned and his assistants entered the Council Chamber and sat down in some of the Assembly members' seating.

On the screens, the rows of binary code were fading, to be slowly replaced by a laughing green dragon. Then the pixels faded to be replaced by a hand making a one finger salute. The terminals reverted to showing replays of Wales' last rugby victory over England and Linda closed the audio channels.

"Auntie, my necklace has won," gloated Linda, refastening the ward around her neck. If jewelry could look self-satisfied, the ward was an exemplary example.

In the doorway of the Chamber appeared the statuesque figure of the police sergeant, with his PC in support.

"'Ello, 'ello 'ello!" announced the sergeant, looking around at the quiet scene. "Do you lot have an explanation for all this?" The official notebook came out of the pocket of the sergeant's knife-proof body armor, and he waved his biro in a threatening manner.

The glass and chrome doors of the Welsh Assembly buildings flew open, the two orange clad-monks hurried out, and ran around the frontage and down the steps, until they could turn towards the back of the building. Moments later, the senior monk stopped dead in his tracks.

"Where now?" panted the accountant.

The senior monk looked wildly all around. "The hire car's gone! It was here when we came past in the *Volvo*, now it's gone!"

"Then lets' get the *Volvo*!" panted the accountant, fishing in his pocket for the keys.

The two monks turned, and moments later reached the forecourt car park, and leaned on their *Volvo*. The accountant's complexion now resembled his orange robes, for he was not used to such exercise.

"You aren't fit to drive!" snarled the senior monk, grabbing the keys.

They both jumped into the car. The senior monk started the engine, selected reverse gear, and drove smartly forwards over the edge of the car park and into the dark waters of Cardiff Bay. Bubbles rose from the sinking *Volvo* and were shortly joined on the surface by two shaven headed monks.

"Maybe I wasn't up to the drive but at least I can swim," gurgled the accountant.

"Any more ideas?" asked the senior monk, when he had finished blowing bubbles.

"Just one," answered the accountant and, turning in the water, struck out and swam across to the moorings in front of the pier.

"I arranged for this cruiser, just as a backup," panted the accountant, as he pulled himself out of the water with the aid of a ladder left projecting over the stern of the orange cruiser. Neither noticed the wet footprints already in the cockpit.

"Good idea, this was," agreed the senior monk, rapidly undoing the mooring lines, and pushing the cruiser away from the moorings.

"There are changes of clothes in the cabin and I had the galley stocked, too," said the accountant, dripping water all over the cockpit as he looked for the keys. Finding them, he started the engine, and the cruiser moved slowly out towards the center of Cardiff Bay.

The accountant looked back over his shoulder at the striking frontage of the Welsh Assembly buildings. As he watched, the doors opened wide and Grizelda, Ned, Ben, Linda and Ned's staff poured out of the doors, which were being held open for them by two saluting police frogs. Grizelda and Ned ran to the front of the foreshore and leaned on the railings. Chris and Erica walked towards them from the gates that led to the moorings. The accountant waved and turned to face the front of the boat, and the scent of the open seas and escape ahead. He pushed the throttles wide open. The engines roared, the cruiser moved forward, and the engines coughed and died. The senior monk rounded on the accountant. "Don't tell me we've run out of fuel!" he yelled.

The accountant was frantically slapping buttons and tapping gauges. "The tanks are full!" he shouted back.

The cruiser rocked in the quiet swell in the center of the bay, as the senior monk grappled with the sails, with which he was unfamiliar. But the cut ropes that slithered through his fingers, allowing the mainsail to slip over the side of the cruiser, needed no experience to be identified as a problem.

"Any ideas?" asked the accountant sarcastically, looking over the side of the cruiser at the dark waters drifting past.

"Suppose we could whistle for a wind," answered the senior monk, sitting down at the cockpit seating and gazing morosely across the bay to the shore.

"What do you recommend? *'Don't pay the Ferryman'?*"

Back on the foreshore, Chris was smirking. "Sugar in the fuel tanks." He explained to his aunt, as they all gazed at the stricken yacht, wallowing in the bay despite the frantic efforts of the two monks.

"Right," Grizelda announced to her troops who were now congregating. "Back to the coach, an' back ter my place. Are yer comin' Ned?"

"Better not. I'm gonna be in enough trouble wi' me boss as it is. We're goin' back north."

"What are yer goin' ter do about them policemen that are after yer?"

"No bother. Before we left, I got that daft sergeant to report in that we were innocent of any wrong-doin' and clear the police computer of all of our details."

Grizelda nodded and, with an imperious wave, swept up her party to head for home and a celebration.

Ned looked around at his staff. "Come on you two. Let's be off."

The three dark wizards wandered off across the waterfront of Cardiff Bay, by sheer coincidence arriving at the collection of pubs and eateries.

"Right," said Ned. "Anyone know how ter manage a boat?"

"You what?" asked the junior, concentrating on a menu posted on a wall.

"We're goin' ter go an' get those two mad monks. The Grey Mage will have a good use for them, I'm sure. An' that will get us off the hook fer not getting' in the way of Fungus an' that new throne."

"Good thinkin'," said the assistant assistant. "I've used a boat before, we'll borrow one of those over there. Ned an' I'll go, an' you can get the car ready fer our getaway."

Ned and his assistant assistant wandered down through the open gates and onto the moorings. A small boat with a large engine was quickly selected and Ned by-passed the ignition key by muttering a spell at the engine, which promptly started.

"Yer must teach me that one," said the assistant assistant. "With the state of the taxi's our boss buys for me, I could use it in me day job."

Slowly, they sailed out towards the floating cruiser.

"Ahoy, there!" shouted the assistant assistant, who was feeling nautical.

The Mystic Accountant and the senior monk sat in the cockpit of their drifting vessel and watched them come alongside.

"Are you police?" asked the senior monk, with resignation.

"No. We're accountants."

"What a coincidence."

"Right," said Ned. "Either yer can stay here an' wait fer the police, or come wi' us."

"Where to?" asked the accountant.

"Well, wi' your skill set, there's a chance our boss will offer yer jobs. An' a hiding place."

The two drifters dived into the cabin and came out a moment later dressed as accountants in shirts and trousers. The orange robes they threw over the side of the cruiser, to drift away.

"I quite fancy a bit of honest dishonesty," remarked the Mystic Accountant, as the assistant assistant tweaked the throttle and headed for the shoreline, and the waiting getaway car.

"It's not a bad life, if yer don't weaken," the assistant assistant said.

CHAPTER FIFTEEN

The Banned waved goodbye to Santa's Little Helpers, and Eddie turned north to drive back to the Helvyndelve.

"So, our quest is nearly over," said Fungus leaning back in his seat.

Haemar was rifling through the collection of CDs for something suitable.

"But Fungus," worried Scar, "what's Lakin goin' ter say when he sees 'is new throne?"

"Look, that's not our problem. He gave us a budget, we spent the budget, an' got what we could for what we had."

"I sort of see what Scar's worried about though," agreed GG.

"Well, if he doesn't want ter sit on the throne, he can always sit on the terms an' conditions instead." Haemar said, still shuffling CD cases.

"That's true," agreed GG. "They are as tall as the seating."

"Probably not as comfy though."

"And it all comes with a genuine certificate of authenticity from *Waccibacci Enterprises*. I've got the paperwork here," said Fungus.

"An' I made sure we had copies too, just in case," muttered Haemar.

"In case of what?" worried Scar.

"Just in case," said Haemar irritably. "Who's bin in the CDs? I can't find the one I want."

"Which one were it?" asked GG.

"Some Leonard Cohen. I wanted cheerin' up."

"Der!"

"I agree with Eddie. You can't expect him to drive while being depressed," objected GG.

"Der."

"He fancies some Stones, and he's drivin'."

Haemar grumbled briefly, then put on *Get Yer Ya Yas Out*, and they all settled down for the long drive, except for Felldyke who had not really woken up since the gig, and was already settled.

More Stones followed on the CD, then Haemar started feeding older blues into the player and The Banned were sung back to the Lake District in a state of bliss. From which they were rudely awakened by Eddie's rest stop at the motorway services.

Despite much traveling on the road, The Banned had rarely stopped at the Services in case their appearance caused some controversy. But Eddie, who had once been a taxi driver, was accustomed to them.

The tour bus and its trailer pulled into the car park and Eddie switched off the engine. Slowly The Banned awoke within the bus.

The next paragraph, describing the scene in some detail, has been deleted on the grounds of taste and decency. Any reader wishing to see the more prurient detail is redirected to the various memoirs of touring rock bands, in particular The Faces, The Rolling Stones and Led Zeppelin.

Eddie opened his door and left the bus.

"Der," he called out as he walked across the car park.

With some disfavor and concern, The Banned looked through the windows at the grey concrete monstrosity before them, garishly hung with signs in primary colors which alleged that food was available within.

"OK," said Haemar slowly, "let's try it lads."

"Suppose we'll have to try it sometime," agreed Fungus dubiously.

"Do yer think it's safe?" asked Scar.

"In absolute terms, or compared ter that gig we did in Glasgow last year?"

"The one where the promoter got the advertising wrong, an' we got a crowd expecting Justin Bieber?" remembered GG with a shudder.

"Yeah. First time in years I were actually in fear fer me life," Scar recalled.

The Banned slowly climbed out of the *Sprinter* and headed for the cavernous doors before them. As they reached the doors, they opened with a loud hiss. The Banned hesitated.

"Dragon-powered doors?" wondered GG.

"Oh come on," said Haemar, "there's bound ter be food an' drink inside there somewhere."

At that point, a group of shaven-headed louts spilled out of the shop, and through the doors, pushing the dwarves to one side as they left.

"Move it, short stuff!" one said to Haemar as he passed, tapping the lead singer twice on his head as he did so, and pulling at the long hair while making a sarcastic comment to his peers.

In one swift move, Haemar grabbed the lad's wrist, twisted it around in the same fashion as he wielded the mic stand onstage, before jumping on his assailant's back, and using his helmet and bad attitude to good effect.

"Never say that to a singer again!" he snarled.

The rest of the louts turned back and jumped at Haemar, but Felldyke (or, to be more accurate, Felldyke's stomach) got there first, and the leader bounced off onto his second, both of whom fell to the floor. Scar and GG then jumped on them, while the remaining lout squared up to Fungus. The lout threw a vicious punch, which landed on Fungus' chest, and so caused no damage to the bog troll.

Fungus retaliated with a wild slap, which echoed across the car park, almost as far as the lout flew across the tarmac. Several passers-by stopped to clap and one took a picture on his mobile phone.

The leading lout made some noise and Haemar, courteously, lifted the lout's face away from the target long enough for the former to breathe for a while.

"Did you say you were a singer?" asked the recumbent one, after a bit of heavy breathing.

"Yes," answered Haemar, shortly.

"In a band?"

"What do yer think this lot are? Scotch mist?"

"Can I say sorry, then?" asked the lout. Haemar relaxed his grip and both Scar and GG released their victims, too.

"If we'd known you were a band, we wouldn't have had a go, mate. Just thought that you were... " the voice trailed off under the weight of Haemar's glare.

"Yer thought we were what?"

"Well, just a bunch of dwarves."

"Can't argue wi' 'im there, Haemar," said GG.

"Excuse ME," Fungus objected.

"Sorry, Fungus. But yer know, well, the rest of us are."

"Can we get up now?" asked a voice by GG's feet.

The Banned slowly moved back, allowing the bunch of louts to get up, and regroup while counting bruises. The one Fungus had slapped was slowly walking back across the car park, while looking very confused.

"No harm done," said the leading lout while pushing tissues up his nose to stem the bleeding. His fellows looked a little less convinced, and The Banned remained on edge.

"What do you play?"

"Blues, rock 'n' roll, jazz," replied Fungus shortly.

"Tell you what, we'll buy you some lunch and talk," suggested the leading lout. "I'm Adam," he introduced himself.

At that point there was a short hiatus, while Eddie hurtled out of the doors to the aid of The Banned, and had to be hastily prevented from renewing hostilities.

Hostilities were indeed almost renewed when the food arrived. Haemar tapped his bacon buttie with a knife and the bacon pinged across the room, landing, with perfect serendipity, back in the serving trays behind the counter, to be swiftly re-sold.

Adam, who was in fact used to dealing with vocalists, quickly pushed his own bacon buttie across the table, and Haemar simmered back down.

"So what's the craic?" asked Fungus, inspecting a cup of almost coffee.

"We're just starting our own record label," said Adam. "It's called Council Industrial Unit Records at the moment, but the name needs some work."

Interest quickened around the table.

"What are yer lookin' for?" asked GG.

"Well, we've decided that we'll only put out live recordings. Can't stand all this manufactured stuff, we want bands who can actually play something, for a change. And if you can play as well as you fight, then we might offer you a contract. When could we see you play?"

Haemar and Fungus exchanged long looks.

"Well, actually – " started Fungus.

" – We're on our way to a gig now, in the Lake District. Where are you based?" finished Haemar.

"Reading," replied Adam.

This meant nothing to The Banned, who didn't read much, apart from bar menus.

"Near London," Adam added.

"Oh. Southerners, then. No wonder we won the scrap," muttered Scar the international peacemaker.

"Whatever. Look, our van has a mobile recording studio. If we can come to your gig and do a test recording, then we could talk about a contract if we like what we hear."

"A contract!" exclaimed Haemar.

"Yeah. We've been out looking for a decent live blues band, but haven't found one yet," Adam told them.

"So where's your gig?" asked his chief assistant. Shaven-headed he might be, but once he had donned his glasses, The Banned had no difficulty in picturing him as an accountant. Or as a Don, of course.

"In the Lake District," said Haemar, vaguely. Fungus frowned at him.

"Look, to be straight," Haemar told Adam. "The place is, well, a bit secretive. I'm not too sure we could get you in."

"Lakin might moan about it," worried Scar.

"He moans about everything else," agreed Felldyke.

"We can get Eddie in," pointed out Fungus.

"Der."

"Yes, but that's Eddie. He's our roadie, part of The Banned, now."

"Der."

"That's quite all right Eddie, you deserve the compliment."

"Well, we could try, couldn't we?" asked Fungus.

Adam had some experience of dealing with the problems bands could have and hence knew the way to get any lead singer onside.

"We could film the performance for you," he told Haemar. "Quality wouldn't be fantastic, not up to TV broadcast standards, but as good as the DVD gigs about."

Haemar froze, the image of a recoded, filmed gig playing across the inside of his head.

"We owe it to our public," he said slowly.

"What public?" asked Felldyke, who only associated the word *public* with conveniences.*

"The audiences," Haemar said, irritated.

"Oh, them."

"What we need," Fungus said to Adam, "are some CDs that we can sell at gigs."

"We can probably help you out there," said Charles, the accountant.

"Der."

"Well, yes, there will be some costs but you will make money out of each one you sell. Let's record the gig first, see what we get, then talk about contracts."

Adam had said the magic word, 'Contracts'. The Banned's eyes glazed over.

"What we'll do," said Fungus slowly, "is... "

"What?" asked GG.

"Is... "

"Yes?" asked Haemar.

"We'll get up there, park up near the back doors, an' sneak this lot in. We'll give them some of those t-shirts we had."

---

* Unlike politicians, who only associate the public with inconveniences.

Haemar looked up, and up a bit more, at the tall figures of Adam and his technicians.

"Never get away with pretending that they're dwarves," he mused. "We'll have to call them some of the Edern."

"Back to the bus," called Fungus, but pulled Haemar back, as the others jogged back to the *Sprinter*.

"Sounds great," he hissed, "but what happens back at the Helvyndelve? When Lakin sees his new throne?"

"A DVD of us being arrested on stage will not showcase our talents."

"Probably sell pretty well, though," Haemar answered. "But what can we do about it? Best chance we've had in ages, this is."

"All right," Fungus agreed. "I'm just worried, that's all."

"Well, don't tell the others. No point in worryin' them."

"GG?" asked Scar.

"Yeah?"

"Look at Haemar and Fungus whispering. That worries me."

"Scar, everything worries you. Be more like Felldyke, he's not worried."

"GG, as long as he's got a drumstick to gnaw at, Armageddon could be going on all around us, and Felldyke wouldn't worry."

"I worry about him, too."

"Doesn't it worry you that all you do is worry?"

"No. Should it?" worried Scar.

"Forget it, Scar. Here they come, now."

"No worries!" announced Haemar.

"We've worked it out," said Fungus. "We'll claim that they are a bunch of Lady Hankey's security staff and nobody will want to bother them then."

"Der."

"Eddie's ready to go," called GG, and The Banned all climbed into the *Sprinter*.

Across the car park, Adam and his cronies jumped into their *Mercedes* van which sported blacked-out windows and a front bull bar, giving the vehicle a disturbing appearance.

"What about Dai?" asked GG.

"Before we left, I put in a quick call to Malan of the Tuatha, he's gonna sort it out fer us," answered Fungus.

The Banned relaxed and leaned back in their seats.

"What's on the CD?"

"Chris Rea. *The Road to Hell*."

"Seems appropriate."

Inside the Helvyndelve, Lord Lakin's temper was as short as the Lord himself.

"Have we not heard from them yet?" Lakin demanded of his guard captain.

The captain swallowed hard. Normally, he picked on a guard who was guilty of a minor misdemeanor for the unpleasant duty of reporting nothing to the King under the Mountain. As a result, the guards had reached a state of alertness and efficiency, and had such spotless armor, that he had been reduced to doing the job himself.

"Sorry, Lord," he muttered.

"Well, today is the last day that I am prepared to wait. After today, I shall declare them to have absconded with the funds entrusted to them. And send you to go and find them."

The captain brightened up considerably.

"And how much would the budget come to, Lord? I mean, there's wear and tear on boots, disguises, we would have to go into various disreputable drinking dens and Blues clubs, them sort of places, to find them. And we'd have to drink a lot, to fit in, you know?" his voice trailed away at the look on Lakin's face.

Lakin waved most of the dwarves around to go further down the chamber, leaving him and the guard captain alone to have a private discussion.

"Lissen." Lakin hissed. "The Amulet of Kings is startin' to run out of juice. I've cut back a lot of the services it runs." They both turned and looked at the huge stack of used pizza boxes stashed behind the dais of the throne, dwarfed, (if you will pardon the expression) only by the pile of empty beer cans.

"When they call me King under the Mountain, it isn't meant to be short for King under the Mountain of Rubbish Nobody Can Be Bothered to Shift."

"Um."

"And it will get worse, captain. The Grey Mage is probing the power of the Helvyndelve. If the amulet was to become too weak, then he might be able to force open our doors."

"He'd be lucky, Lord. Even our maintenance teams can't do that when it's rainin'. They stick something wicked, you know."

"Well, I can feel the forces of evil gathering around us again."

"Most likely that's the Council. I keep telling the lads not to do it but they will keep pretending to be traffic wardens and collecting on-the-spot penalty fines from tourists whenever they want to go out for a curry. Probably been some complaints."

"Whatever. But I need that new throne now, urgently." Lakin sat back in his chair, with a dark expression. At the entrance to the Chamber of the Throne, there was a small commotion as a small, or possibly bijou, dwarf forced his way through the doors and tramped up the hall at his best speed. Stopping before the dais, he saluted his Lord who stared, with some disbelief, at the shining bright armor before him.

"What did you use to clean that?" asked Lakin.

"Special recipe, sir!" answered the dwarf.

"Brown Sauce an' Coke," advised the captain.

"Doesn't the coke scratch the armor?"

"He meant the fizzy stuff in cans, not the coal the lads used to dig up for the fires," explained the captain.

"An' we've gone smokeless now, anyway," put in the guard, hiding his smokes in a back pocket.

"That's the Council's fault, too," grumbled Lord Lakin. "Anyway, what do you want?"

"We had a message from The Banned Underground, Lord."

"Where is it?"

The guard offered a piece of paper that might well be described, in book terms, as seriously foxed. Possibly beared and wolved as well. Anyone who has recovered a letter from the local Post Office sorting centre would recognize the effect at once.

"What's this, then?" asked Lord Lakin.

"Erm, that's the message, Lord, as it came in to us at the Entrance Chamber."

Lakin examined the paper minutely.

"Six onion bahjis. One lamb Korma, twelve poppadums, two chutney trays, one garlic naan and three chicken Tikka Masalas, all with half rice, half chips. Is it a code?"

"Sorry, Lord. We was a bit short on paper, so we used our dinner order. The message is written in the bottom corner, look."

"Bak tomoz. Got throne. Need gig, quick, tell Lakin 2 sell tickets fast."

The guard captain winced.

"How many of you are there in the Guard Chamber?" asked Lakin, looking at the take away order again.

"Just the two of us, Lord."

"Better get back there, then. And get ready for the usual suspects turning up for a gig tomorrow night."

"Yes Lord."

"And Milim?" called Lakin, after the retreating guard.

"Yes, Lord?"

"This time, wait until the guests have gone home before you sell their weapons to Ugly Fred, him with the scrap metal yard in Keswick."

"Yes, Lord. But at least it meant that they had no weapons to fight with when they left last time."

"I know. But I still had that idiot from the police come round moaning at me, so think on."

"Yes, Lord," said Milim, departing thankfully.

"Right," said Lakin forcefully. "Guard captain, we need to arrange for a ceremony to install my new throne here on the dais, and also get the Cavern of A Thousand Knights ready for a gig. I did promise that to Fungus, so it will have to happen. Cancel all guard leave, make sure everyone's on duty."

"Yes Lord."

"And send someone down to the printers, we will need some tickets and posters pretty damn quick. And get the fly poster team out again."

"Yes Lord."

"And have someone ring the Council and get them to send a couple of skips to the back doors. When the amulet is back in the throne, we can get some of the rubbish shifted."

"I'd best ask for the biggest skips they have, then."

Across town, the word was spreading. Before the printers had finished the fly posters, news of the gig was flying into a certain accountant's office.

"Boss, I have urgent news!" announced the dragon receptionist.

"Not now, Gloria," replied The Grey Mage, absently. "I'm just working out how much to bill this client."

"Whatever you had in mind, just double it and call it extra research," she suggested.

"Not a bad idea. Now, what is this news? Any word from Ned?"

"No. But the printers are making up posters for a gig at the Helvyndelve tomorrow night: The Banned Underground will be back."

The Grey Mage leaned back in his chair. "That can only mean that they have got a new throne for the king."

"Elvis? Isn't he dead?"

"No, Lakin. And Elvis isn't dead, the CIA have got him in hiding. Why else can no one get into Area 51? It's just so that the US Presidents can have private gigs."

"Did you see that in your scrying bowl?"

"No. It's all over the internet." The Grey Mage thought for a while.

"Try and raise Ned. Then summon the Black Coven, we will try and intercept them ourselves, and stop the new throne getting to the Helvyndelve. And you are coming, too."

"Yes, Boss."

The Grey Mage pulled his keyboard forward and called a map of the Helvyndelve onto his computer screen, leaned back in his partner's comfy chair, and began plotting. "They always bring the customers in through the front door, so that they are knackered by the time they have walked all the way to the central caverns," he mused.

"But they won't bring the throne that way – too far to carry it. That means the back door, in the old mines."

His finger reached out and stabbed a point on the screen of his computer.

"So, we'll meet in this car park and get them on the bend. We'll force them into the Ullswater Lake and that will be the end of the new throne."

His receptionist put her head through the door. After shaking bits of wood away in irritation, (dragons so often forget to open the door first) she spoke:

"Ned's called in. They had a run in with the police and missed Fungus. But they are close behind on the motorway, and he says that he's got two willing recruits for the coven with him. Oh, and one of them's a qualified accountant too."

"Aha!" gloated The Grey Mage. "So, we'll be ahead, they'll be behind, we'll have them caught in a sandwich."

"That reminds me," said his receptionist. "Got any of those chocolate digestives left?"

Chapter Sixteen

"Der," announced Eddie.

"Eddie says we've just left the motorway!" called GG to the snoozing Banned.

"Not far, now, then," yawned Fungus, waking up and adjusting his sunglasses.

Beside him, Haemar also yawned, and then swung his head round on his neck to remove the cricks. Felldyke tapped his fingers in time to the rhythm of the crackling sounds, then winced as Haemar's helmet fell from its owner's head and landed on his toes.

"Sorry," muttered Haemar. He reached back, grabbed the helmet and then disappeared from view as he jammed it onto his head – the wrong way round. Scar and Felldyke together managed to release the helmet from Haemar who then released some choice language.

"Are that record lot still behind us?" asked Fungus rapidly, to distract Haemar before his face turned purple.

"Der," Eddie told him.

"Good."

"Where's Dai goin' ter meet us?" asked GG.

"I told Malan ter meet us at that car park near the turnin' up ter the back door," Fungus replied.

They all swayed as Eddie negotiated some sharp bends on the road.

Shortly afterwards, the *Mondeo* swayed wildly as the assistant assistant took the same bends. He was finally enjoying himself after the long, boring drive north on the M6, while the others had slept or meditated according to personal choice. The satnav had become considerably more cheerful after the car had crossed the Severn Bridge and the happy humming noise it made had driven all five occupants to the edge of insanity.

Suddenly, the efforts of the satnav to sing *I'm Walking on Sunshine* for the four hundredth consecutive time were interrupted as the screen glowed in a myriad of arcane colors, and dissolved into the face of The Grey Mage.

"Oi!" screamed the satnav, "that hurts!"

"Not as much as yer singin' does," muttered Ned. "That you, Boss?"

"I will be brief, Ned," said the image of The Grey Mage.

"That'll make a first, then," muttered the junior from the back seat. Being squashed between two depressed monks was not one of his reasons to be cheerful.

"I heard that."

"Sorry, Boss."

"I'll see you later about that. Now, I have got my old *Mercedes* and a few of the lads here ahead of you. We are going to ambush The Banned at the car park close to the dwarves' back door and, when we do, you lot pile into them from behind."

"Right, Boss," said Ned, waking up. "Lissen, Boss, there's another van with them now as well. But we don't know who – or what – is in there."

"You sure?"

"It's been with them all the way up 'ere since we caught up wi' them. Black van, blacked-out windows."

"Right. Then I'll bring the dragon receptionist as well, for a bit more firepower."

The assistant assistant shuddered.

The image wavered.

"I'm l... ing si... l," announced The Grey Mage.

"Sorry Boss, you're losing signal!" Ned shouted. But the image in the satnav screen wavered and was gone.

"Ugh!" said the satnav. "That was awful. Like someone else pushing into your brains."

"'Ow would you know?" asked the assistant assistant. "I thought that yer had chips in there, not brains."

"Wouldn't mind some chips," muttered the junior.

"Well, you are not having mine," insisted the satnav.

"Wouldn't taste the same. We've no vinegar."

"Shuttup," said Ned. "You two in the back, we are about ter 'ave a bit of a scrap. If yer help out, then the Boss will certainly take yer on. 'E's good like that."

There was some rumbling of disagreement from the other two dark wizards in the car.

"Well, he's not sacked you two yet 'as he?" asked Ned.

The *Mondeo* slowly closed the gap between them and the vehicles ahead.

Inside the blacked-out black van, there was some tension. The sound technician had put in a bid for a union-sponsored pub break, seconded by the cameraman. However, Adam had put his foot down hard (on the sound technician's head) and clinched the argument with a head clench for the cameraman. Charles, the accountant, had needed no convincing to follow whoever signed the checks, and the driver knew he wouldn't be allowed to drink anyway, so didn't care.

"Why are you slowing down?" demanded Adam, reluctantly releasing the cameraman and allowing the latter to fall to the floor of the van.

"The *Sprinter's* pulling into that car park."

"OK. Follow them in."

As the tour bus and the van stopped, the *Mondeo* pulled into the car park behind them, and the doors were flung open. Across the car park, from the shadows, The Grey Mage stalked from his old *Mercedes* estate with his receptionist and two other Dark Coven members.

"Der!" yelled Eddie, trying to turn the *Sprinter* around. But, with the trailer on the back, he had no room. Ahead of them, the receptionist threw off her coat, and changed shape into a green dragon six feet long and four feet high.

"We need to get out!" panicked GG.

Felldyke and Scar threw open the doors and jumped out of the *Sprinter*.

"I meant out of the car park!"

Fungus and Haemar exchanged a glance, then Haemar grabbed a long tire lever from underneath the dashboard, and he and Fungus climbed out. Eddie was there already. Adam and his lager louts joined them.

"What's going on?" asked Adam, who couldn't tear his eyes away from the dragon.

The cameraman had already dived back into the van and was feverishly grabbing his kit.

At a shout, they all looked behind, to see that GG, Felldyke and Scar were already scrapping with Ned and his crew who were trying to get to the trailer.

The Grey Mage smiled, in triumph, and raised his staff.

"Who's the old git?" asked Adam, as his cameraman pointed the lens at the dragon receptionist.

"An Evil Wizard," replied Haemar, pronouncing the capital letters.

"He looks just like my bank manager. And is that really a dragon?"

The receptionist blew a very hot flame at the sound technician, who dodged.

"I'll take that as a yes, then."

"We're in a bother this time." Haemar said to Fungus. "What are you lookin' for?"

Fungus was looking wildly around the deserted car park, but didn't answer.

The receptionist sent another blaze of flame, this time at the shrouded shape on the trailer, but the flames failed to catch hold and burn.

"What do they want?" demanded Adam.

"For starters, they want to burn that thing we've got on the trailer," Fungus told him.

"And then we'll be fer seconds," Haemar added grimly. The fighting noises grew louder from behind.

"Get stuck in can't yer?" yelled Ned at the monks. He had a tight hold of Scar's leg but, as Felldyke was sitting *on* Ned and trying to insert a drumstick (wooden variety) into Ned's left nostril, Ned was unable to capitalize on this advantage.

"We always preach non-violence as a form of dispute management," replied the senior monk, glaring at the accountant, who was trying to brain GG with his abacus, an attempt foredoomed to failure.

"Just help out!" Ned shouted, as Scar freed his leg with a vicious kick, and jumped on the tax junior from behind. As they fell to the ground, the assistant assistant tripped over them, and GG paused – fending away a wildly swinging abacus to put his boot into a strategic spot. The Watches were no longer a threat.

"XL5"* yelled The Grey Mage, waving on his Dark Coven, and the two extra evil wizards (that is, they were additional numbers, not superlatively evil) started throwing fireballs at the shrouded shape of the throne.

"Why are those fireballs not working?" wondered The Grey Mage.

"Why are those fireballs not working?" Adam asked, as one bounced off the throne and set fire to his foot. Adam started hopping about the car park.

"Why are those fireballs not working?" Haemar asked Fungus, while stamping on Adam's foot to put out the blaze. Adam continued hopping around the car park and started yelping in pain.

"Why is everyone asking me?" Fungus wanted to know. "Maybe Waccibacci put some protection on the throne, like goods-in-transit insurance?"

The next fireball bounced off the throne and set alight the front tire of the black van. Thinking quickly, the sound technician extinguished the

---

*   Trying to amuse the older reader there.

blaze with the nearest liquid source available. His nervous state, enhanced as more dragon fire removed his eyebrows, helped to increase the flow.

"We'll have to get the cover off it." The Grey Mage decided and he waved his minions forward. But they ran into Adam, his driver and the sound technician, and a brawl developed. The Grey Mage sighed and strode forward towards the *Sprinter*.

"We've got two options," Fungus told Haemar, as he eyed the wizard's approach.

"Good. Isn't that a chocolate drink with different flavors? Just what we need now."

"Actually, I meant we can try an' hold him off, or we can run away," Fungus said.

"I like run away. I like it a lot," Haemar said, backing away to the *Sprinter* as more random dragon fire burst across the car park towards them, setting fire to a parking meter and thereby incurring the wrath of the Council and a substantial fine. (But, on the plus side, incinerating a fly poster announcing a particular forthcoming concert.)

"I just don't think that I could be fast enough."

Haemar passed the tire lever to Fungus and drew his short sword. (All dwarves carry short swords. It's probably a cultural thing.)

"We need a good battle cry," Haemar said. "It could be our final fling."

"Then how about 'Last orders at the bar'?"

"Good one! Fungus, why do you keep looking around?"

"For help."

"Fungus, no one's coming. Come on!"

Haemar gave a blood curdling yell and leaped forwards. But The Grey Mage just sneered and waved his staff. Fungus and Haemar fell to the ground, bound fast together with magical chains.

"Well, it was worth a try," groaned Fungus.

Haemar shook the iron chains, which for some arcane reason were covered in pink fur. The dragon receptionist stopped breathing flames everywhere and examined the chains with some interest. The Grey Mage changed color in embarrassment, as he blushed.

"Those handcuffs are covered in glitter, too," she observed.

"Yes, well, I bought that spell second-hand from a solicitor," The Grey Mage muttered. His receptionist looked disbelieving.

"Right," said The Grey Mage, striding over his bound protagonists towards his goal. Haemar tried to bite him on the leg as he passed, but missed: the shrouded throne lay on the trailer, at his mercy. But then there came a loud, single, perfect note (possibly A-sharp) and a large golden globe appeared on top of The Grey Mage's *Mercedes* estate, causing another sound. (B-flat, probably.)

The average *Mercedes* estate is a well-built, solid vehicle, somewhat reminiscent of a World War Two tank. But that didn't stop the roof bending inwards under the weight of the globe, causing a scream of rage from The Grey Mage.

The globe shimmered, and vanished, leaving in its place Malan and Finn of the Tuatha, Grizelda the witch holding her broomstick and Dai looking confused.

"Are we too late?" called Malan.

"Only we heard someone yell 'Last orders' and got a bit worried," added Finn.

"What's goin' on here then?" demanded Grizelda.

"Were you expectin' this lot then?" Haemar asked Fungus.

"Well, yes. But only Malan and Dai, the other two are like a bonus."

Grizelda did not resemble a free gift, as for example, the plastic toys that used to be included in cereal packets. She had not enjoyed the Tuatha's transportation methods, having spent most of the journey squashed up against Dai who maintained quite a high body temperature.

The sight of Dai had also raised the receptionist's temperature, but in a different way, and she stopped sending jets of fire at the throne, and tried simpering instead. The Grey Mage averted his eyes in horror.

Finn and Malan jumped down from the roof of the *Mercedes*, leaving boot imprints on the bonnet as they passed, then helped Grizelda down more modestly.

"What do we do now, Adam?" asked the cameraman.

"Just keep on filming, until I tell you to stop!" Adam hissed back. The sound technician and the driver joined them, leaving the two Dark Coven members groaning on the ground. The two orange-clad monks at the rear quietly slid behind the *Mondeo*, out of view.

"I asked, what's goin' on?" repeated Grizelda.

"These Caer Surdin idiots ambushed us, an' have been tryin' ter set fire ter the throne." Haemar explained to Grizelda.

"Them chains suit yer," she replied and then glared at The Grey Mage.

"This one's a draw now that we've got here in time," she told him.

The Grey Mage looked around the field of battle. His dark coven had not yet recovered from the record producers' attack. His receptionist was simpering at the drunken, red dragon in a manner he had never seen before, to Dai's intense interest. Ned and The Watches had succumbed to the rhythm section of The Banned Underground, and the monks were cowering from Grizelda. He himself, was confident he could overcome Grizelda, and Haemar and Fungus were immobilized. But that left two of the Tuatha to fight at the same time as Grizelda, and he knew he was outnumbered.

"OK, Grotbags," he replied. "You win... for now."

Grizelda turned brick red – she did not care for the open use of her nickname.

The Grey Mage beckoned to his forces and they all limped or crawled back into their respective vehicles, and left the car park. The receptionist peered sadly out of the back window of the *Mercedes* as they drove away.

Grizelda inspected the chains that bound Haemar and Fungus and sniffed loudly.

"No wonder he's no good in a fight if those are to his taste," she commented, and then muttered the charm that vanished the offending manacles.

"Thanks, Grizelda," said Haemar, standing up slowly. "What are you doing here?"

"Besides saving you?"

"Well, yes."

"Malan told me he was bringing Dai up here fer yer next gig, so I hitched a lift. Could do with pickin' a couple of bits up from me old cottage. There's some herbs I want ter plant down in Wales, ter go in the curry."

Finn had more important issues on his mind.

"Never mind all that, Grizelda. What about last orders?"

The Banned all brightened up at once.

"The pub's only a mile away," Haemar said and, in record time the car park was, again empty, except for a forlorn and discarded abacus.

CHAPTER SEVENTEEN

Haemar had somewhat relaxed after his second pint.

"Suppose we should be getting up ter the Helvyndelve, now," he said to Fungus.

"Umm. Yeah, you're right. Don't want any more problems, do we?"

"Rivet," remarked the barmaid, who had made the mistake of asking Grizelda to remove her hat.

"Der."

"Yes Eddie, we know," Haemar told the roadie, "but it's not far and Dai looks as if he is properly refueled now, so he can fly it."

They all looked at Dai, who was deep in conversation with Adam at the bar.

"I think we should do something about that camera though," Fungus observed.

"I'll mention it to Grizelda. We don't want footage of that ruckus making the news or the internet." Haemar wandered off to speak to Grizelda, while Fungus drained his beer.

"Come on guys, time to go!" he called.

The landlord looked disappointed.

After some issues with finding GG, who had gone to sleep in the toilets and needed rousing with cold water, the motley group collected outside.

"Listen up," Haemar said to them all. "We are going up ter the back door. But we need ter be a bit discreet in getting there."

Scar looked worried.

"Haemar, we've got a van that looks like it belongs to an MI5 hit man, a witch on a broomstick and a drunken red dragon, and the *Sprinter* is towing a giant toilet. How, exactly are we goin' ter be discreet?"

"Who says I'm drunk?" demanded Dai, but spoiled his effect by staggering sideways into Malan, who fell over.

"Oh, sorry." Dai helped Malan get up, while Finn laughed.

"Dai, we all know you're drunk," sighed Fungus.

"Who is likely to see?" asked Grizelda, who had never been to the back door of the Helvyndelve before.

"Let me see. We go through the center of the village, past a holiday caravan park, then there's a youth hostel, and then some cottages beside the mines where the entrance is hidden." Haemar told her.

"Oh, what a great location to have a secret door," Grizelda observed.

196

"Unfortunately, it's the only one with a road leading up to it," Scar explained.

Grizelda sighed.

"OK, well, I can deal with this. These gentlemen, whoever they are, with the black van: they can lead."

"We don't know the way," objected Adam.

"Der."

"Eddie doesn't know it either," said GG.

"We knew that," said Haemar. "I can ride with Adam, Eddie follows us, an' everyone else follows Eddie."

"An' I will cover everyone wi' a mist, so that we stay unobserved," said Grizelda, smugly. She raised her arms and chanted a short spell.

"Perhaps I've overdone that a bit."

"Maybe," agreed Fungus, who could now see less than three inches in the thick white mist that surrounded them all.

More mystic chanting followed and the mist thinned to manageable levels. The convoy set off, pausing only to extract Dai from a tree he had inadvertently flown into and set on fire.

"Sorry. It's the mist," he apologized.

"Yeah, 'mist' as anything, that's you." Scar called up to him.

"Suppose that no one's got any choccie bikkies?"

"Shut up and fly."

The cavalcade, at length, drew up before the hidden back door and Haemar climbed out of the black van and walked up to the pile of discarded slates that hid the entrance.

"I'll just unlock the door," he called.

Adam and Charles watched, fascinated, as Haemar carefully selected his spot, then kicked a particular piece of slate as hard as he could and commenced a complicated tap dance.

"Must be like a key code," said Charles.

"Wonder how he remembers the steps?"

The driver wound down the window and the sound of the dwarf's belligerent swearing at his sore toes came into the van. The driver wound the window back up.

The pile of slate shimmered and turned into a large pair of wooden doors, clasped with rusty iron. In the center of the left door was fitted a flat metal plate, which comprised the lock. Haemar put his palm against the plate and the doors creaked and groaned from unaccustomed effort as they opened.

Haemar limped back to the black van and climbed in.

"We don't usually open the big doors, there's like a small entrance further on, but we'd not get the van or the minibus inside."

The record company staff all looked at him in silence.

"Drive on, "said Haemar.

"In there?" asked the driver, looking at the dark tunnel ahead.

"Well, yes."

"But that's a mine," pointed out Adam.

"Well, yes."

"Underground," said Charles.

"Well, yes."

"Is it safe?" asked the driver.

"Compared to pitching against an evil-tempered witch like her behind us?"

The driver quickly let in the clutch and drove forward. Once the last of the party had entered, the aged wooden doors closed with a clang, shutting out the last of the daylight. Behind them, the slate pile magically slid back upwards, hiding the doors from common view.

"That's better," said Fungus as the lights came on dimly within the entrance chamber.

The dwarves all got out of the vehicles.

"That's as far as we can drive, now," Haemar told the party.

"How do we get the throne to the Chamber, then?" worried Scar.

Haemar waved his hand at the ferociously-armed dwarf guards who were now becoming visible in the growing light.

"They can push the trailer."

"What do yer think yer up to then?" demanded the guard captain, fingering his huge bushy beard, and stamping up to Haemar.

"We're on a mission, so you'd better help out," replied Fungus.

"I'll help yer out, all right. Lads, kick this lot back out the – rivet, rivet, rivet!"

Some of the guards looked bemused. The Banned were not in armor and so wore no rivets. From underneath his helmet, which was now spinning gently on the floor, the guard captain made certain complaints, suggestions, and requests.

"Not 'til yer take that back!" sulked Grizelda.

The second in command approached, cautiously.

"Yer must understand, we are under orders from the Archlord of Helvyndelve, an' we're not supposed ter let ordinary people in."

"These aren't people," retorted Haemar, giving the still spinning helmet a surreptitious kick. He had never liked that particular dwarf and was quite content to see him frogged for a while.

"We're The Banned Underground. Fungus here is a personal friend of the Archlord. These over here are from the Tuatha and this is Grizelda, the witch you will have heard of."

The guards had indeed heard all about Grizelda and backed away quickly.

"Now, we are here returning from a quest imposed upon us by the Lord Lakin, so yer can all just help out."

"Rivet, rivet," observed the helmet from the floor.

"See? Even he agrees."

Before long, matters were settled to Haemar's satisfaction. Grizelda had received a fulsome apology ("rivet, RIVET, rivet, rivet") and restored the guard captain to both his natural shape and almost to his sanity. Adam had agreed that his technical support team would carry all their kit. And the guards were grumbling (their default state) as they pulled the trailer deep into the Helvyndelve, followed by several guards struggling under the weight of The Banned's equipment.

"Der."

And being ordered about by Eddie.

The long column at last reached the heart of the Helvyndelve, to find preparations well advanced.

"Set up in the Chamber of the Throne," ordered the captain of Lakin's personal guard as he met them at a passage-meet.

"I thought that we were playin' in the Cavern of a Thousand Knights," objected Fungus.

"Lord Lakin has decided to be generous," replied the guard captain.

The Banned all looked suspicious.

"He has decided to celebrate the inauguration of the new throne with a gig in the Chamber of the Throne, so that all can admire the new throne, and then allow you to play a second gig the next night in the Cavern of a Thousand Knights."

Haemar and Fungus each grabbed one elbow and moved the dwarf captain away from all the others.

"Now. Tell me the truth," hissed Haemar.

The guard looked furtively all around.

"The amulet has nearly run out of power now. Lord Lakin sold so many tickets that he needs to spread the crowd over two nights, cos he needs to recharge the amulet in the new throne to power the gig, power the bars, and run security all at the same time. He's worried that if too many are here on one night, the power might run out and plunge the Helvyndelve into darkness."

"What about the candles?"

"Too much like Barry Manilow. The crowd wouldn't wear it. They're arriving already, so let's push on with setting up."

Indeed, over at the Bowder Stone, security was again in full swing.

"Where's yer tickets?" demanded Milim, glaring at the line snaking down the hillside.

"Er. I've got this t-shirt," said the one at the head of the line.

Milim sighed.

"You again. Just pay me now, or get lost."

"Do yer know what time it is?" demanded the second-in-line. There came a growl of agreement from behind him.

"Why?" asked Milim, as the line pressed forwards. Behind him, Daran – also in full armor – drew his sword.

"7:30 it says here on me ticket, an' we've got ter walk the whole length of the western passage, an' buy drinks cos you won't let us bring our own!" shouted one further down the line.

Milim took a step backwards.

"Listen, I'm only followin' me orders. Stay where you are!"

The line pressed forwards, and the Doors of the Dwarves opened wide under the pressure.

"Stampede!" yelled a stone troll further back down the line.

Soon afterwards, Milim managed to get to his knees. His helmet, stamped flat, was some yards away, and clearly unusable. His sword was bent into a u shape and his armor showed signs of the trampling he had received.

"Daran? Daran? Where are you?" he called.

"Bits of me are over here," came the reply. Daran's head emerged from behind the security desk, which he had used as a refuge.

"There's a few more bits over there, too," Daran added, his eyes revolving in different directions.

The two guards pulled themselves together and looked at the cloud of dust at the entrance to the western passage that marked the passing of the horde.

"Should we tell them that the audience is on its way?" wondered Daran.

"I wouldn't bother. I think that they'll find out soon enough when that lot hit the bars."

"Yeah. Let's lock up an' go and find a drink."

"Or two."

"Or, as you say, two."

"Each."

"At least."

Fungus was peering through the curtains slung across the dais.

"We've got a great crowd again!" he reported excitedly, pushing his sunglasses back into position.

"Who cares?" asked Haemar. He sat on a huge bag of coins, which the guards had reluctantly left with them.

"I'm finished with the wiring, anyone want a last sound check?" called GG.

"It's too late for that now," replied Fungus, looking again at the audience.

"I did mine earlier," called Felldyke. A guard with a drumstick in his ear glowered his agreement.

"What's a sound check?" asked Dai, giving his bass a last clean and trimming his front claws.

"Ah, er, I did yours for you," muttered GG quickly.

The guards stiffened to attention, as Lord Lakin entered the backstage area.

"Ah, The Banned Underground." Lakin smiled. "And you have brought me my new throne."

Fungus pushed a large block on wheels over to the Archlord.

"What is this?" asked Lord Lakin.

"That's the receipt from Waccibacci, the genuine Certificate of Authenticity he wrote for us on the back of a bar menu, and the manual/terms and conditions of use."

Lakin examined the block of documents, which rose as high as his waist.

"It's a bit big to be small print," he observed.

Fungus shrugged.

"Well, that seems to be in order. You have been paid for tonight?" asked Lakin.

Felldyke moved over and sat on the bag beside Haemar.

"So, here is the deal," continued Lakin.

"You play the first half of your set, then we reveal the throne, I place the amulet in the socket provided so that it recharges. You play the second half of the gig and then we have a party once the audience has gone. Tomorrow, you get to play a second set and get paid again."

"Suits us," agreed Haemar, picking up some whisky and gargling.

"What is that roped off area in front of the dais, with those suspiciously human-looking beings fussing around some strange equipment?" asked the Lord of the Helvyndelve.

"Ah, we're recording the night for posterity," replied Fungus.

"That sounds very right and proper," agreed Lakin. He nodded to the guards and moved towards the curtains.

"Here we go," said the Archlord.

"That's my line," complained Haemar reaching for his scarf.

The excited hubbub in the hall rose then fell in disappointment as Lakin, Archlord of the Helvyndelve and King under the Mountain pushed through the curtains to the front of the stage and seized the microphone.

"Is this thing working properly? Whoever's doing the sound, see me later," announced Lord Lakin. The crowd cheered and carried on drinking.

"Right!" yelled Lakin and silence spread out around the hall. At the desk, Adam and his assistants were frantically adjusting the volume levels.

"The program will commence now," Lakin continued.

Thinking that he had said enough, the crowd cheered wildly.

"After the first half of the set, we will have the main part of the program."

"The second half of the set?" called one of the crowd and the guards marked him out for later.

"The inauguration of the new throne!"

There was a muted cheer, the volume levels markedly increased in those regions of the crown within reach of the pointy end of a guard's spear.

"Now, the warm up," said Lakin, offended, and walked off the stage.

Fungus and Eddie pulled back the curtains and the noise rose.

Haemar strutted to the front of the stage and sucked for a moment on his beer-soaked scarf.

"Here we go!" he yelled into the mic, and The Banned roared into their set.

Going Underground was followed by *Please Don't Touch, Come On Everybody, Shaking All Over, Please Don't Go, Gimme Some Lovin', Sunshine of Your Love, Oh Well, Black Magic Woman* and then *Start Me Up* and *Jumping Jack Flash* to end the first half of the set.

The crowds were ecstatic. Whatever they had paid for the tickets was well worth the money.

"Tell you what, that's a good first half," Adam said to Charles, who wasn't paying attention.

"I said that's a good first half! Mick, you'd better have that recorded," Adam told the engineer who was still bent over his console.

Away at the bars, business was brisk, and the lines enormous. Some, however, seemed able to reach the front easily.

"I'll have a Port an' Lemon, barman."

"No port luv...Rivet! Rivet!...Coming straight up madam. On the house."

"Ten pints of bitter, mate," called Malan, over the bar.

"And I'll have ten too. Will that be enough between us, Malan?"

"Should be, Finn. No, put them on The Banned's tab, please. Proof? Well, I've got this t-shirt that they gave me... "

Malan glared at the dwarf behind the bar, who shrank a little further.

"An' I'll vouch fer them," added Grizelda. That seemed to be a clinching argument as far as the barman, whose face still bore a green tint, was concerned.

"Boys did well, I think," she added.

Malan nodded. "They're getting better. Maybe having the bass player helps the sound, do you think?"

Grizelda was unconvinced that having Dai around could help anyone but a brewery, but did not say so. On stage, preparations were in hand for the great unveiling. Heavily veiled at the far end of the bar stood a shadowy group, keeping to themselves.

"It were good of yer ter buy us all these tickets fer the gig, Boss," said Ned.

"Yeah, thanks, Boss," came a chorus.

"Om, yes, indeed."

"That's all right," replied The Grey Mage. "Treat it as a work outing, lads, and have some fun. I'll dock the cost from your wages at the month end."

"Thanks, Boss," came a less appreciative chorus.

"Now, observe. The ceremony may yet go wrong, and the new throne fail to recharge the amulet. I have arranged that we will have an army of fire trolls, rock trolls and our Bodgandor ready to attack if that happens."

"Om. Please, what are Bodgandor?" asked the Mystic Accountant.

"Evil goblins from a parallel world, who will do our bidding," replied Ned.

"Om. Handy, if they do not cost too much."

"Remind me to offer you a job when we get back to the office," The Grey Mage told him. The saffron-clad accountant bowed and smiled in relief.

"ORDER. ORDER!" yelled a guard from the dais.

The audience, largely clustered around the bar, ignored him.

The guard seized the microphone and yelled "ORDER! ORDER!" again.

This time, the amplified sound filled the Chamber of the Throne, vibrating tired revelers off the chairs onto which they had collapsed at the end of the first set, and causing seismic vibrations deep within the heart of the mountain of used pizza boxes stacked high along one wall near the dais. Glasses shattered in the drinkers' hands, spilling more beer onto the floor.

The guard, disappointed at the apparent lack of reaction, filled his lungs and prepared to shout into the mic but, fortunately, Haemar appeared through the backstage curtains with an angry expression and a shattered glass.

"Keep off the kit, yer muppet!" he snarled, and snatched the microphone from its stand and vanished backstage with it.

The guard turned purple from the effort of holding his breath and there would have been a nasty accident had Felldyke not chanced to lose his grip on a drumstick at that moment. The drumstick (wooden) flew over the curtain and bounced off the unfortunate guard's helmet. With a whoosh, the held breath was released.

The captain of the Archlord's guards sneered at the antics and, himself, climbed onto the dais. When he shouted for silence, he got it. A tribute to the power of his lungs, honed over years of command, and his reputation as a nasty piece of work it didn't pay to offend. The Chamber of the Throne quietened down and even the small fights breaking out wherever a dwarf had been covered in second-hand beer were carried on with discretion. And unnecessary violence, of course.

"Right you lot!" yelled the captain, his voice carrying effortlessly without artificial aids.

Beside the dais there was some unscripted movement, a shimmering in the air. Even the assault and battery being carried out at one end of the bar paused, fascinated. The captain swelled up until, in Grizelda's expert opinion, he resembled a Mississippi bullfrog.

"Now show your respect for the Archlord Lakin, King under the Mountain!" thundered the captain. "Now," continued the captain, "SILENCE for the Archlord of the Helvyndelve!"

To ironic cheers, Lord Lakin made his way onto the dais. However, his voice lacked the projection of his guard captain and it was clear that he was unlikely to be heard at the far end of the chamber. As the guards formed up around the dais, a hand carrying a microphone was thrust through the curtains hiding The Banned.

Lakin grabbed the mic and strode – resplendent in his polished ceremonial armor – to the front of the stage.

"Now," he announced, "the purpose of tonight is to unveil officially the new throne of the King under the Mountain. This throne has been made especially for us by the last known maker of magical thrones. The world shall never see its like again."

Lakin turned and clasped an ornate piece of rope attached to the shrouded throne.

"I can tell you all that the Amulet of Kings has been placed in the niche prepared for it, and the fact that the bars are serving you chilled beer proves that the new throne has the same magical powers as the old one."

The room echoed with cheers and more calls for drinks.

"Our power over the Helvyndelve is restored and, with it, our security!" Lakin announced.

Security looked extremely satisfied and The Grey Mage pulled a face.

"Looks like we've lost this one, again," he complained.

"Never mind, Boss," Ned reassured him. "At least we're in the warm, wi' decent beer an' The Banned are playin' a good gig. There will be a next time."

The Grey Mage cheered up. "And if there's nothing going down, then I don't need to pay you any overtime."

The Watches looked unsurprised. In fact, the junior pulled out his wallet and gave the assistant assistant ten pounds.

"What's that for?" asked The Grey Mage.

"We had a bet on how long it would be before yer worked out how not ter pay us," answered the junior. "He won."

"Serves you right for not having more faith in me," glowered The Grey Mage.

The junior looked over at the assistant, who had gone back to the bar.

"No, I bet you'd need until the second half ter do it. He reckoned the interval."

The Grey Mage looked offended, then shocked, as Ned also pulled out his wallet.

"I didn't think it would take yer this long," Ned complained.

They all winced as feedback echoed all around the Chamber.

"Be upstanding for the new throne!" shouted Lakin and pulled on the cord.

As if pulled by another chord, the audience rose to their feet, cheering. Lakin was speechless, for a moment, and then started yelling for the guards.

"Arrest them all!" he yelled. "Instead of a new throne, I've got a wooden toilet with a canopy!"

"Tell you what the opener is for the next set," Fungus said the Haemar, as the guards burst into the backstage area, waving their swords importantly.

"*Jailhouse Rock.*"

"Again," agreed Haemar gloomily.

Epilogue

Eddie the roadie coasted the *Sprinter* tour bus down the gently sloping lane. He had turned the engine off as Fungus had impressed upon him the need for silence.

In the back of the van, thrown carelessly among the drums, the drunken victim lay unconscious and naked.

"Are you sure we have to be so careful?" asked Haemar.

"Listen, I've met her," Fungus replied. "She's even scarier than Grizelda."

The rest of the group shuddered, as Eddie pulled on the handbrake, and the bus shuddered to a halt outside the silent house, in darkness, owing to the very late, or rather very early time of day. Fungus nodded to the dwarves in the back of the van. GG and Scar slipped out and grabbed the still-unconscious author, panting a little as they dragged him across the road to the porch, and dropped him by the front door. As a friendly gesture, they left his clothes in the pond by the gate.

Eddie started the *Sprinter* and Scar booted the front door as hard as he could – then ran for it – GG was already climbing into the bus. Eddie floored the accelerator, as the porch lights sprang on. Pulling up at the end of the lane, they could hear shouting and abuse through the open windows.

"Was it really necessary to do that to him?" asked Felldyke.

"Yes!" said Haemar firmly. "I've seen what he's thinking of doing to us in the next book!"

Eddie wound up the windows, and The Banned Underground drove away, chuckling.

If you liked *The Mystic Accountants*, rock on with Fungus and The Banned, Chris, Linda, Grotbags – rivet, rivet – *ahem*, **Grizelda**, Edern and the Tuatha (if they ever get off their pub crawl) on Facebook at

www.facebook.com/pages/The-Banned-Underground/222107091139685

or on the Safkhet book page at

www.safkhetpublishing.com/books/fantasy/9781908208088/TBU2.html

The Banned Underground Series

The Amulet of Kings
The Mystic Accountants[*]
The Vampire Mechanic (late 2012)
Bass'd Out (2013)

---

[*]   This book, in case you were wondering.

Lightning Source UK Ltd.
Milton Keynes UK
UKOW051832140412

190767UK00001B/1/P